ORGANIZED GRIME

Squeaky Clean Mysteries, Book 3

By Christy Barritt

CHRISTY BARRITT

Organized Grime: A Novel
Copyright 2011 by Christy Barritt

Published by River Heights

Cover design by Palko Media.

This ebook is licensed for your personal enjoyment only. This ebook may not be re-sold or given away to other people. If you would like to share this book with another person, please purchase an additional copy for each recipient. If you're reading this book and did not purchase it, or it was not purchased for your use only, then please return to Smashwords.com and purchase your own copy. Thank you for respecting the hard work of this author.

The persons and events portrayed in this work are the creation of the author, and any resemblance to persons living or dead is purely coincidental.

Acclaim for the Squeaky Clean series:

Christy Barritt's novel, *Hazardous Duty*, is a delightful read from beginning to end. The story's fresh, engaging heroine with an unusual occupation hooked me, and I couldn't put it down. I highly recommend *Hazardous Duty*. ~ Colleen Coble, bestselling author

The next time you're tempted to watch CSI reruns, read this book instead! Spunky, sassy Gabby St. Claire sparkles in this new series. She'll keep you turning the pages. ~ Siri Mitchell, INSPY award-winning author

With Gabby St. Claire, Christy Barritt has created a fun sleuth in a unique profession. *Hazardous Duty* provides both humor and an engaging mystery. The twists and turns of the whodunit are matched only by the surprises of Gabby's spiritual growth and romantic entanglements. ~ Sharon Dunn, multi-published mystery and suspense author

Stay tuned and watch for more from this gifted, talented author. You'll love it. ~ Cheryl Wolverton, multi-published author

Crime scene cleanup should be a safe enough occupation, right? It comes after the crime is over. Not necessarily! Come enjoy this fun romp through the complications . . . men, mold, mayhem and murder . . . in

Gabby St. Claire's rollercoaster life. ~ Lorena McCourtney, author of the Ivy Malone mysteries

Crime scene cleaning is dirty job, but Christy Barritt has made it hilarious. Amateur sleuth Gabby St. Claire is back, and in trouble again! *Suspicious Minds* delivers a riveting mystery, but it's Gabby's irrepressible charm as she engages a zany cast of characters that keeps readers turning pages. Put this series on your must read list! ~ Claudia Mair Burney, author of the Amanda Bell Brown Mysteries

Suspicious Minds is witty, punchy and fast-paced. Kudos to Christy Barritt for an entertaining and intriguing read! ~ Janice Thompson, award-winning author

Suspicious Minds plays havoc on the nerves and the funny bone as crime scene cleaner Gabby St. Claire wisecracks her way between dead bodies and flying bullets. A treat not to be missed! ~ Jill Elizabeth Nelson, author of the To Catch a Thief series

Dedication and Thanks:

This book is dedicated to my readers. Writing wouldn't be nearly as fun without you there to live out my stories with me. Thank you for living my dream with me!

A special thank you to Ruth, Kathy, Idalia, Evelyn, and Pat for your encouragement with this book.

Other Books by Christy Barritt

Squeaky Clean Mysteries:
#1 Hazardous Duty
#2 Suspicious Minds
#2.5 It Came Upon a Midnight Crime
#3 Organized Grime
#4 Dirty Deeds
#5 The Scum of All Fears
#6 To Love, Honor, and Perish
#7 Mucky Streak
#8 Foul Play
#9 Broom and Gloom
#10 Dust and Obey
#11 Thrill Squeaker
#11.5 Swept Away
#12 Cunning Attractions (coming soon)

Squeaky Clean Companion Novella:
While You Were Sweeping

The Sierra Files
#1 Pounced
#2 Hunted
#2.5 Pranced (a Christmas novella)
#3 Rattled
#4 Caged (coming soon)

The Gabby St. Claire Diaries (a tween mystery series)

#1 The Curtain Call Caper
#2 The Disappearing Dog Dilemma
#3 The Bungled Bike Burglaries

Holly Anna Paladin Mysteries
#1 Random Acts of Murder
#2 Random Acts of Deceit
#3 Random Acts of Malice
#3.5 Random Acts of Scrooge
#4 Random Acts of Guilt (coming soon)

Carolina Moon series
#1 Home Before Dark
#2 Gone by Dark
#3 Wait Until Dark (coming soon)

Suburban Sleuth Mysteries:
#1 Death of the Couch Potato's Wife

Standalone Romantic Suspense:
Keeping Guard
The Last Target
Race Against Time
Ricochet
Key Witness
Lifeline
High-Stakes Holiday Reunion
Desperate Measures
Hidden Agenda
Mountain Hideaway
Dark Harbor

Standalone Romantic Mystery:
The Good Girl

Suspense:
Imperfect
Dubiosity
Disillusioned (coming soon)

Nonfiction:
Changed: True Stories of Finding God through Christian Music
The Novel in Me: The Beginner's Guide to Writing and Publishing a Novel

CHAPTER 1

Slam!

I glanced at the clock above my TV. 11 p.m. Way too late for visitors. The five residents who lived in our converted Victorian apartment complex knew better than to let the front door slam shut at this hour. Otherwise, they'd face the wrath of Sierra, who hated to be woken from her beauty sleep, which lately had been starting promptly at 9:30.

The detective in me woke up as more noise downstairs caught my ears—literally. Like a magnet being drawn to a refrigerator, my right ear gravitated toward my door and didn't stop until my skin plastered the grooved wood there.

Someone entered the apartment building. The front door had a tendency to slam shut with a reverberating thud each time someone entered or left. Who could it be?

Someone must be visiting. My upstairs neighbor, Mrs. Mystery as I affectionately called her, was taking a rare vacation to the Bahamas. Rare because I don't think her skin has ever seen the sun except in five-minute increments. My downstairs neighbor, radio-talk show host Bill McCormick, was on a huge tour to promote his show and not due back in town for two more weeks. Sierra had left at four this afternoon and I hadn't seen her since then. And Riley, who lived across the hall, was up in D.C. visiting his parents for the weekend.

It had been a very slow evening for me. Even my friend and business partner Chad Davis had decided to go meet his college buddies for a weekend ski trip in the mountains of Virginia.

That's why the door slamming downstairs had me even more intrigued.

Footsteps pounded upward, bypassing Bill's apartment.

I puckered my lips in thought.

Maybe Riley had returned from his parents early. But he wouldn't let the door slam, especially not at this hour.

Someone rapped at my door. At the very place—only on the other side—of where my ear suctioned to the wood. I jumped away and cradled my poor lobes, wondering if the eardrum had burst.

"Gabby? You in there? I saw your van outside."

I released my ear. Parker? My ex-boyfriend? What was he doing here?

I grabbed the knob and jerked the door open, forgetting that I was supposed to make him want to eat his heart out and realize what he was missing every time he saw me. The tattered flannel pants and faded

"Meat is Murder" T-shirt that Sierra gave me wouldn't do the trick. Nor would the curly red hair that frizzed away from my ponytail in stubborn poofs around my face.

I hadn't expected an overly friendly Parker. I hadn't spoken to him in months. But I really didn't expect the brisk man in a suit who flashed an FBI badge and attempted to barge into my apartment.

Parker craned his head to see beyond me and tried to charge forward. "Is Sierra in here?"

I raised my hand into the internationally known sign for "stop." "Where do you think you're going?"

Parker ignored my upraised hand until his chest collided with my palm. He looked down and scowled. "We need to talk, Gabby."

I peered around Parker long enough to eye the two other suits accompanying my ex. "About?"

"This isn't a conversation you'll want to have in the hallway."

I contemplated my options a moment before dropping my hand and nodding. The three men filed inside. I shut the door behind them before turning their way in curiosity.

"Wilkerson, FBI," the blond said.

"Stephens," said the bald one.

Parker, with his Brad Pitt good looks, stopped his roving security camera-like inspection of my home and zeroed in on me. He nodded curtly, as if we'd merely been acquaintances in the past. "Gabby." His gaze began roaming again. "Where's Sierra?"

"Sierra?"

"Yeah, your neighbor."

I jerked my head back. Sarcasm was my job, not my ex's. I ignored his comment when I saw the other two men approaching and realized this was no time for jokes. "I haven't seen her since this afternoon. Why? What's wrong?"

"I need to talk to her."

"About?"

"The fire at the housing development in Chesapeake that's been all over the news. It looks like an act of ecoterrorism."

"Ecoterrorism?" I nudged my jaw back into closed position. But only for a moment. "Sierra would never—"

He held out a hand to silence me. "If you know where she is and don't tell me, then you'll be impeding a federal investigation."

I tried to hide my agitation. I hate to be bossed around. And I really hated to be cornered. "I don't know where she is, and when did you become a fed?"

"Last month." He stepped closer and lowered his voice. "This is serious, Gabby."

"I know. I heard there was a fire—"

"Gabby, three people are dead, and Sierra is our prime suspect."

CHAPTER 2

"Sierra would never murder someone. She believes in preservation of life." I pointed to my T-shirt. "Meat is murder."

Parker cocked an eyebrow up. "Yeah, only if you've got fur, walk on four legs and like to sniff people."

"That's not true. Remember when she set those crabs free last year? They weren't furry." I winced at the weakness of my argument.

Parker scowled. "How could I forget?" He lowered his voice and leaned toward me. "Gabby, Sierra was seen at the development earlier today. She was arguing—very heatedly—with the contractor and threatened to 'light a fire' on the issue if he insisted on expanding the neighborhood anymore."

I shrugged. "It's an expression. People say stuff like that all time. It doesn't mean they're actually going to do it."

"When did you see her last?"

I resigned myself to answer his questions. He'd find out Sierra was innocent. All he had to do was talk to my friend. She'd have an alibi. "She left to meet a friend at around four."

"Did she say what she was doing?"

I swallowed, my saliva burning my dry throat. "They had to talk about some kind of plan they were developing." I paused, realizing how incriminating those words sounded. "Parker, Sierra is a protester. She's a debater. Sure, she's done some stupid things in the past. But never murder. Never."

Parker turned his back on me and the three suits huddled together for some quiet talk. All I could think about was Sierra—who was like a sister to me—being guilty of murder. No way. She was extreme, but not that extreme. Finally, Parker turned around and approached me.

"Do you mind if we wait here for awhile?" He nubbed his thumb back at his henchmen... er, partners. "If she's innocent, she should be returning home soon, wouldn't you agree?"

"She *will* be returning home at any time because she *is* innocent. Please do wait. I want to be here when you're proven wrong. And when you are proven wrong, I'm not going to let you leave unless you write 'Gabby was right' one-hundred times on the chalkboard for all the world to see." There was nothing better than knocking down cocky confidence a notch.

One suit sat in an orange tweed chair, the other on my second-hand couch. Both looked like they might have their clothes disinfected when they left. Was it my furniture or was it the roll of biohazard tape they'd had to move before seating themselves? Or maybe the fake blob of blood on the coffee table that someone had given me as a joke? Parker still glowered at me from my apartment's entryway.

He rubbed his chin, and his gaze flicked behind me to the kitchen. "Do you have any coffee?"

"Sure do. You know where it is. Help yourself." No way was I going to fix coffee for someone accusing my best friend of murder. Traitor.

He went into my kitchen and opened the cabinet over the sink. After pulling down a canister of Maxwell House, he began a brew. It was obvious that he'd done it in my apartment a million times before. Out of the earshot of his comrades in arms, I leaned against the kitchen counter and crossed my arms.

"A fed, huh? Not surprising." He'd always been the uptight type.

He pulled a mug from one of the hooks beneath the cabinet. His favorite one—the blue and red logo proclaimed "Superman." "Yeah, Charlie encouraged me to go for it."

Charlie. The woman he'd started dating after we broke up. "How's she doing?"

Parker grinned for the first time. "Great. I'm going to be a dad."

I pulled my head back in surprise. "A baby? Wow. Congrats. When's the big day?"

"Not until this summer." He removed the glass coffee pot and stuck his mug directly under the stream of brown liquid coming from the percolator.

I did a quick check of his hand for a wedding ring. "Did you...?"

He followed my gaze, nearly spilling his much sought after coffee in the process. "Nah. Not yet. We'll see. We're not in a hurry, you know?"

People rarely call me a prude, but at the moment, I felt like one. Kids should have a mom and dad who were committed to each other and to them. As someone who grew up in a dysfunctional home, I knew all about the importance of a stable home life.

I attempted to swallow my judgments. "Lots of changes."

"Yeah, how about you?" His gaze ran up and down the length of me. "What's new? You find yourself a saint who can handle you yet? Or maybe I should say a superhero?"

I scowled. "Ha ha. Very funny. I don't need a man, thank you very much. I'm perfectly content with my career." Most of the time. Okay, fifty-percent, at least.

"How's the crime scene cleaning?"

I shrugged and pictured myself alphabetizing my cleaning supplies earlier this week. "Booming."

He did his trademark eyebrow quirk. "Strange, because we've been slow."

I took a sip of my coffee. I was drinking it black, something I rarely did. Right now, I needed the extra dose of caffeine, though. "Yeah, the big-time criminals must be hibernating. That's a good thing, right?"

He smirked. "Not for Sierra. It just means we have more time to focus on her."

"You're barking up the wrong tree, Parker." Why, oh why, did I always think of animal expressions when I talked about Sierra? "You'll find that out as soon as she gets back."

"Tell me—what friend was she getting together with?"

The blood drained from my face. "I don't know. She didn't say." It was the truth, if you defined "truth" by its loosest definition.

He cocked an eyebrow again. He knew me better than I wanted to admit. "But you have an idea."

"I only have guesses. Guesses don't mean anything."

"Give me a name."

I narrowed my eyes at Parker as he sipped on his coffee mug like he belonged in my apartment. "Why are you acting like this? I'm on your side—the side of the law. I always have been. But I'm not going to incriminate my friend."

He set down his coffee mug on the counter with a loud clank. "I just want a name, Gabby. Maybe the name will help prove her innocence."

I sighed, my breath ruffling my hair. "I think his name is Henry. I don't know his last name."

"What do you know about him?"

I shrugged, trying to be nonchalant. "Not much. He's a freegan."

"You mean vegan?"

"No, a freegan." Sierra's long, long speech on the definition of a "freegan" came back to me. "He only eats free food. They're called freegans. They go dumpster diving and stuff."

"Why would he do that?" Flashy Parker actually looked stupefied at the thought.

I sighed again, suddenly feeling like I was the suspect *and* a freegan. "Apparently, the U.S. wastes about half of the food it produces. Freegans don't want to support an economy that wastes so much so they only eat food that others discard."

Wow, I'd said it and sounded convincing. I was good.

"They sound like freaks."

I shrugged. "Call 'em what you want. They're out there."

He picked up his coffee mug again. "How long has she been hanging out with this Henry?" Long sip.

"Two, three months."

"What's your impression of him?"

A picture of Henry flashed in my head. I'd given him the nickname "The Smell." Yeah, enough said. "Aside from the fact that he looks homeless?"

"Homeless?"

A picture of Henry flashed into my head. "Apparently freegans don't shower very often or buy clothes either. Nor do they own cars because he's always trying to hitchhike or riding his bike. He's talked Sierra into getting a car that runs on used vegetable oil." I shook my head at the thought. "Whatever floats your boat. Peels your wheels. Moves your hooves. Propels your—"

"Are they romantically linked?"

The thought made me forget my poetic aspirations. "I hope not." I relaxed my shoulders as I realized how uptight I sounded. "I mean, if he makes her happy, then they should be together." I paused. "Romantically." As soon as the word left my mouth, I wanted to throw up. Who would want to kiss someone who ate trash and didn't shower?

Maybe people said the same thing about me. Who would want to date someone who cleans up blood and smells like death?

I pressed my hands into the counter behind me and focused my thoughts. Sure, Henry was extreme when it came to the environment. But that didn't mean Sierra, simply by affiliation, had burned down a new housing development. Not Sierra. But if she was associated with the wrong people—people who were involved with this crime—then she could still be in trouble…

I shuddered.

"You can't assume she's guilty until you have more evidence. It's the American way."

Parker took a long sip of coffee, his eyes never leaving mine. "We just want to ask her some questions."

"It sounds like you already have your mind made up."

Parker reached down and grabbed the newspaper from my kitchen counter. His eyes scanned the article there before he looked up, his eyes sparkling. He began to read aloud.

"Gabby St. Claire knows how to clean up scum. She can get blood out of carpet, pick shattered bones from plaster, and clean up other less-than-enticing fluids from nearly any surface. St. Claire also knows how to clean up another kind of scum— the scum of the earth. She's known around town as the girl who cleans up crime. The crime isn't always blood and guts. She's also cleaning up the streets by helping to put the bad guys behind bars. How does she do it? By using her training in forensics at the very crime scenes she's cleaning." He nodded and took another sip of coffee, his eyes still fixated on the newspaper. "Nice article."

I shrugged. "So I've been told."

Yes, the article—which came out two months ago—was still on my kitchen counter, but I'm not an egomaniac. But when someone finally acknowledges that the work you do is valuable, you've got to hold on to it. This article had helped solidify my business in the community. It had made me a bit of a folk hero in some circles. And it had gotten the attention of the medical examiner's office, the very place where I would love to be employed once I finally finished my degree in a matter of a few months.

Parker's cell phone rang. He pulled it from his belt and flipped it open. His voice became softer. It must be Charlie. He wandered down the hallway, talking.

Again, I was so glad he'd made himself at home in my apartment. Just what I wanted my ex-boyfriends to do.

An ex-boyfriend who was now having a baby with his new girlfriend. Weird. Very weird.

And here I was, alone.

Okay, not really alone. I mean, Chad would date me if I said the word. And Riley, well, half the time he acted interested in me and the other half like he was having second thoughts. It doesn't do much for a girl's ego, but I take what I can get. Besides, I've sworn off dating for awhile. Thinking about Sierra kissing Henry was enough to make me swear it off for good.

Parker's phone rang again, this time a good old reliable jangle instead of the softer chirp he had for Charlie. With the phone still to his ear, Parker charged toward my door. Uh oh. I stepped out of the way so quickly I nearly toppled my halogen lamp.

Parker held his hand over the mouthpiece. "We've got to go. When Sierra comes home, call me. Got it?"

The three men rushed from my house like floodwaters escaping a dam. I rushed after them, swinging myself around the doorframe in time to see their figures trotting down the stairs.

"Wait! What's wrong? What happened?" Had they found Sierra?

Parker didn't even bother to glance back at me. "A bomb just went off downtown."

"Oh." A bomb was terrible, but at least that had nothing to do with Sierra.

Parker paused at the bottom of the stairs and looked up at me. "At the office of Harrison Developers."

CHAPTER 3

I felt like a bomb had just gone off inside my head as I walked back into my apartment. Parker was way off base with this one. No way was Sierra involved in any of this craziness. She was crazy, but ... I shook my head. No, she wasn't *this* crazy.

Henry, on the other hand...

Sierra, I hope you didn't get yourself involved with the wrong crowd.

I leaned against the door, my legs feeling like they might buckle any time. My temples suddenly started throbbing. My stomach turned in a not-so-appealing manner.

Sierra. Where are you?

My little friend had a big heart. Really she did. So what if she protested circuses and sent nasty letters to fast food restaurants and refused to eat eggs. So what if she'd been arrested for freeing crabs and coerced my friends and me into eating acorn brownies.

She was a decent human being. Graduated from Yale. She was smart enough to stay away from federal investigations. Right?

I wiped my forehead, noticing the moisture there. Darn it, Parker. He'd made me nervous enough that I was sweating.

Sierra was in trouble. I could feel it.

I propelled myself across the floor and grabbed my phone from the kitchen counter. I dialed Sierra's number. I had to talk to her.

The phone went straight to voice mail.

Where had Sierra said she was going when she left earlier today? I closed my eyes, trying to remember the conversation. I pictured her and Henry leaving together. Where did they say they were going? If it was up to Henry, they'd probably be dumpster diving. But I couldn't help but think that she'd said something about having a planning session...

I closed the phone and then flipped it open again. I tried Sierra's number. Again I got her voicemail.

"Pick up the phone, Sierra!" I flipped the phone closed and slammed it on the counter. I had to get a grip, not assume the worst.

I forced myself to sit on the couch and try to relax, to pick up where I'd left off thirty minutes ago. Assuming things and speculating would get me nowhere. I needed to watch some late night TV and mind my own business.

Who was I kidding? When did I ever mind my own business?

I couldn't just stay in my apartment by myself while my ex-boyfriend hunted down my best friend and caged her in jail like one of the poor little animals she fought so hard to save. I grabbed my keys, hurried downstairs and toward my van. I would go downtown and see what all the fuss was about.

The brittle nighttime air froze the breath in my lungs as soon as I stepped outside. I pulled my scarf tighter around my neck and ran to my van. I cranked the heat. Cold air blew through the heating vents.

"Come on!" I pulled my hands away from the vents, wishing more than anything that I'd remembered my gloves. There was nothing I could do about it now. I grabbed a towel from the back and threw it over the steering wheel, so the plastic wouldn't feel like ice against my hands.

I started down the street like a bloodhound on the scent for quarry. As soon as I turned out of my neighborhood I spotted the plume of smoke rising between the towers of downtown. My heart went ice cold, joining in the rest of my body, as the severity of the situation fell over me. A bomb had gone off—and it had been a big one, not the chemistry class variety. In the distance, sirens wailed. A police car blurred past.

Harrison Developers. That's where Parker said the explosion happened.

The company had been in the news a lot lately. James Harrison, the company's CEO, had deep pockets and a huge ego. A performing arts center in neighboring Virginia Beach was named after him, as well as a minor league baseball stadium.

I'd met the man once, by accident really. I attended a benefit dinner with Riley and, in a moment of oblivion, spilled my punch right on the man's tuxedo. The rich fifty-something had twittered around—his grey comb-over never moving once during the process, I might add. He'd stared at his stained shirt before proclaiming me a "stupid woman." I'd tried to tell him a great solution for getting out stains, one I used all the time at crime scenes. That's when he started muttering that he was going to call the police. Riley had politely led me away, doing his customary headshake.

Riley and I have known each other seven months, and I still don't think he knows what to do with me. Of course, he is Mr. Straight Laced, one who gave up a prestigious job with a top law firm in order to help the less fortunate. Sometimes I wish I could just have a touch of his goodness.

Headlights glared in my rearview mirror. I readjusted it and cast aside my not-so-nice thoughts about tailgaters and what I'd like to do to them. I took side streets around traffic, following the smoke as far as I could. Roadblocks stopped me at least six blocks before I reached the scene.

I circled back around and found a parking space on the street. As I pulled into the parallel spot, the car with the glaring headlights sped past. Was someone following me? *Why* would someone be following me? I had one answer: Parker. I bet he had one of his men tailing me, hoping I'd lead them to Sierra.

I slammed my car door shut and stomped away from my car, ready to give Parker a piece of my mind. But as I approached the roadblocks, the reality of what had happened hit me. I prayed no one had been inside the building when the explosion happened. Whoever was behind this had set the device to detonate at night, when everyone was at home with their families.

That sounded like... something someone with a heart would do. My throat tightened. Not Sierra, though...right?

I walked through the downtown business area. Several tall office buildings stood along the streets. Some of the structures were old, faded and chipped while others were newer, sleeker and more ornate. I knew from being down here before that none of the other buildings were as tall or eye-catching as the Harrison Developers building. The building, finished in marble and sculpted in detail in everything from the windowsills to the ritzy front entryway, had stood like a crown in the downtown area.

A crowd had already gathered to watch the tragedy unfold as if it were a TV crime drama. I couldn't quite understand people's fascination with the morbid. My theory was that we'd all become hardened and desensitized to it because of the gruesome crime shows on TV. We'd confused reality with fiction.

A fire truck, several police cars and some unmarked sedans were parked at various angles around the building. The smell of smoke and dust and ashes hung heavy in the air, tingling my nose and making me cough.

I craned my neck to see more and gasped at what stood—or didn't stand, I should say—in the distance. The seven-story building in front of me looked like it had been part of a war zone. I supposed it had. Half of the structure lay crumbled at the ground. The building's innards—where the offices used to be—were now exposed, along with metal beams, concrete and wires.

I closed my eyes a moment. *Lord, what kind of monster would do something like this?*

I opened my eyes again as an ambulance screamed onto the scene. In the distance, I spotted Parker on his cell phone again and the two other suits—Wilkerson and Stephens, I think—chatted with police officers. I shoved my hands into the pockets of my puffy coat, just then noticing how my fingers felt like ice cubes.

Everything seemed surreal, like something out of a movie. Only this movie wouldn't be over, and I wouldn't return to life as always when I stepped from the theater. Tragedy had occurred. Lives would be changed by this. Certainly the landscape of the city had been.

If the building had been one other than Harrison Developers, I might have wondered if this was an act of terrorism. The people around me wondered that also.

"Is this another 9-11?" someone behind me whispered.

"A holy jihad maybe. I knew an attack would happen on American soil again. I just knew it," a female responded.

"Why would someone hate America so much?" still someone else whispered.

If I had to bet, this wasn't your traditional terrorism. If anything, it was eco-terrorism.

Again, Sierra's face flashed through my mind. I desperately hoped my friend had nothing to do with this, that people had witnessed her this evening at some march for animal rights. I'd even take one of her why-people-are-stupid stories over this.

Chills raced up my spine but not from the cold. I still had that feeling of being watched. I turned and scanned the crowd but saw no one who looked particularly villainous. Mostly the crowd consisted of college kids who'd probably been out clubbing, a few businessmen, a man walking his bulldog, a teenage girl standing with a camera around her neck.

Could the person who'd done this be standing in the crowd right now? Were they watching their destruction unfold? We'd read case studies about this in one of my forensic classes at college. The smartest criminals were those who blended in, which could mean anyone in this crowd could be guilty. I swung my gaze back to the devastation in front of me.

Parker spotted me and scowled. He purposefully strode my way. "What are you doing here, Gabby?"

"I had to see for myself." I rubbed my nose, which felt like an ice cube. "It's horrible, Parker. Heartbreaking that someone could be this twisted, and it's a near miracle that no one was killed. Sierra could never do something like this."

He scowled again and looked both ways. Finally, he pulled me over the police line where no one could hear our conversation. "If you know anything..."

"I don't. I swear." I dropped any pretenses and spoke from my heart. "All I know is that Sierra would never do this. She's too smart and her heart is too big."

"That's not what the evidence is telling us. You're a scientist. Think about it, Nancy Drew." Nancy Drew dripped with sarcasm.

I bit my lip. I didn't want to think about what the evidence was saying. Nor did I want Parker calling me by my old nickname. He'd lost that right when we broke up. This wasn't the time for that discussion, though. I looked back at the building. "Is everyone okay? Was anyone inside?"

"No, thankfully everyone was gone for the day, except for a janitor but he wasn't hurt. He was working in the other side of the building and managed to get out in time." Parker rubbed his chin. "Do you have any idea where Sierra is?"

I shook my head. We'd been over this before, hadn't we? "None. Why do you look like you don't believe me?"

"Because I know how loyal you are."

"Being loyal is a good thing."

"Not if it impedes an investigation."

"I'm not impeding an investigation. And while I'm thinking of it, you really don't have to have one of your men following me."

His gaze flickered. "I don't."

"Then what was up with the headlights on my way here?"

He shrugged. "You tell me. Have you gotten yourself in another pickle?"

I feigned shock. "I would never. And there was a car following me. I still think you put one of your men on me."

"You should go home, Gabby." His voice sounded weary and maybe a touch concerned.

"I'm fine." I rubbed my arms again, thinking about how bitterly cold the weather felt.

"No, I mean you should go home in case Sierra comes back."

I scowled. Of course. I should go home because that fit his plan, not because he was concerned about me. The exact reason we'd broken up. Maybe I would go home, but it wouldn't be because Parker had told me to.

He placed his hand on my elbow and led me back to the other side of the police line.

"There's nothing to see here," Parker growled.

Did he say that to me or to the crowd or both?

I took one last glance at the building, one that had once stood like an urban masterpiece on this busy corner. All it had taken was one little device called a bomb to cause the whole structure to crumble.

I decided to get out of the cold and go home. I'd return to my original plan of snuggling under my blanket and doing happy feet air dances. Staring at these ruins would do me no good.

Back in my car, I noticed those headlights behind me again. If it wasn't one of Parker's comrades, then who was driving that car? And should I even go home and show whomever it was where I lived? Or maybe I was beginning to lose it, imagining all of this.

I swerved to the left, taking a side street. I held my breath, watching the car behind me. The sedan continued straight.

I slowed down, shaking my head and chuckling. Maybe I *was* losing it.

I circled the block until I pulled up to the old Victorian that had been cut up into five little apartments. Home sweet home.

When I stepped inside, I couldn't help but think about Sierra. The battle raged inside me. Was she guilty or not? And why wasn't she home yet? It was, I checked my watch, past midnight. The girl should be home by now. She was not a night owl, by any stretch of the imagination. Without sleep, she turned into Mrs. Cranky Pants.

I stared at Sierra's door to my left. I had a key to her place, and I'd never used it before. How would she feel about me going into her apartment? In this situation, I think she'd be just fine with it.

I fingered her key on my oversized ring. I was going to do it. I just needed to check inside her place to make sure everything was okay, to make sure there were no signs that something terrible had happened to her. I was doing this to look out for her best interests, not to snoop. If something was wrong, Sierra would thank me for this.

I slipped her key into the lock. The door clicked open. I pushed past the beads that my friend had strung from her doorframe. Immediately, the scent of incense hit me. And she'd left her whale music playing in the background.

Strange, very strange.

I closed the door behind me and scanned the room. Everything appeared to be in place. There were no signs of struggle, though the music and earthy-smelling sage incense made me think she'd left in a hurry. Why would she leave in a hurry?

Because she wanted to escape the authorities before they caught her maybe?

What kind of friend was I, questioning Sierra's innocence? Friends didn't question friends like this.

I'd just take a quick peruse through her place to make sure everything was okay, then I'd leave and mind my own business.

Like I ever minded my own business.

I quickly checked her bedroom, where everything was in place. I ignored the images of injured animals that plastered her walls. Apparently, those pictures compelled her to fight even harder for animal's rights. Maybe it was the same reasoning that caused Christians to hang crosses on their walls, a reminder of Christ's suffering and our need for a life change.

Her bathroom looked as clean as ever. I even checked her closets. All clear.

There was no sign that a killer lived here.

I'd leave and go back to my evening.

As I breezed through the living room, a paper sticking out from under the couch caught my eye. I backed up and tugged it from under the cushions. It was probably nothing.

I caught my breath when I read the title of the paper packet.

"Building Bombs and How to Use Them. Published by the National Federation for a Cleaner Earth."

Holy schnikies. What had my friend gotten herself into?

CHAPTER 4

I shoved the papers under my arm and decided my best option was to simply escape Sierra's apartment, go upstairs to my couch and sit dumbfounded there for a bit until reality sunk its sharp teeth into my hard head.

In my haste to evacuate, I didn't even notice the looming figure stepping into my apartment building until I collided with him. The telltale papers in my arms scattered everywhere.

"Whoa, where's the fire?"

I looked up and relief momentarily softened my uptight muscles as Riley came into view. He wore jeans, a sky blue sweater and a sporty black leather coat that accentuated his broad shoulders. His brown hair looked tousled, like the wind had whipped through it on his walk from the car. His blue eyes looked as piercing, yet soft as ever. At his feet sat a small black suitcase.

I was so glad to see him that I threw my arms around him. "Riley. You're not supposed to be here."

He wrapped his arms around me a moment before pulling back. His gaze searched mine a moment before he took a step back. "I heard we might be getting some snow so I decided to come home early. What's going on?"

"Going on? What makes you think something is going on?"

He shrugged. "Oh, I don't know. The suspicious look in your eyes as you snuck from Sierra's apartment maybe?"

I decided to go with the truth. You knew the situation was serious when I abandoned my snarkiness in favor of acting mature instead. "I think Sierra's in trouble. Big trouble. Trouble that I'm not sure I can help her out of."

An amused sparkle lit his gaze. "Let me guess. But you're going to try by stealing evidence?"

How'd he know? "Something like that."

His eyes widened, and he grasped the sides of my arms until I locked gazes with him. "I was kidding, Gabby. But I have the feeling you're not. What's going on?"

I nodded toward the floor. "Help me pick up these papers before the feds get back and then I'll explain."

He blanched. "The feds?"

"Long story." I let out the breath I held, wondering if perhaps this was just an awful dream. I knew it wasn't.

I couldn't ignore the tinge of electricity that zapped me as our hands collided on the floor in my mad rush to pick up the papers I'd dropped. Riley had always had that effect on me, like it or not. I equate Riley to chocolate—a habit I try to break myself of, but my willpower is never quite strong enough. Nothing seemed to deter my heart from beating double-time whenever I saw him.

Riley paused and narrowed his eyes at a piece of paper in his hands. "Building Bombs and How to Use Them? What is this?"

If only I knew... "I don't know but it doesn't look good."

"I'd say." He sounded awfully lawyer-ish.

I paused—froze, really, as my conscience finally caught up with my impulsiveness. "I have to call the FBI." My heart felt heavy as the words scattered from my mouth. I couldn't betray my friend. There had to be another way...

"Why do you need to call the FBI?"

My gaze skittered up to his. "They think Sierra is responsible for the explosion downtown, as well as the fire at a housing development in Chesapeake."

"What?" Surprise showed across Riley's face, from his wide eyes to his gaping mouth.

I nodded. "It's true. I can't take these things and pretend they don't exist. But I know Sierra didn't do this, Riley. I know it." I lowered my head. "I don't know what to do."

He took my hands, which were now trembling, causing the papers to clap together. "Let's go talk first. I need to know what's going on. All of it."

We trudged upstairs to my apartment, and I spilled everything to Riley. He was just that kind of guy. The kind that I could easily share my entire heart with, if there was ever the proper invitation. But Riley was out of my league. I knew that. We were on different levels however you looked at it. Every day, I tried to kill that nagging bit of hope that remained in me concerning a relationship with him. Why was it that the things that were unobtainable were always the things people wanted the most?

Riley soaked in everything I told him, his gaze turning more serious by the moment. "You're right. You do need to give this to the FBI. You don't want to find yourself in trouble for taking potential evidence. But I'm with you about Sierra. She wouldn't do this."

"Then where is she? What if that Henry guy pulled her into the middle of something?"

"She's smart, Gabby. This is all going to be okay. But if you get yourself implicated in any way, you won't be of any help to her."

Riley knew me all too well. Probably all of those times I'd almost gotten him killed along with me had made him a quick study.

The important thing at the moment was that he agreed with me. Sierra couldn't be responsible for any of this. My racing heart slowed for a moment. It was going to be okay. Everything would be okay.

My phone jangled. I snatched it from the end table beside me and shoved it to my ear. "Hello?"

A crackle greeted me. Bad connection. "Hello?" I repeated.

"Gabby, it's me."

I sat up straight. I'd hardly recognized the quick, whispered voice. "Sierra?"

Riley leaned toward me, straining his ear toward the phone.

"Listen, I –" Static broke through. "...name's Lydia."

"Lydia? What about Lydia? Lydia who?"

Syllables of words broke through, but nothing I could make out.

"Sierra, I can't understand you. What's going on? Where are you?"

"I...Gabby—sorry."

"Sorry? Sorry about what—?"

Sierra didn't answer. The phone line went dead.

I looked at Riley and bit back a frown. The bad feeling in my gut turned into an all-out disaster. What had Sierra gotten herself into?

CHAPTER 5

I ran my hand over my face, flabbergasted, exhausted and curious, all in one huge gust of emotions. "Lydia. That's the only word I could make out. How am I supposed to find some random woman named Lydia?"

Riley leaned toward me, the picture of calm, cool and collected—as always. "Maybe she was talking about Lydia Harrison, the wife of James Harrison."

I perked, even more enamored with the man in front of me. "You're brilliant. Now, how am I going to track down Lydia Harrison?"

"You've tracked down people who were far harder to find, Gabby. I'm sure you'll locate Lydia."

I cast a quick glance at Riley, unsure if I'd heard him correctly. "I can't believe you're not discouraging me from this."

He shrugged. "I know you well enough to know that discouraging you will do no good."

I threw my head back into the couch, disbelief settling over me. Riley held out his arm. "Come here."

I gladly fell into his arms. Images of our rocky relationship played in my mind. Just as we'd been on the brink of a relationship—or so I'd thought—his fiancée had shown up. Okay, she was an ex-fiancée who hadn't gotten the message yet. Good old Riley had to give their relationship another shot, though. That's when I started dating Parker. But then Parker fell for his new partner. Then I met Chad, who's now my business partner. Our relationship is comfortable and flirty, but deep down I know that Chad isn't Riley. Sounds like a confusing mess, huh?

And I know I need therapy. Lots of therapy. Maybe some electric shock. Water boarding?

Of course, my relationship problems were the least of my concerns at the moment. Nice distraction, though, Riley. For just a moment, I'd forgotten the problems at hand as I relished Riley's strength.

"I'm sure Lydia's address is unlisted. Her husband's office has now been demolished by a bomb, so I can't snoop there. And the feds are swarming anything vaguely connected with the company. They'll never let me get close."

Riley said nothing. Which made me pull my head back and look him in the eye. "You know something?"

He hesitated. "She's on the board for the nonprofit Arms of Love. I'm sure you can get in contact with her through that."

I sat up straight. "You know her?"

Riley shook his head. "No, but I've seen her at different events around town."

I leaned toward him, curious now. "What do you know about her?"

"She's one of those mover and shaker types. There's something about her that I've never quite trusted, though, Gabby. I can't put my finger on it. On the surface, she seems like the perfect citizen. But there's something in her gaze that makes me cautious."

"Your gut feeling is rarely wrong."

He twisted his lips like he needed to say something but his mouth wasn't cooperating. "There's something else, Gabby."

"What's that?"

"Arms of Love has a fundraiser tomorrow evening that I'm going to be participating in."

Delight sizzled up my spine. "A fundraiser? What is it? A concert? Dinner?"

He licked his lips, suddenly looking ill at ease. "It's a bachelor auction."

I pulled back in surprise. "A bachelor auction? You're being auctioned off?"

He ran a hand through his hair and left half of it standing on end. "I didn't want to do it, but Lydia convinced me that I should. It's for a good cause."

"Lydia convinced you? It sounds like you do know her." *Tamp down the jealousy, Gabby. Tamp, tamp, tamp.*

He shook his head. "No, not really. Like I said, we've rubbed elbows at a few of the same events. That's it."

I leaned back into the couch, a little too hard. "Well, I'll be. I would have never guessed in a million years that you'd participate in a bachelor auction." I hoped he caught the glimmer in my eyes when I tilted my head toward him. "Is it too late for me to get a ticket?"

***

How did one find ecoterrorist groups? I couldn't simply look them up in the phonebook and give them a call. Nor did people generally hang signs on their doors or put titles on their nametags proclaiming that they were environmental freaks. However, wouldn't someone who was crazy about keeping the earth clean possibly belong to what looked like a peaceful, save-the-planet group?

An Internet search last night had led me to one such group, and it just so happened that they were doing a presentation at a local library today on "Ways to Live Greener." Of course, I'd decided that I needed to attend that meeting, scope out the people who attended and maybe befriend the instructor afterward. I needed to find out if Sierra was associated with the group and, if so, if anyone knew where she was right now. It was the only place I could think of to start my investigation. I narrowed my options down to the facts that I either needed to find Sierra or find who'd bombed Harrison Developers.

As I drove to the meeting, I reflected on the first time I ever met Sierra.

I'd just moved into the apartment building. My mother had passed away two months earlier from cancer. My crime scene cleaning business was just taking off, and Sierra'd just been hired by a local nonprofit—Paws and Fur Balls. I walked down the stairs of the apartment building wearing a new leather jacket and eating a hamburger. She'd just come from picketing a local restaurant and wore a chicken costume. We'd stared each other down for several moments. Finally, I'd said, "What's up with the chicken costume?" just as she'd said, "Why are you dressed in a cow?"

"I'm not dressed like a cow."

"I didn't say like a cow. I said *in* a cow."

I looked at my jacket. "Really? In a cow?"

"There are kinder ways of doing things."

"And there are more dignified ways of doing things." I pointed to her costume.

She looked down at her outfit and finally started laughing. "You're right. I do look ridiculous. It's always the newbies in the company who are stuck looking like chickens."

"Remind me not to ever work for your company."

She extended her hand. "I'm Sierra, an animal rights activist. And I'll remind you not to work for my company if you remind me not to work for yours."

"You don't even know what I do."

She waved a hand in front of her face. "No, but whatever it is it's left you smelling terrible."

I'd just come from a particularly gruesome scene—a knife fight between two men in a kitchen. One of them had died, and tile floor didn't exactly absorb anything leftover from the battle, so I'd had puddles of—never mind, actually. It's pretty gross. Needless to say, the smell there had seeped into my hair and skin. Even after scrubbing myself clean and protecting my clothes with a Hazmat suit, the smell remained. Some scenes were just like that.

"That's rude."

"Tell that to the cow you're wearing."

I couldn't help but laugh. And laugh. I don't know what it was about the situation that struck me as so funny, but it tickled my funny bone. Sierra's tough façade cracked also and she began laughing with me.

Finally, I returned the gesture and reached for her outstretched hand. "I'm Gabby, your new neighbor."

"It's about time we got someone normal living in this building."

Normal? She thought of me as normal? I pointed to myself in shock.

"Living next door, I've got the self-absorbed radio talk show host who thinks he can get any woman he wants when he really can't. A crazy woman who writes mysteries and likes to act out her murder scenes lives upstairs. The man who used to live in your apartment claimed to be a comedian, only he wasn't funny—unless there's something hilarious about chicken nuggets that I'm totally missing. And the empty apartment across the hall from you? A mime."

"Really?"

"Really. Even without make-up on, he used to only communicate using his body language. Finally one day I communicated with him using my body language and plucked him on the forehead."

"You plucked a mime?"

"I figured it was the only way I'd ever get him to talk. Besides, he'd just flushed a goldfish down the toilet—only the fish was still alive. How can someone live with themselves after doing that?"

"Did it work? Did he talk afterward?"

"No, he just acted like he was crying."

And that was it. After that day we were best friends. I knew if I found someone who thought I was normal that I needed to hold tight to them. Sierra and I didn't always see eye to eye, but we'd been there for each other in tough times—through breakups with no-good boyfriends, low crime rates (also known as high unemployment in my circles) and the death of a pig at the local zoo.

Back in the present, I walked into the library and surveyed the merry group of contentious people there. Eight people had gathered, sipping on coffee in Styrofoam cups as they waited. Styrofoam? Really? Earth-conscious people sipping on drinks from a product that clogged up the landfills should have been my first sign that something was off.

Just as I walked in, the instructor stood and walked to the podium. She was a heavyset woman in her thirties probably. Her clothes appeared to be made of henna and her hair was held back with an off-white scarf that made it appear more like she had a head wound. No make up, hippie-style sandals on her feet, and she drank out of a sensible, re-usable coffee mug.

Would Henry be here? He was one of those people passionate about the environment. But he was smart enough not to show his face here when the authorities most likely would look for him in connection with what had happened yesterday. Sure, he seemed like a freak on the outside, but I knew the guy had once worked in construction until the economy went south. Apparently now he took odd jobs to pay his bills. And he began going overboard with the dumpster diving, Freegan mentality.

Don't get me wrong here. I'm all for being responsible when it comes to taking care of the earth. I just think some people can go overboard with it. For instance, I really had no desire to set my thermostat to 78 degrees in the summer or to boycott drinking straws because they weren't biodegradable or to even start using public transportation to ease up on carbon emissions. And that's that.

The instructor—I think her name was Fiona?— began her lecture. I grabbed the water bottle from my purse and took a sip. I stared at the bottle for a moment, feeling guilty for a fraction of a second that I hadn't brought a reusable one. Next time, I assured myself. Next time.

Instead of listening, I watched the crowd. A few people nodded enthusiastically as Fiona preached about Mother Earth. A couple looked bored. Two people took notes.

The thing about passionate people was that, even though they had their ideals that they stuck with most of the time, everyone messed up sometimes. Environmentalists used Styrofoam cups. Animal rights activists ate something made with an egg. Christians told a lie. Politicians kept a promise. It was human nature, I'd learned. Not that I excused the hypocrisy. I simply had to acknowledge that it exists everywhere, no matter how good the intentions or the person.

A man sitting at the back of the crowd caught my eye. He was what I referred to as a "mouth breather." Instead of breathing through his nose—like most people—he sucked in air and expelled through his mouth, giving him a slightly dazed appearance with his mouth constantly agape. Why did he look out of place? What about him caught my eye?

Perhaps it was his leather shoes. The disposable water bottle at the base of his chair. The sweat across his forehead. The way his foot tap-tap-tapped the floor.

"And you in the back? What do you plan on doing for Mother Earth this week?"

I snapped my head toward the voice and saw Fiona staring at me. Great. This is where it would have come in handy to pay attention. I cleared my throat and brushed a crumb from my "It's Not Rocket Surgery" T-shirt.

"Well..." Well, what? I tried to think fast. "This week I will," I looked at the bottle in my hands, "throw all of my water bottles away?"

At least three people in the room gasped, and I realized what I'd said.

"I mean, I won't throw them away. First I'll drink them. Then I'll throw them away. I mean, recycle them. Then I'll only use reusable bottles for the rest of my life. Unless I'm on a road trip and forget one, and then I'll be forced to buy one at the gas station. But you get the point."

Not believable, Gabby. Not believable.

The people giving me dirty looks turned their attention to the man at the back. "And you, sir?" Fiona asked him.

He wiped the sweat from his forehead using a tissue. "I'm going to get a compost bin for my backyard."

His answer seemed to please the masses, because smiles stretched over their faces now. Compost bin? Really? What was he going to put in that bin? Evidence of a crime, perhaps?

I had no reason to believe he was guilty of any crime, other than the fact that he appeared nervous and out of place. I needed to find out what that man was doing here at this meeting because I had a feeling his intentions weren't simply to pick up some tips.

The meeting couldn't have ended quickly enough for me. The man at the back stood and started toward the door. I reached out to touch his arm and stop him, but Fiona called to me. I froze, quickly trying to think of some quick responses in case she asked me for more ways I could help the environment this week. Solar panels? Not on my apartment building. Compost pile? I was sure that was against my landlord's rules. I could tell her that I'd cut down on the chemicals I used when cleaning up after dead bodies. That usually shut people up pretty quickly.

"I can't help but think you seem out of place. Is there something I can help you with? You're not a reporter, are you?"

"A reporter? No. Why would you ask that?"

She tried to shrug it off. "No reason, really. I've just gotten a couple of phone calls after everything that's happened in this area over the past few days."

Casual. Appear casual, Gabby. "Everything that's happened?"

She waved her hand in the air, trying too hard to appear nonchalant. "With the housing development fire and such. You know everyone thinks it was done by an environmental group protesting the use of wetlands."

I glanced at the door and saw the man slip out. Rats. I'd missed him. Had there been a class sign-in sheet? Had he signed it?

"That fire was terrible. Was it done by an environmental group?"

"Of course not! That's ridiculous. Do you know how bad fires are for the environment? It just wouldn't make sense, not with global warming and all." She studied my face, an edge of distrust creeping in. "So you are a reporter?"

I shook my head. "Nope. Not a reporter. I am trying to track down some information, though."

"What information would that be?" The woman looked tenser than a tightrope. Her voice had inched upward in pitch with each response, and lines had formed around her eyes now.

I pulled out a picture of Sierra. "Do you know this woman?"

The woman didn't even blink. "That's Sierra Nakamura. Yes, I do know her. Why do you ask?"

"Was she a part of this group?"

Fiona picked up a Styrofoam cup someone left on the table and crushed it with her hand before tossing it in the wastebasket. "No, not at all. Being involved with animals and the environment would have spread her too thin. She did great work for the animals in the area."

"How did you know her then?"

Her eyes shifted a moment. "I try to help out the nonprofit she works for. I go to their fundraisers and such. Plus, sometimes the environment and animal rights can go hand in hand. Take that housing development, for instance. By them building there, they endangered the environment, which then endangered wildlife. By destroying those wetlands, we're losing all hope that oysters, trout and even river otters will ever return to the area. In fact, there have been fish kills and we believe it's been caused by wetland destruction in the area."

Well, that would explain Sierra's involvement. This wasn't about the environment for her. It was about the animals affected by the environment. The rest of the group filed out, so I readjusted my stance, in no hurry to leave now. "If I wanted to find out if there were ecoterrorists in this area, how would I do that?"

Fiona shook her head and raised her hands in the air, causing all of her beaded bracelets to tumble toward her elbows. Exasperation strained her voice "I wouldn't know. Why are you asking me?"

"Don't you have any fringe members of your group, members who go a little overboard sometimes?"

"Every group has those, I suppose." Not only had her voice risen in pitch, but now all of her words tumbled together. I was getting to her. The question was—why?

"Of course they do. Who in your group is like that?"

She narrowed her eyes at me before shifting her gaze to the door. I knew that look. She was plotting her escape. "Who are you again?"

I took a slight step to the right, blocking the exit. "I'm Gabby St. Claire."

"Are you a detective?" The way she said "detective" made it sound like a bad word.

I shook my head, knowing I needed to put her at ease if I hoped to get any information from her. "I'm a crime scene cleaner."

Her eyes flashed with recognition simultaneous with her shoulders drooping in relief. "That's why you look familiar. I read that article in the paper about you a while back."

Ah, the article again. The local newspaper had actually used it on the front page. A photographer had tailed me for a day, taking pictures of me in my Hazmat suit. It mentioned that I'd helped the local police in a couple of cases recently. They'd even gotten comments from some local police detectives who had surprisingly kind things to say about me.

I was surprised by the number of people who'd read that article. I still had people telling me how much they enjoyed the piece, as if I'd written it myself. The coffee shop across the street from my home, The Grounds, had even framed a copy and put it on the wall there.

I didn't complain. Any way I could spread the word about my business would help me. Even a couple of my college professors had seemed impressed.

Fiona lowered her voice. "I don't want any trouble. No one I know was behind the fire—at least not to my knowledge."

"Are there any names you want to give me?"

She looked from side to side again, even though we were the only ones in the room. "You're a friend of Sierra's, you said?"

I nodded. "She's my best friend, and I want to make sure she doesn't get blamed for something she didn't do."

She stepped closer, the smell of herbs drifting upward with her. "Look, I wouldn't tell just anyone this, but since you're a friend of Sierra's, I can assume you're trustworthy."

"I like to think so."

She leaned even closer. "Bruce Watkins. He's over the top sometimes and seems to have some kind of vendetta against anyone who does anything he deems inappropriate. I want to see a cleaner earth, too. But not at the expense of people's lives."

"So he's said something that would indicate he's capable of violence then?"

She stepped back and shrugged. "Maybe he's all talk. You know how we can all say foolish things in the heat of the moment sometimes. I can't prove he's ever actually acted out on any of his threats."

"Where can I find Bruce Watkins?"

"He works for a gas station in Norfolk. That one on the corner of Tidewater Drive and Ballard Street."

"Thanks, Fiona. One more thing. Do you have any idea who that man was who sat in the back?"

She shook her head. "Never seen him before. Let me see if he signed up for my newsletter." She plucked a sheet of paper from the table nearby and her gaze scanned the list. "I can't be 100 percent sure, but I think his name is Clifford Reynolds."

Great, I had two names. It was a start.

I glanced at my watch. I didn't have time to track them now, though. Right now I had to get home and get dressed for the bachelor auction this evening.

CHAPTER 6

Pushing my way through the crowds milling around the convention center that evening, I felt unusually alone. Most often when I went on these sleuthing expeditions, I had Sierra, Chad or Riley tagging along with me. Right now, it was just me in a maze of people who wore expensive perfume and flaunted their money with more pride than a peacock spreading its feathers. There was just as much schmoozing as there was boozing, and people seemed more than willing to throw their money at anything that might gain them attention including expensive finger foods and a crazy-expensive raffle. All the profits did go to a local children's hospital.

I smoothed the little black dress I wore—a simple, sleeveless number with an elegant v-neck and a hem that stopped above my knees—and pulled a loose red curl behind my ear, praying my French twist would hold until the evening was over. This wasn't my thing. I was more of a baseball game and hot dogs kind of girl. Here, I felt out of my league.

I sipped on some punch and tried to blend in and look casual. I kept my eyes open for Lydia Harrison in the process. I'd found a few photos of her from various past events on the Internet, so I had an idea of what she looked like—like every other blonde, beautiful, rich woman who was out there. From the pictures I'd seen online, she had shoulder-length hair, pleasant, unremarkable facial features, a trim body, and impeccable taste in clothing. She was what was known as a "mover and shaker" in the community, involved in several nonprofits and charities. As chairperson of this event, she was no doubt fluttering around backstage, trying to get everything organized.

I'm doing this for you, Sierra. I don't know what you've gotten yourself into, but I'm going to figure it out, my friend.

My inner circle was like family to me, and I didn't like it when people messed with the people I loved. When Parker had come back to my apartment last night, I'd had no choice but to turn over the bomb-making manual, along with offering my insistence that there was an explanation for why Sierra had it. Maybe she'd bought it at the thrift store to use as kindling for her fireplace—only, Sierra didn't have a fireplace.

I still didn't know why Sierra might have had the manual, nor could I fathom an acceptable reason.

I eyed the crowd, wondering if someone in the room knew something about the explosion yesterday. After all, many of those attending had connections with Harrison Developers. I'd gathered that much from a few of the conversations I'd overheard. Lydia had done a good job recruiting her circle of influence.

Before I had a chance to ponder very long, the band stopped and Lydia Harrison appeared behind the microphone to announce the start of the bachelor auction. She wasn't one to tap the microphone before she started. No, she was the type who was confident that the equipment would work for her and, if it didn't, that someone would jump in to fix it while she remained unflustered.

"We're here tonight to raise money for some great children over at our local hospital," she started. "What better way to raise money than by giving all of you the chance to win dates with some handsome men." She paused. "And women, we do have some handsome men. I mean, wow. You're going to be blown away."

I studied her a moment. She looked just as I remembered—pretty with coiffed blonde hair, perfect skin and a well-kept body. If I had to guess, she was probably in her early 40s. What could this woman know about the explosions? About Sierra? The two didn't seem the types to interact with each other.

She excused herself as an auctioneer came onto the stage. All of the women crowded toward the front, bidding paddles in hand. Myself included, though I felt ridiculous, like I was at some kind of grown-up sorority party.

The first few bachelors had fun with the auction. One was a doctor, the next a model. They'd obviously brought little fan clubs with them, women who offered wolf whistles as if this were a strip club instead of a

$100 a ticket event. I hardly noticed, though. I wanted to see Riley. As a participant in this event, he'd gotten one free ticket—and that's how I'd gotten in.

Finally, he appeared on stage. Just the sight of him in a tuxedo nearly took my breath away. Tall and lean with the build of a runner. Dark hair that was just a little too long for his profession. Blue eyes that could melt my heart. I could spend the rest of my life with that man. I'm pretty sure I was destined to be the best friend, though. Always the best friend.

I bit my lip, watching Riley carefully. No, he wasn't the flashy type who liked to be center of attention. But he was confident and smart and down to earth. I couldn't help but blink in surprise as he swerved on his heel, put his hands to hips and grinned, looking as if he'd had a past career walking the runway or something. The women around me loved it. They offered catcalls and whistles.

What had gotten into my Riley?

He lowered his head and laughed at the reaction of the crowd—but only for a second. Then his head popped back up again. That one action had shown his character though—handsome, but humble; confident, but kind; fearless, but centered.

The bidding started fast and furious. My eyebrows flickered up. It wasn't usual that I was frozen in shock. Right now, I was. Who was this person Riley had been hiding from me?

I held up my paddle. "$500."

Another paddle shot up in the distance. "$550."

I cut my gaze in the direction of the other bidder. Was it Lydia Harrison? I couldn't be sure. I raised my bidding tool again. "$600."

"$650." It was the same woman. Lydia, perhaps?

I'd come into this not knowing what to expect and not entirely expecting to bid on anyone. But $700? I knew it was for a good cause, but I was on a budget. I couldn't compete with the wealthy women around me. Nor could I give up my rent money just to prove myself.

Despite that, my hand shot up. "$700."

It almost seemed like a collective gasp sounded around me. The other men had only garnered a couple hundred dollars each. Riley was a hot commodity, apparently.

The other woman—Lydia, I was sure of it now—outbid me again. "$1000."

With firm resolve that I couldn't beat this woman, I crossed my arms, another plan stewing in my mind. Maybe Riley should go on a date with Lydia. It was terrible the ulterior motives that poked their ugly heads up, begging for my attention. But I needed to talk to Lydia, and Riley had just been auctioned off to her.

I glanced around and noticed that people were watching me, waiting to see if I was going to bid again. With a grin, I held up my hands in surrender. People cheered as Lydia darted on stage, grabbed Riley's hand and raised it in victory. Riley laughed and gave her a side hug. I had to admit that a surge of jealousy rushed through me.

Jealousy. Hm. I wasn't supposed to be jealous, now was I? I was new at this Christian thing, but I'm pretty sure jealousy had no place in my life. I'd do my best to douse it out.

Lord, any help here would be awesome, though.

Another thought hit me. Lydia was still married, wasn't she? Mr. Perfect Christian Riley Thomas couldn't go out on a date with a married woman…right? Hm. The moral dilemma echoed in my mind as the next bachelor appeared. The rest of the auction was a blur.

As soon as the bidding ended, I wove through the crowd toward Lydia and extended my hand to her. "Congratulations."

She raised a thin, finely plucked brow. "I guess the best lady won."

There was a part of me that wanted to rip the smug look right off of her face. But I didn't. Instead, I smiled. "I'm sorry to hear about your husband's troubles lately."

Her smug look disappeared without any violence on my end. Perfect. "Soon to be ex husband. And yes, it was tragic. Thankfully no one was hurt, right?"

I caught Riley approaching in the distance. My opportunity to bring up Sierra was quickly diminishing. I opened my mouth to say something—I wasn't sure what, only that it would undeniably be brilliant—when Riley appeared with a grin. I thought the grin was directed toward me, but suddenly Lydia slipped her arm around him. I stopped my mouth from gaping open. I'm pretty sure Riley did the same. Or did he?

"I got the best looking guy up there. That was my plan all along. That and to give away as much money as I could to help the kiddos."

How generous of her.

"I'm flattered," Riley muttered. "But I thought the agreement when I signed up for this was that married women weren't allowed to participate. You've put me in an awkward position, Ms. Harrison."

Go Riley. Go Riley. I mentally did the Cabbage Patch dance. I knew he'd stand up for his principles.

"I sign the divorce papers this week, darling. I'll make sure our date is after that. You've got morals. Just one more thing that makes you adorable." She placed her hand on his chest and a husky giggle escaped. Or was it more of a growl, like that of a lioness claiming her territory?

"Well, I'll be more comfortable with the arrangement after the divorce is finalized."

She ran a finger over his cheek. "Oh, it will be. I've been counting down the days until I can distance myself from that man, and it's finally in reach. I can already taste my freedom."

I crossed my arms over my chest. "He couldn't be that bad, could he?"

The scowl appearing on Lydia's face was all the answer I needed, I suppose. "You have no idea. All he cared about was his work. He treated his stupid cars better than he treated me."

My arm muscles softened some. "I'm sorry to hear that. It must have been very difficult."

The scowl disappeared. "It's nearly done with now, and I don't want to talk about him anymore." She looped her arm through Riley's. "I'll be in touch. Thanks for being such a good sport."

As she sashayed away, I glanced up at Riley and we shared a shrug.

I cleared my throat, trying to swallow the bitter taste in my mouth. "As Lydia said, I guess the best girl won."

Riley looked down at me. Was I just imagining it or did his eyes soften? "Then why am I going on a date with Lydia instead of you?"

My cheeks actually warmed. Was Riley flirting?

"You're obviously too expensive for a girl like me."

He titled his head. "It depends on how you define wealth." He squeezed my arm. "There are things far greater in life than money."

I felt myself blush and knew I had to change the subject before my I-could-care-less-who-you-date façade crumbled. "She's too old for you."

Riley didn't break eye contact. "She's too married for me."

"What are you going to do?"

He looked away to sigh. "I don't know. I'll figure it out. I just have to preserve my integrity and character in the process."

I looked around for a second, trying to collect my thoughts. My best friend would soon be on the FBI's most wanted list and here I was daydreaming about romance. Why did men make women do stupid things? I straightened, pulling myself out of airhead mode. "I've got to get out of here. This is not my kind of function."

Riley loosened in his tie. "Me neither. Let's go."

He put his hand on my back and led me from the pack of cougars toward safety.

CHAPTER 7

I got a call at nine o'clock that evening to go to a crime scene and clean. Some people considered getting their houses back in order after a tragedy a top priority. No waiting until the next morning. They wanted all evidence of the horror committed to be gone as soon as possible, as if scrubbing away the blood would somehow wash away their pain. If only it was that easy. But if me cleaning up for them would give them some peace of mind, then why not?

I hesitated as I started down the steps of my apartment building, trying to be quiet and not disturb Riley. But I'd only gotten three steps down when his door opened and he popped his head out.

"Where are you headed at this hour?"

I pivoted. "Going to a job."

"Is Chad still out of town?"

I nodded.

He scowled. "Then I'm going with you. I thought we'd already discussed this. Going to crime scenes alone isn't a good idea. Especially if your name is Gabby St. Claire."

I shrugged. "I know you have a busy week. I didn't want to bug you."

"You never bug me, Gabby. Can you wait a couple of minutes for me to get my shoes? I want to go with you."

"Only if you insist."

"I do. What's the job this time?"

"Homicide. Stabbing, to be more specific. I don't think it's going to be pretty. At all. You sure you're up for this?"

"I won't be able to sleep tonight if I think you're there alone."

"You might not be able to sleep at night if you see this crime scene."

"I see a lot of stuff every day on my job, Gabby. Ugly stuff. I'll be okay."

Yeah, but lawyerish ugly stuff was a lot different than the ugly stuff I saw. I kept my mouth shut, though, grateful to have someone come along with me. Crime scenes at night could be ... spooky, to say the least. And I had almost been killed at a couple of the locations, so there was that consideration also.

"I'll be right back." He disappeared into his apartment.

"I'll be waiting in the van."

Riley knew that I had a nose for trouble and, bless his heart, he tried to look out for me. It was a big job, one that very few people were equipped to do. He made it so easy to fall in love with him, even though I knew we were so different as people.

As I passed Sierra's door, my heart panged. Where was my friend? What was she doing? Was she okay?

The more I thought about the situation, the further I concluded that something was very wrong. Sierra was smart. She would turn herself in if she'd done something wrong. She would allow herself to be questioned rather than hide from authorities. The only reason she might be hiding was because...because she was in danger. I was convinced of it.

I climbed into my van, shivering down to the bone at the cold temperatures outside. I must have left something in the back of the van because the stench inside was enough to make me gag. No sooner had I started the van and cranked the heat did someone stick his head between the seats.

"What's up, Gabster?"

I screamed and clutched my heart. That's when I got a good look at the "intruder." I lowered my hands and my racing heart slowed. "Henry? What are you doing? Why are you in my van?" The smell. I should have known.

"I don't have anywhere else to go. The FBI is looking for me."

I gave him my best "duh" expression. "You think? So you thought you could hide in my van? Where's Sierra?"

"I don't know. I was hoping you could help me find her." He smacked his bubble gum. I didn't even want to know where the freegan got that. Underneath a desk?

I swiveled so hard in my chair that my neck nearly twisted off my head. "What do you mean? What do you know, Henry?"

He shrugged, and I noted that he looked just as unshaven and homeless as ever in his oversized coat and faded ball cap. "I know she's in trouble."

Irritation pinched my spine. "Yeah, I gathered that also. Why's she in trouble? What did you get her into?"

He threw his hands in the air as if I was the crazy one. Was it my imagination or did some wilted lettuce and soggy tomatoes fly out of his sleeves at the action? Just where had he been dumpster diving now? "I didn't get her into anything. I'm just as clueless about all of this as you are."

"I have a hard time believing that's true."

"It is. I just want her to be okay." His eyes softened, but I didn't buy it. The action looked too purposeful and not all that natural and sincere.

"I'm pretty sure you were the last person to see her. That makes you my first suspect."

"I'd never hurt Sierra. Never. I did meet with Sierra for a while yesterday. It wasn't to bomb any buildings or burn down any housing developments, though. We were going to go protest at a pet store. She canceled on me at the last minute. Said she had to go meet with someone."

I sat up straighter as my internal clue-o-meter began registering. "Who?"

"She didn't say. I haven't heard from her since then. But she wasn't acting like herself."

"That's all you can tell me?"

"It's all I know."

I tapped my fingers on the steering wheel, wondering how much time I was wasting by having this conversation. "I'm going to do a job right now, Henry. I can't take you with me. I can't even let you stay in my apartment because I, for starters, don't want to get arrested. Secondly, I'm still not sure I believe you."

"I'm innocent, Gabby. You'll see." He grabbed the door handle. "I'm going to run now. I'll be in touch, though."

He disappeared out one side, as Riley slipped into the other.

Riley froze, as if contemplating whether to chase the person who'd just escaped or check on me. His eyes shifted back and forth in confusion and suspicion. Finally, in an even tone, he asked, "Who was that?"

I bit my lips a moment. "That was Henry."

"Henry?"

I nodded. "Yeah. He thinks Sierra is in trouble, too." I relayed our conversation.

Riley's eyes met mine. "I don't like this, Gabby."

The weight on my shoulders felt even heavier just then. "I don't either. I don't either."

***

Riley paused in the center of the dimly-lit living room, his gaze scanning the crime scene around him. A heaviness seemed to settle over him at the sight. The spot where a life had been taken from this earth could do that to a person. "You were right, Gabby. This scene is grisly."

I paused from my spot on the floor where I worked a scrub brush with enough skill to make a custodian jealous. "I warned you."

"That you did."

I leaned back on my heels, concern for Riley spreading over me. Not everyone was cut out for this, not even tough guys. I considered it a calling. "You don't have to stay, you know."

His gaze cut toward me. "But I do. I don't want anything happening to you."

Certainly, I was simply imagining the affection and concern I heard in his voice. To protect my heart, I latched on to that idea. Yes, I'd imagined it, and I kept scrubbing. Of course, setting my mind toward cleaning up blood and guts didn't quite have the same appeal as letting my mind run wild at the thought of Riley and me having a future together.

We scrubbed in silence for a few more minutes until finally I stood, pulled up my mask, snapped off my gloves, and wiped my forehead. The Hazmat suit I wore could make an Eskimo going ice-fishing sweat.

Riley followed my lead and also took a breather. We wandered away from the scene and into the next room—the kitchen.

"Terrible thing that happened here," Riley muttered before chugging down some water.

I leaned against the counter and grabbed my own water bottle. Condensation from the plastic trickled down my fingers. "I know. These are the hardest crime scenes to clean up after. Apparently, this was a home invasion gone wrong. The homeowner was supposed to be out of town, but he decided to stay home at the last minute. The robbers probably weren't expecting anyone to be here. And now someone's dead."

I knew I shouldn't do it, but I abandoned my water bottle, wiped the extra liquid off of my fingers and onto my suit, and then thumbed my finger down the stack of books and papers on the kitchen counter. The man who died had worked for a solar energy company, or so I gathered. Sometimes I had to go searching for information like this, but, in this case, the man's mother had poured out her pain to me before I was hired. I wanted to reach through the phone and hug the woman. I couldn't even imagine her grief.

Absently, I tugged at a piece of paper from the stack. A word in the corner caught my eye. Why did the format of the paper look familiar?

"What are you doing?" Riley stepped closer.

I froze up a moment at Riley's closeness. "What I do best. Snooping."

His hand covered mine a moment—not in affection, but to stop me from doing something I might regret. It didn't work. "Is that a good idea?"

"The police have already been here and collected all the evidence. The crime scene has been cleared." I yanked out the paper. My eyes widened when I saw the words at the top of the page.

Building Bombs and How to Use Them.

The same papers that Sierra had in her apartment.

Was there a connection between this crime and the others?

I lifted my gaze to the ceiling. *Lord, what has my friend gotten herself into? Protect her. Please.*

CHAPTER 8

"Tell me one more time where you found this," Parker demanded. He stood in the kitchen at my crime scene, again looking like he owned the place. He was good at that false ownership thing.

I pointed to the same stack of papers and books that I'd already pointed at twice. "Right there, wedged between the pages of that notebook."

He scowled. "And how did you discover it?"

"My natural nosiness was at work again. Of course. I don't know what else you want me to tell you." I threw my hands in the air in frustration. Riley stood behind me, a hand on my shoulder—again, not out of affection, but as a way of keeping me grounded.

Special Agent Wilkerson approached Parker. "I just got off the phone with the mother. She said she pulled that stack of papers and books from the shelf in the victim's room. Someone at his company asked if he could take a look at them for a special work project."

Parker raised a brow. "Convenient. Did she remember who that person was?"

"Someone named Daniels. Mark Daniels, I think."

I tapped my foot, appearing not to pay attention but secretly storing away all of the information. Someone had to be an advocate for Sierra. I'd chosen myself to be that person, and I'd do whatever I could to ensure my friend was okay. "Please tell me you don't think that Sierra is responsible for this crime also?"

"The evidence will tell the story." He leaned toward me. "Isn't that what you would say?"

I nudged my chin out farther. "Of course the evidence will tell the story. It will prove that she's innocent. There has to be another explanation for this. I know there is."

"You're loyal, if nothing else."

I scowled this time. "And you're annoying, to say the least."

He chuckled, shook his head and took a playful swipe at my chin. "I love your spirit. I really do. Never lose that."

"I hear ya." I grabbed my air scrub, a piece of the standard equipment I used when cleaning. The industrial piece helped to take away the smell often left at crime scenes. I needed to use it in my van after Henry's visit. "Anything else? I've gotta get some shuteye."

"Yeah, one more thing. Stay out of trouble. I don't know what's going on here, but I know this is no joke. Whoever is behind these crimes—whether they're connected or not—they're dangerous."

I resisted a shudder. I believed Parker. Only, I wasn't going to let the danger stop me.

Riley's hand moved to my ... waist? "You ready?"

I nodded, not missing the glance Parker bounced between Riley and me. "Yeah, let's go."

Outside, the nighttime seemed startlingly quiet. Had the cold killed all the little nocturnal insects that chirped? The late hour apparently kept any pedestrians and traffic at bay. Still, something about the silence made me shiver.

And then stop.

There was that feeling again. That feeling of being watched.

I let my gaze wander over my surroundings. I saw nothing unusual. Just a few cars parked on the side of the street, neighbors whose windows glowed with light from inside, some branches waving in the slight breeze.

"What's wrong?" Riley paused beside me.

I continued to stare at everything around me. "Something feels off."

"Off how?"

"It's just a feeling. The feeling that someone's watching all of this unfold."

Riley scanned the area also. "I don't see anything."

I drug in a deep breath and took another step across the cracked concrete. "Yeah, I don't either." I let my gaze soak in everything around me once more as I approached my van. I held my breath as I opened the doors, half expecting to see Henry again. Thankfully, cleaning supplies greeted me. Riley and I loaded everything into the van. As I climbed into the driver's seat, a piece of paper there caught my eyes. Riley and I exchanged a glance as I picked it up. Carefully, I unfolded it and saw the typed words there.

Watch your back, Gabby St. Claire. This is no amateur's game. Are you sure you're cut out to take this on? Or are you too green?

Green? That word couldn't be a coincidence. I looked at Riley. "What does that mean? Are they challenging me to get involved and encouraging me to stay away at the same time?"

"How about 'threatening' you to stay away?"

"They were here, Riley. Whoever is behind all of this was here tonight. Maybe the person who left this is the same person who's following me."

"Someone's following you?" His voice sounded low, serious.

"It's just a gut feeling. The thing is that my gut feeling is usually right. I'm tired of discounting it."

"You're right. God gives us those instincts for a reason. You should trust your gut." He paused. "Have you told Parker?"

I shook my head. "I know Parker. He'll just think I'm crazy."

"You have to show him this note, you know. There could be fingerprints."

"I doubt it." I sighed again and opened my door. "But here goes nothing."

***

I've been going to church for about four months now and, if truth be told, I still wasn't 100 percent comfortable there, even if the church I was attending met in a high school cafeteria and had a pastor that I'd affectionately—and secretly—nicknamed Pastor Shaggy because of his resemblance to the character from Scooby Doo.

I officially became a Christian two months ago—on New Year's Day, to be specific. After Thanksgiving, I'd gone to church with Riley. I'd been promising to go for months, and I finally decided to keep my word. I'd surprised myself when I actually liked it there.

I'd been wrestling with the whole faith versus science thing for a while. But I knew that I was ready to take the plunge into Christianity. And plunge I did. Even though it was forty degrees outside, as soon as I decided to become a Christian, I wanted to be baptized—in the ocean.

Pastor Shaggy had agreed to it. The day was cold and windy, but the sun shone brightly. All of my friends—Riley, Sierra, Chad, Sharon, plus a few others—gathered at the beach, huddled up in coats and blankets. Pastor Shaggy and I waded out into the icy ocean water and, after offering up a beautiful prayer, he plunged me into the surf. I loved the symbolism of being dunked under the water and coming up washed clean. What a beautiful picture of my new life in Christ.

My friends had applauded. A few rushed into the water to hug me. And we'd sung some worship songs and prayed—after I changed clothes, of course. Then we'd all gotten coffee and eaten pie and laughed together at a little oceanfront diner. My theme song had changed from "I Still Haven't Found What I'm Looking For" to "Amazing Grace."

I'd felt like a new person. I was a new person, and I was so grateful for the change in my life. I'd merged my thoughts between faith and science. I knew the two could go hand in hand. And I was ready to accept that there was a creator who loved me, who made all things work for his purposes. I also believed that he'd given us knowledge of certain things in life that we could use in order to prove that God was real.

Riley'd had a big influence on these life changes of the past couple of months. He was the one who hadn't given up on me and my continual skepticism about God and Jesus. He encouraged me to stay strong and not to be as narrow-minded as the people I criticized. He'd met with me early on after I was baptized, and we'd read the Bible together, prayed together.

The thing I liked the most about church was that the more I grew in my relationship with Jesus, the less I thought about myself. I'd come to the conclusion that putting others above yourself was the true prescription for happiness.

I'd also been learning that faith was just that—faith. It wasn't concrete. There were no lab tests I could implement to determine whether or not my faith was real. It simply was. And I was okay with that. The scientist in me often rebelled, but I knew in my heart—and through careful research—that faith and science could merge into one.

Believe it or not, I'd even brought some people to church with me. There was Sharon who owned the coffeehouse across the street from my apartment building. Bill McCormick, my downstairs neighbor, also came with me sometimes, though I had to wonder if he simply came as a means of networking and trying to gain more fans for his radio talk show…or maybe even to pick up women. But who was I to judge?

Perhaps most striking for me was that my father had begun to come with me. Yep. My father, the alcoholic who'd claimed for years that he couldn't work, was now sober. He was coming to church, along with his new girlfriend Teddi. And he was working as a painter, a job he'd held for three months. That might be a new record for him. Not that I was counting.

The fact that this was the church Riley came to still amazed me. When I'd first met him, I'd assumed he'd go to the uptight variety. But instead, here he was in a congregation of blue-collar workers, college students and artists. I liked to think of the group as closely aligned with the twelve disciples. After all, the disciples were a ragtag group and hardly seemed upright and overly righteous.

The sermon today had been on the Prodigal Son. I'd heard the story before, but today, it struck me fresh as I realized that God forgave me the same way the father had forgiven his youngest son in the story. Accepting forgiveness in my life had felt like layers of burdens had been peeled away until the core of my personhood was revealed. Sometimes those layers began to curl back up, and I had to remind myself that someone else was in control of my life—God—and that he was going to take care of me. That wasn't an easy concept for someone who had trouble loosening her grip on the reins.

Everyone stood to sing the last song before church dismissed. As the guitarist started strumming the strands of "Here I Am to Worship," I closed my eyes. Worship. This was my favorite part of each service. I wasn't one to often express my admiration for people—or for God, for that matter. But singing allowed me to do just that without feeling self-conscious.

God was working in my life. I never thought I'd say that, but he was.

Life seemed to be falling back into routine with church today. I already had two jobs lined up for the week. Riley would go back to work tomorrow. Chad should be back from his ski trip this evening.

But how about Sierra? How could we return to normal with Sierra missing? Shouldn't the police be out searching for her? She was the victim here. Would they ever realize that?

And why was someone playing games with me? Why were they pulling me into this mystery? More importantly, who was that person?

I had so many questions and so few answers. I needed a game plan for how I was going to figure all of this out.

The answers had to start with Lydia. I'd tried to patiently wait for her date with Riley, but that wouldn't be until after this week when her divorce was finalized. I couldn't wait that long. Sierra's life could be on the line, so this was no time to be patient.

"Gabby?"

"I have to do it," I blurted.

Riley cocked his eyebrow. "Do what?"

I shook my head, trying to come out of my stupor. "Huh?"

He tilted his head, a no-nonsense expression gracing his perfect features. "I asked you what you wanted to do for lunch, and you said, 'I have to do it.' Care to explain?"

Why bother concealing my plan? Riley would find out anyway. He always did. "I have to talk to Lydia. Today. Can you help?"

He paused a moment, saying nothing, before he finally nodded. "I have her phone number. I suppose I could pass that along to you."

"Thank you."

He touched my elbow. "What are you thinking?"

"I'm really worried about Sierra, Riley. Something's wrong. I feel like I'm going on with my life as if nothing has happened. What if she's hurt somewhere? Or in danger?"

"You're doing what you can, Gabby. The FBI is even working on this case. I'd venture to say that plenty is being done."

I shook my head. "Not by me. I've got to talk to Lydia. And Mark Daniels."

"Mark Daniels?"

"The man who called and asked for those books to be set aside at the crime scene last night," I reminded him. "Those two are the only leads I have."

"Let's go then."

I raised a brow. "You're coming?"

"How many times do I have to tell you, Gabby? I don't want you trying to conquer this alone. I know I can't stop you, but I can at least tag along and try to keep you out of trouble."

"He's right, you know." My dad appeared in our little circle. Surprisingly, I didn't feel the initial resentment I usually did when he came around. We had so many issues from the past to work through. I just didn't know how to approach most of them, which was pretty unusual for me. I had a track record of diving into things headfirst.

"Well, father knows best." I tried to keep the edge out of my voice, but I'm not sure it worked.

"You're not going to come by the coffee shop for a sandwich?" Sharon, the owner of The Grounds coffee shop, as well as a friend, approached us. She wiped a pink strand of hair out of her eyes, revealing the multiple piercings that graced her eyebrows, nose, upper lip and ears. Sharon was quiet, a good listener and had more creativity in one iced latte than I experienced in a lifetime.

I shook my head. "I can't right now. There's something I have to do. But I'll take a rain check on it."

"We've got these new paintings that you have to see. I think they're right up your alley, Gabby. The artist is local and edgy and almost has a bit of mystery about her work. I thought of you when she hung them up for display."

"I'll definitely check them out. I've just got to do something for Sierra first."

Sharon's gaze scanned the crowds. "Where is Sierra?"

"I wish I knew." I bit my lip. "Pray for her."

Sharon's smile dropped. "It's that serious?"

I nodded. "Yeah, unfortunately."

"I just saw her yesterday morning."

I straightened. "Yesterday morning? Are you sure?"

"Positive. I thought she was up to her strange antics again. She was climbing into her apartment through a window. I saw it from the coffeehouse."

"Are you sure it was Sierra?"

"Pretty sure. Short Asian chick with dark plastic framed glasses."

I looked at Riley. "I've got to check out her apartment. That's where I need to start first."

Riley and I hurried from the crowd and outside to his car. The school was close enough that we could have walked, but the biting cold remained so we'd taken his car. As soon as I slipped inside, I saw the paper on the windshield.

"Not again," I muttered. I stuck my hand out the window and snatched the paper, hoping it was simply a local restaurant advertising its daily specials.

As soon as I saw the typed words on the other side, I knew it wasn't.

For I know the plans I have for you, declares the Lord. Trust in God's plan. But remember, I am God.

I looked at Riley after reading it out loud. "What does that mean? Someone is playing God?"

"People who end the lives of others often think they're God. I think there's a killer who wants you to play his game. This is serious, Gabby."

I felt chilled to the bone. "Yeah, I know." I tucked the paper into my purse. One more thing to give Parker. Why couldn't I just get that man out of my life? Did God want to teach me some cosmic lesson by having me interact with Parker daily now? "Let's not waste any more time. I've got to check Sierra's apartment and see what's going on."

The drive home took three minutes. I couldn't even talk the whole way there, which only proved how serious I felt since I, by most accounts, was never quiet.

I pulled Sierra's apartment key from my messenger bag and gripped it as Riley pulled into the lot. As soon as the car was in park, I threw the door open and hurried into the apartment building. As I opened Sierra's door, the wooden beads hanging on the other side began their clacking. The sound made me miss Sierra even more.

Sure, Sierra could be a little hard to take sometimes, but so could I, so who was I to complain? I missed her acorn brownies, the moaning—supposedly relaxing—whale music she listened to, and her constant soliloquies on the evil of humanity toward the animal kingdom.

I pushed aside the beads and stepped into her apartment. I could feel Riley behind me. When I stopped in my tracks, he collided into me.

"Someone's been here." The place was ransacked. Not a table or book had been spared. Her plants had been turned upside down and dirt scattered the floor.

Her posters had been ripped in half. Her couch cushions had been gutted.

Riley stepped around me to survey the damage. "Did Sierra do this yesterday when she snuck inside?"

I shook my head, staring at the mess around me. "I can't imagine she would do this. What purpose would it serve?"

"If it wasn't Sierra, then who?"

"Whoever is behind all of these crimes." It seemed a reasonable deduction. "Maybe they want to find Sierra. Maybe she has something they want. Maybe that's why she snuck back into the apartment yesterday."

Riley shook his head, his jaw jutting out to show his disapproval of the situation. "This is getting crazier by the moment, Gabby. I don't like it."

Another thought hit me—a horrible thought, but one I needed to address. "Riley, we need to make sure Sierra's not here. Sharon saw Sierra come in. She didn't say she saw her come out."

Riley's eyes registered my thought process, moving from disapproval to concern. He put his hand on my shoulder. "You stay here. I'll go check everything out."

I didn't argue. I stepped backward into the clacking beads and held my breath. He stepped over some books, dodged a broken bowl and slid around the overturned dining room table. He knew enough to not disturb anything. Evidence could be all around us. Fingerprints, footprints, fibers. If Sierra were hurt, the police would collect all of that in order to find out the person behind the crime.

I held my breath. *Please, Lord, help her to be okay.*

Riley disappeared into the hallway, back toward the bedroom. I waited, the minutes painfully stretching onward. What did Riley see? Was my friend okay?

"Gabby, you're going to want to come see this."

I swallowed, my throat burning. What had he found? I tiptoed along the same path as Riley did earlier and found him in the bathroom.

Raw ground beef—along with its juices—was strung across the sink, creating a terrible stench in the small space.

Then on the mirror were the words "Meat is Murder."

CHAPTER 9

I stared at Parker who, even with his Brad Pitt good looks, couldn't make a scrunched up nose look attractive. He stared at the mangled, raw ground beef in Sierra's bathroom. As quickly as he lost his G-Man composure, the aloof detachment returned

My hands went to my hips as I grew impatient with him trying to process the scene. "What do you think this means?"

He shrugged, still staring at the very visible—and effective—threat left by the person behind this chaos. "I'm not sure. Someone's definitely trying to make a statement, though."

"A statement that they want Sierra dead." I bit my lip, not wanting my thoughts to go there.

Parker shook his head. "Not necessarily."

My eyebrow twitched in curiosity. "What do you mean? What else could this message possibly mean?"

He turned from his examination of the bathroom and stared me straight in the eye. "You said your friend saw Sierra sneaking in here yesterday, correct?"

I stepped back, indignation flashing through me. "You think Sierra did this? No way. Why would she do that?"

He shrugged in such a casual manner that I wanted to sock him. "To take the suspicion off of herself."

"She wouldn't do that."

"She's smart enough to devise a plan like that."

I swung my head back and forth, anger boiling through me. "No, she's smart enough to turn herself in if she's guilty. And she'd never touch raw meat. Never."

"I think she broke in here, picked up any evidence that might point to her, something she might have missed, and then tore the place up."

My finger went in the air. "You're off base. You're way off base. You're wasting valuable time looking in the wrong direction."

Parker didn't back off. He stepped toward me, arrogance saturating his gaze. "Okay, Miss Know-It-All, what do you think is going on here?"

"I think my friend was at the wrong place at the wrong time. I think she's being set up. And I think she's running for her life because whoever is behind these crimes knows that she knows."

"Nice theory. Not likely though."

Riley grabbed my finger, which ever since I'd raised it had been swinging wildly through the air with each word I spoke. "Let's put that away," he mumbled. "Fussing at each other will get us nowhere."

Parker sighed and lowered his voice. "Gabby, we have it on video that Sierra was at the office of Harrison Developers only four days ago. She entered the building with a backpack. She left without it."

The information felt like a slap in the face. Finally, I came out of my stupor. "That means nothing. Another coincidence." But even to my own ears, my words didn't sound right. "I'm going to prove she's innocent, Parker."

His gaze locked on mine. "Just don't get yourself killed in the process, Gabby."

Riley followed me to the door and said nothing as I charged outside, hoping he was behind me. I climbed into his car and, to my relief, he did also. We sat silently a moment until finally Riley asked, "Well?"

"Right now I want to track down someone named Bruce Watkins."

"Who's Bruce Watkins?"

"No one. Just an ecoterrorist."

***

We pulled into a parking space at the gas station, and Riley turned toward me. "And your plan is...?"

I shrugged. "I have no plan. I'm going to wing it."

"Winging usually doesn't equal winning."

"Is that court talk?"

He blinked at me. "Court talk?"

"You know, what you tell yourself before a trial or something?"

Riley shook his head. "No, it's just common sense."

I opened my door. "How about this then? Let's do this on a wing and a prayer."

He groaned but stepped out of the car also. A couple of snow flurries pecked me in the face as I hurried across the parking lot. Just as I pulled open the door to the convenience store, a man breezed out. Just before he was out of my line of sight, I read his nametag. Bruce. This had to be my guy.

I stopped in the doorway, and Riley slammed into my back. I turned toward him, raised my eyebrows and nodded toward the employee who'd just left.

Riley silently mouthed, "What?"

I shrugged and nodded toward the employee again.

He shrugged, his eyes wide in confusion.

I nodded toward Bruce Watkins again, wondering why Riley was having such a hard time reading my brilliant body language.

"Casual," I whispered. "Come on."

I walked back toward Riley's car, keeping my eyes on Bruce as he climbed into an old clunker of a car.

Riley leaned toward me, close enough that I could feel his breath across my cheek. "You don't look casual, Gabby. You look like you were attempting a robbery, but your plan was foiled," he whispered.

"We've got to follow that man before he gets away. This is no time to worry about if I look suspicious." Regardless, I tried to relax my shoulders and slow my gait.

Riley climbed into the driver's seat just as Bruce pulled away.

"We've got to follow him!"

Riley put the car in drive, a little too slowly for my taste. He glanced at me once more, still not moving. "Are you sure you know what you're doing?"

I nodded in fake confidence. "Absolutely." Yeah, so really I had no idea. "Let's go!"

We followed him through Norfolk until he stopped at some townhouses, parked his car and climbed out. I watched as he unlocked the townhouse with the red door, looked both ways, and then went inside.

"What now?" Riley asked.

That was a great question. What now? I made a decision. "Now I'm going to go talk to him."

Riley arched an eyebrow. "Just like that? Go up to his door and demand he tells you where Sierra is?"

I shrugged. "Not exactly." I unlatched the door and waved my head in the distance. "You'll see." Before I slammed the door closed, I grabbed a clipboard from the backseat, jammed a blank piece of paper under the clip, and tucked a pencil behind my ear.

"Do I even want to know?"

"Probably not. You're going to need to stand where he can't see you. Otherwise, he'll never buy my story."

"I'm not sure I want you that close to him alone."

I pointed to a bush. "You just crouch there. You'll be close enough to spring into action if I need you."

He drug in a breath. "I'll have to trust you on this one." He gave me one last look before taking his place out of sight.

I tucked a hair behind my ear, threw my shoulders back and rang the doorbell. A moment later, Bruce answered the door, already clad in an undershirt and flannel pants. His dirty blond hair looked a touch greasy at the part and his beard had a few crumbs in it. "Can I help you?"

"The question is, can I help you?"

He twisted his head in confusion. "Excuse me?"

I extended my hand. "I'm Gabriella, and I have a cleaning service. I'm trying to drum up business in the area, so I'm going around from house to house and offering one free basic cleaning in hopes that you'll consider my services."

He paused. "You want to clean my house? For free?"

I nodded. "That's right."

"Do I have to sign something? Buy something? Commit to anything?"

"Absolutely not. I only ask that if you like my work that you'll consider me for the future or tell anyone you may know, who's in need of a cleaner, about me."

He looked from side to side again, and my heart stopped a moment as I feared he'd seen Riley. Finally, he looked back at me. "You're really a cleaner?"

I nodded again. "I am. I was a teacher, but I lost my job when the economy went south. So now I'm cleaning houses, and I find I quite enjoy helping people get their homes back in order."

I waited for his reaction. He continued to try and size me up. Finally, a grin broke across his face. "I like that. I lost my job too awhile back, so I know what that's like. I work at a gas station now. What can I say? It helps to pay the bills, even if I am helping to deplete the ozone layer by selling a product that's bad for the environment."

I nodded. "I know. I hope the new government regulations will make it harder for people to buy those gas-guzzling vehicles. It should be a felony."

"I agree. It's like they enjoy torturing Mother Earth."

"You gotta take care of Mama E."

He grinned again. "I like you. And I'd like you to come spiffy up the place. I can't promise you I'll be able to hire you afterward, though I could try to recommend you to some friends." He shifted his weight. "Do you use environmentally friendly cleaning products?"

I used my most incredulous expression. "Of course. Vinegar and water. Sometimes some lavender oil. All natural stuff."

"Can you come tomorrow?"

"You name the time."

"Eight o'clock. I have to leave for work at nine. Will that be okay?"

I nodded. "Of course. I'll do what I can in the time I'm here."

He reached over and touched one of the overgrown shrubs in front of his house. My throat went dry as I wondered if he would see Riley and this whole operation would be uncovered. My heart pounded in my ears as I waited for what would happen next.

"You don't do lawn work too, do you?"

I wanted to laugh in relief. Instead, I said, "All I have to do is look at a plant and it dies. Sorry."

"I understand." He looked me over and smiled again. Chills raced over me at his obvious interest. What was I doing? He could be a dangerous man. "I'll take what I can get."

Sierra, I reminded myself. I had to think of Sierra.

I tried to offer a winning grin. "I'll see you tomorrow then."

"I'll see you then."

                                           ***

"Are you crazy? You can't be alone with that man in his apartment!" Riley crossed his arms over his chest and stared at me from the moment we climbed into the car.

"It's the only way I can think of to find out what he knows."

"Gabby, I don't like this. Didn't someone tell you that they think he could be an ecoterrorist? Doesn't the word 'terrorist' have any meaning to you at all?"

"Of course it does. I'm going to be careful."

"I can name a million other times in the past when you were 'careful' and you almost died."

"A million? You're exaggerating just a little, don't you think?"

"You know what I'm saying, Gabby. This is a bad idea."

I put my hand on his knee, trying to get his neurons to stop firing at such a rapid pace. "I'm going to be fine. I'm going to clean, look around a bit, and then leave."

His jaw twitched as he drove, and I knew he wasn't happy. Silence stretched between us. I tried to think of something to say that might snap him out of this mood, but not a thing came to me.

Finally, I noticed that we turned in the opposite direction of our apartment. "Where are we going?"

He continued to look straight ahead. "We're meeting Lydia Harrison for coffee."

"Lydia Harrison?"

"I took the liberty of calling her to see if we could talk."

"That was... awfully nice of you."

"Yeah, at least I can be there with you when you talk to her. I'll have some measure of comfort in that fact."

"Riley..." Again, I didn't know what to say. Finally, I settled for "thank you."

***

I stared at Lydia Harrison, and I suddenly knew what it meant when people said, "to shoot daggers with your eyes." The woman had such an air of confidence about her that I wanted to throttle her. Instead, I gripped my chair so hard that my knuckles hurt. "So you have no idea who Sierra is? Are you sure?"

Lydia shook her head, her hair not moving even a fraction of a centimeter with the action. She took another sip of her fancy coffee—which she did indeed drink with her pinky raised—and kept her eyes on Riley. "I'm positive. Why would I know this Sierra you're speaking of?"

I closed my eyes and willed myself to remain calm and collected. Maiming someone at an expensive coffeehouse wasn't on my bucket list. "She said you had answers."

Lydia circled her French manicured finger in the air and looked at me blankly...or was she just acting? "Rewind some. The answers to what?"

"Who bombed your husband's office building and set fire to his housing development."

Her composure broke, but only for a moment. Immediately, she snapped back to her intensely controlled demeanor. She obviously wanted to call the shots in this conversation. Most likely, she wanted to call the shots all the time. She just seemed like that kind of person. "Why would I know that information? I have nothing to do with my husband's company. It doesn't concern me."

I leaned toward her. "Your divorce is about to be finalized. Do you stand to gain anything from these incidents?"

"I beg your pardon? What are you accusing me of exactly, Ms. St. Claire?" Lydia's thin eyebrow popped up, arching with more skill than a gymnast at the Olympics.

Riley put his hand on my arm, effectively stopping me from answering. That was probably a good thing. "Gabby isn't accusing you of anything, Lydia. She's just concerned about her friend. Her friend indicated that you had some answers."

"I don't know what exactly these elusive answers are. I have no idea why someone would blow up my husband's business." She paused and tapped her finger a second. "Well, that's not exactly true. He does have a lot of enemies."

"Like who?"

"Well, there was the environmental group who claimed he was wasting our nation's natural resources by building on the property where the fire occurred."

Check, I knew that. I'd add them to my list of people to question, though.

"And there's that community group who already thinks we have enough traffic in the area where he wanted to build. A bunch of conspiracy theorists if you ask me."

"Okay." I could check them out, I supposed.

"Oh, and don't forget that Native American group."

"Native American group?"

"Right. They found some bones when they began to prep the area for the housing development. Turns out it was the ancient burial ground for a local tribe. James went through all the hoops to get the remains moved. There were some natives who were not happy about all of that, though."

"Interesting."

She smirked. "I'd say."

"Can I talk to your ex?"

"You'd have to ask him."

"Where can I find him?"

She shrugged. "I couldn't tell you. I haven't spoken with him in weeks."

I bit my lip and leaned back in my chair.

I had to find Sierra. But how would I do that when every road led to a dead end?

***

"What next, detective?" Riley asked as we walked back to his car. The snow had never really started. The sky just seemed to randomly release cold spittle at will. Every once in a while, a piece of chilly ooze would find my cheeks.

Otherwise, a brisk wind slapped any exposed skin it could find—mostly my toes, which, unfortunately, were exposed in my flip-flops. Flip-flops in the winter? Don't worry. These were my wool-lined ones, designed especially for crazy people like me who wanted to wear the shoes year-round.

"So many choices, I hardly know where to start. I want to know more about this Native American group. Can I use your smartphone?" I climbed into his car, embracing the shelter from the wind and elements.

He slid into the driver's seat and cranked the engine. Heat poured out from the vents as he handed me his phone. "Here you go."

"Perfect." I waited for the Internet to load. "I'm so glad you make enough money to have a phone with 4G."

He pulled out of the parking space, the light from the gray sky outside outlining his profile. Just seeing him and having him beside me brought such a measure of peace. "I remember when 4G was my seat at a baseball game." He ran a hand through his hair and stole a glance at me. His eyes twinkled. "I think I'm getting old."

I shrugged, knowing better than to pass up an opportunity. "You do still have a landline phone, so the odds are stacked against you in the age department right now."

He cut his gaze toward me. "What's wrong with a landline phone?"

"Nothing's wrong with it, other than the fact that only people over thirty have them." I didn't really have room to talk since Riley was only three years older than me. But I did it anyway.

He scowled and pointed to his phone. "Did you find anything?"

"There's one mention of the group here in a newspaper article. The tribe is the Mishcosk. There's one person who acts as the group's spokesperson. He's quoted here in the article. Let me see if I can find his contact information."

I did a quick search and, what do you know, he was listed online. I made a quick call and he agreed to meet us at the housing development in thirty minutes. Easy enough. Too easy?

"We're not any closer to having answers, are we?" Riley gripped the steering wheel so hard that his knuckles were white.

"I don't even know if we're looking in the right direction. I just know I have to keep looking."

We pulled up to the housing development and stepped out of Riley's car. I squinted against the deceitfully bright sun, a sun that made it seem warmer than it really was. The wind bit through my clothing as its breezes swept across the river beside us.

The land really was lovely, located on the banks of the Elizabeth River with tall marsh grasses jutting upward. The construction crew had started to build three houses on prime spots along the river. Now, only one of the houses stood. The other two were ashes.

A lone truck, one in desperate need of a paint job with its dull gray finish, sat at the end of the lane. A tall, broad man leaned against the back, his arms folded over his chest, and his eyes watching us. He didn't move as we approached, he only stared. His long dark hair was swept back into a neat ponytail, and his honey-colored skin gave him an exotic look.

"That must be Broken Arrow," I whispered.

"Broken Arrow?"

I shrugged. "That's his Native American Name. His real name is Wayne Wood."

"Broken Arrow is way cooler."

I held out my hand as I approached. "I'm Gabby St. Claire and this is…" I glanced at Riley. How should I introduce him? My friend? My neighbor? My… "… my male secretary, Riley Thomas."

Riley's eyes widened until he shook his head, a hint of a smile playing at the corner of his lips. Just as quickly, he pulled his lips back down in a respectable non-expression.

I turned back to Broken Arrow. "Thanks for meeting with us."

Broken Arrow didn't smile or take my hand. He only glared at me, as if I'd done something wrong. I'd done lots of things wrong, but none so specific that he would know about them.

"You have some questions about the burial ground?"

I jammed my hands into my pockets, trying to keep them warm and to erase the awkwardness from the unreturned handshake. "We wondered if it had something to do with the fire here."

"I'll tell you like I told the police. We're a peaceful people. We wouldn't do this. Why is it your concern?" He spoke slowly, as if he chose each word with precision.

"My friend is being implicated for the crime. I need to prove her innocence."

He showed his first sign of emotion. He blinked. "Sierra? Your friend is Sierra?"

"You know her?"

He nodded once. "I met her once. She was trying to get a meeting with James Harrison at the same time I was trying to get a meeting with him. We chatted for a few minutes afterward. You don't easily forget someone like Sierra."

Not forgetting her was one thing, but ... "How did you know she's being implicated?"

"Her name and picture were on the news today."

I gasped, but the rush of cold air into my lungs caused me to cough. "What? They can't do that!"

"They said she's a person of interest."

"I can't believe Parker would do this." I jammed my fists into my hips.

"He has to do his job, Gabby," Riley said. "Right now, his job is to find Sierra and get some answers."

One thing was growing more and more certain by the moment—I had to find Sierra before anyone else did. Her future depended on it.

CHAPTER 10

The car ride as we pulled away from the housing development was silent. I chewed on my thoughts, trying desperately to make sense of some of them as the landscape and traffic blended together outside my window. It was no use. Logic eluded me.

Sierra was on the news. Really? Parker had to know she didn't do this, even if she did look as guilty as sin.

I stared out the window, trying to keep my spirits up, to hang onto that fighting spirit I was known for. As I stared into the side view mirror at the traffic behind us, I straightened.

"Riley, you see that car behind us?"

He glanced in the rearview mirror. "I see a lot of cars behind us."

"The maroon, economy type car." I craned my neck around. "Three cars back."

His eyes flickered up. "Okay, yeah, I see it."

"It's following us."

Riley quirked an eyebrow at me. "Are you sure?"

I nodded, a little too adamantly. "Positive. And that's the same car that was following me on the night Harrison Developments was bombed."

Riley sighed. "Splendid."

"Pull over right here. Get into the right lane."

"Why?"

"I want to lose them from behind us. Then *I* want to follow *them*." The hunter becomes the hunted. Okay, maybe I watched too many movies. But still, I had to find out who was following me.

Riley looked over at me, his eyes widened in shock. "Why would you want to do that?"

"Maybe they're my connection to Sierra. Maybe whoever is driving that car knows where she is."

Riley's jaw twisted, and I could tell he wasn't keen on my plan. But, to my surprise, he swerved into the right lane and braked. The maroon car didn't have room to swing into the turn lane. It sped past. I craned my neck trying to get a look at the driver.

Tinted windows. Rats. I could only see an outline.

Riley jerked back into the left lane and began tailing the car. I loved this man. I did.

"I hope I don't regret this," he muttered

"If it helps us find Sierra, then what will there be to regret?"

The driver of the maroon car seemed to sense what we were doing. He accelerated toward a yellow light. I gripped the armrest as I pondered what Riley would do. Run the red light? Slam on brakes?

The maroon car squealed through the intersection, causing oncoming cars to slam on their brakes. My eyes widened as the scene unfolded in front us. I waited to hear the crunch of metal. I waited to feel the impact of a crash.

Riley pressed on the brakes until we came to a screeching halt. My racing heart pounded in my ears as the car froze.

"Sorry, Gabby. I couldn't do it."

"It's okay." I glanced over at him. "Something's going on here, Riley. I have no idea what it is. I can't talk to Mark Daniels until tomorrow when he gets to work. I hate feeling so helpless."

"You're doing everything you can, Gabby."

"There has to be something I'm missing. I just don't know what it is."

My cell phone beeped. I didn't recognize the number so I answered with, "Trauma Care."

Someone else needed me to clean a crime scene as soon as possible. I supposed I had nothing better to do at the moment—at least, I couldn't think of what it was. I wanted to track down clues and follow the evidence, but I'd come to a dead end. I might as well earn some money.

"Another job?" Riley asked.

I nodded. "Yeah, another one."

"I'm going with you."

"I'm going to have to put you on payroll if you keep coming with me."

"When's Chad getting back?"

"He called this morning and said he'd decided to stay all week. I told him I could hold the fort down while he was gone."

"But can you?"

I shrugged. "I just know that forcing Chad to come back here and work instead of skiing is a fast way to get him to quit. He's a free spirit and isn't great at the whole 'being tied down' thing."

"Are you talking about working together or a romantic relationship?"

I glanced at Riley, surprised by his question. He rarely asked me about my dating life, yet he sounded so earnest right now.

"In some ways, both. But Chad and I would never make it dating. I'm convinced that we'd kill each other."

"At least whoever acted first would know exactly how to clean up the evidence."

I couldn't help but laugh. Riley was beginning to pick up on my sense of humor. He'd been hanging around me too long, obviously.

"That's awfully considerate of you to let Chad off the hook."

I shrugged. Did Riley know the real reason? Ever since I'd told Chad I couldn't date him, things had been awkward between us. Working the jobs by myself was just as well...other than the fact that there could be a serial killer out there with my face plastered to his practice target.

Chad really was a great guy, though. When he found the right girl, he was going to make someone really happy. And that would make me happy.

"Did you tell Chad about Sierra?"

I cut a sharp glance at Riley. "No, why?"

Riley shrugged. "Just wondering."

"I figured that would only want to make him come home early. What good would that do?"

Riley pulled up to our apartment complex. "Right. What good would that do?" He patted my knee. "Let's not waste any more time."

***

Raymond Morris was known in the world of contractors as "the plaster guy." How ironic was it that I had to pick parts of a plaster-guy's bones from the once-smooth plaster? Had he spread this plaster himself? How unfair that not only had a gun taken his life, but it also ruined his beautiful work all in one fatal shot.

As I carefully used my tweezers to get bone fragments from the wall, Riley stood behind me watching. We'd already washed down the walls and removed the carpet. The gore was mostly confined to this one small space.

I turned my head toward my friend. "This is really a one-person job, Riley. I'm sorry that your time is being wasted."

He shrugged, handsome even in the Hazmat suit. "It's not wasted. It's with you."

There he went again with those sweet little things he kept saying to me. What was up with that? If it were anyone else, I would have straight-up asked them. But not Riley. I'd rather believe that maybe there was something more to his words than have those dreams crushed by reality.

"Someone's being killed because of these construction projects," Riley blurted.

It was just the sweet nothing I wanted to hear. Only it wasn't nothing. I paused with tweezers in hand. "Come again?"

He began pacing. "Think about it. Housing development burned. Developer's office bombed. The crime scene we were at last night—didn't that man work for a solar energy company? This man is a plasterer. That's the connection."

I abandoned the tweezers and rocked back to a sitting position as his words settled in my mind. "It does look like ecoterrorism, doesn't it? Like someone's trying to send a message?"

Riley shook his head. "I think ecoterrorism is too easy, though, Gabby. They usually take credit for what they do. No one has taken credit for these things."

An eerie feeling crawled up my spine at Riley's implication. "These things? Riley, do you think this man is connected too? You think these murders—that seem random—are actually connected with the fire and the bombing?"

He stopped pacing and shrugged. "It's a thought."

My gaze scanned the man's house. I left my task for a moment and walked around the perimeter of the room. Was there something in this house that would offer a clue to whatever was going on? Would I know it if I saw it?

The man was a hunter. I saw deer heads and lots of camo gear and even some books on hunting. But nothing that would give me a clue as to whether or not he was involved in this whole Sierra/bombing/crazy fiasco.

Riley watched me. "When was this man shot?"

"Friday night, I think. They just released the scene." I stopped at a picture of the man holding a deer he'd obviously just shot. He stood beside another man who also wore camo gear. I squinted at the picture, but finally shook my head. No, neither of the men in the picture was familiar to me.

Riley's pacing began again. "Do you know anything else about this man?"

"From what I understood, he was shot on Friday by an unknown intruder. The man's brother is being investigated because I guess they were seen arguing earlier in the week. That's really all I know."

Riley nodded, obviously still deep in thought. "Who called about the job?"

"The man's estranged wife."

Riley paused. "Estranged wife? So she doesn't live here anymore?"

"That's my understanding. Why?" What was Riley getting at?

He pointed to the room behind them. "There are brownies on the kitchen table."

"Brownies? What's so strange about that?"

His gaze nearly tinged her. "Most single men aren't going to bake themselves brownies."

I had to give Riley props for that one. I walked over to the table and leaned down for a better look at the chocolate treats. When I looked closer, I sucked in a breath.

"Do they smell that bad?"

I shook my head, suddenly feeling nauseous. "Riley, Sierra made these."

His eyes widened as he approached. "How do you know?"

I pointed to the top, where an acorn had been carved into the icing with a knife. It was Sierra's signature. She made acorn brownies, and recently she'd taken to sculpting an acorn on top for flourish. "These are hers. I'm sure of it."

"So Sierra was here? What has she gotten herself into, Gabby?"

I shook my head. "Whatever it is, it's huge."

CHAPTER 11

I rubbed my eyes the next morning, yawning as I stepped from my apartment. I'd spent most of the night searching the Internet for environmentally friendly ways of cleaning homes. I'd spent the other half of the night mixing the proper solutions together, organizing my supplies and printing new business cards before I cleaned Bruce Watkins' house. I was surprised when I stepped outside, bin of cleaners in hand, and spotted Riley leaning against my van, sipping on some steaming coffee. Another cup rested atop the van.

"Riley? What are you doing?"

He grabbed the second cup and handed it to me. "I cleared my schedule this morning so that I can go with you."

I jammed my key into the van door. "That's incredibly kind of you, but I think my cover might be blown if you're with me."

"Why would your cover be blown?" He hurried around to the other side of the van.

"Because you don't look like the cleaning type." I climbed inside, taking a sip of coffee. Its warmth spread through me. Riley needed to be rewarded for his thoughtfulness. Going with me to the home of a possible ecoterrorist was no way to be rewarded.

"What does that mean? What does the 'cleaning type' look like?"

"Not like you. You look...cultured and well-to-do. You can't help it. It's just the way you were raised."

His eyebrows drew together, as if he were offended. "I'm not above cleaning."

I started the van and listened as the engine roared to life. "I didn't say you were. I just don't think Bruce is going to buy it. Besides, I think half of the reason he said yes was because he thought I was cute."

Riley tilted his head. "You think?"

"Sarcasm's my job."

"Sarcasm is just anger disguised as humor."

I tilted my head this time. "So you're angry?"

He released the tight grip he had on his coffee cup. "I'm not angry. I'm just concerned. I don't want to see you walk into a dangerous situation like this. If something happens to you, I'll... I'll..."

"You'll what?"

His voice softened. "I'll never forgive myself."

Some of my anger faded when I heard the sincerity in his voice. "Okay, fine. You can come. But you're going to have to wait in the van."

"Really?"

"It's better than nothing. You'll be plenty close."

"Not close enough to see if something's happening. You could be bleeding to death on the floor, and I'll be sitting in the van twiddling my thumbs."

"Okay, I'll leave my phone on speaker. You'll be able to hear everything I say. And the first thing I'll do is open the curtains so that you can see inside, somewhat at least." I looked at him. "Is it a deal?"

Finally, his statue-like stance broke and he nodded. "Deal. I guess. I still don't like this, though."

"Thank you, Riley, for caring. It means a lot to have someone watching out for me, even if I do grumble and complain about it."

"Of course I care, Gabby. We're... friends, right? That's what friends do."

My smile slipped. Friends. Of course. Why did my mind always go other places? I nodded. "Friends." My throat burned as I said the word.

I pushed those thoughts aside and put the van in drive. We bumped down the road and finally pulled up to the townhouse. "I need you to put your phone on mute. I can't risk any unexpected sounds coming out of my shirt pocket."

"Got it."

I dialed his number, put the phone on speaker, and stuck it in my shirt pocket. "If I say 'hot mama' that's my code word for you to come help."

"Hot mama?"

I shrugged. "Or if I scream like I'm being murdered. Either one of those things."

He scowled. "For the record—"

"You don't like this. I know." I softened my words, seeing his obvious sincerity and concern. "Thanks, Riley. Here goes nothing."

Bruce answered the door dressed in faded jeans and a dirty T-shirt. I wondered momentarily if he was a freegan, too, or if he had something against doing laundry. I asked neither. Instead, I offered my most winning smile, and in return he grinned back at me.

"I thought maybe it was just a scam and that you weren't coming back."

I stepped inside. "Now that wouldn't have been very nice of me."

He pointed to the bottles in the bin I carried. "I see you mix your own solutions."

"Of course. What kind of self-respecting cleaner doesn't?"

He stepped back. "Well, come on in. I just have to answer some emails before I leave for work. Do you need anything from me?"

I shook my head, staring at the untidy—and that was putting it nicely—place. I was going to have my work cut out for me. There was probably a reason I stuck to crime scenes and not general housekeeping. Where did I even begin here? It was kind of hard to clean due to all the messes around me. Nonetheless, I decided to start with vacuuming. He did have a vacuum, didn't he?

I wandered down the hall in the general direction that he'd just come from and found Bruce sitting at a desk in what had probably been intended for the dining area. "Vacuum?"

He stood, setting down a stack of papers. "Oh, right, right. Let me grab it for you."

As he hurried down the hallway, I took a quick glance at his desk. *Making Bombs and How to Use Them* by the National Federation for a Cleaner Earth. Something I hadn't noticed before now stared at me from the paper.

Written by T. Watkins.

T. Watkins? Was Bruce's first name really not Bruce? Or did he have a family member who was an ecoterrorist maybe? I knew enough to deduce that either Bruce or someone Bruce was affiliated with had written this bomb-making manual. And from the looks of things, he was busy writing some other manuals. What were these about? How to kill the masses and get away with it? How to blow up gas-guzzling cars and make it look like a factory defect?

"Here you go."

I startled, trying not to appear as if I'd been snooping. He didn't seem to notice. He was probably too excited to have someone else clean up his filth. I forced a grin. "Thanks."

I tried to make quick work of vacuuming any open areas I could find. When I finished with that, I started dusting. I took my time, hoping he would wander away from his office while I cleaned that room. I needed to snoop more.

When he left to go get another cup of coffee, I seized the opportunity. I noticed that he'd put away the bomb-making manual before he left and everything else was left in semi-neat little piles. I also noticed his smart phone sitting there on the table.

I glanced up and into the kitchen. He had his back to me as he poured himself some coffee. But how long did I have? Did I dare try to look on his smart phone?

My muscles tightened at the idea. Casually, I swept my finger over the device's screen. It lit up.

Bruce still had his back toward me. "So how long have you been doing this again?" he called over his shoulder.

"A few years," I responded. I looked down at his phone and pressed the calendar button with one hand while feather dusting with the other.

"You from around here?"

"Grew up in Norfolk." I glanced at last week. My gaze focused in on last Thursday. There. At 6 p.m. it said S.N.

Sierra Nakamura.

Bruce had met with Sierra before she disappeared. Did he know anything about her disappearance now?

"What are you doing?"

I gasped. I looked up to find Bruce standing at the table. "I'm just dusting."

"My phone?"

"I must have hit it with my duster. Sorry."

He looked at me for a moment, as if trying to gauge if I were trustworthy. Finally, he nodded and grabbed the phone, sliding it into his pocket. "The screen's pretty sensitive."

I had to change the subject and fast. I nodded toward the litter box in the corner. "Have you seen that new eco-friendly kitty litter?"

Kitty litter, Gabby? Really?

"Uh… no, I guess I haven't. Tell me about it."

"It's supposed to be a lot better for the environment. It doesn't contain carcinogens and burden our landfills. It's amazing the products they're coming up with."

"Isn't it?"

"You seem really into stuff like that."

"Yeah, I'm pretty passionate about it. Some people might call me over the top."

"Why would they do that? They just don't understand what it's like to believe in something with your entire being."

He nodded, warmth in his eyes. "That's right. They just don't understand. Everyone should be passionate about something. It helps us to discover our purpose in life, you know."

"Absolutely."

He leaned against his desk. "So, what are you passionate about, Gabrielle?"

Putting bad guys in jail. Probably shouldn't go there. "Animals. I'm passionate about animals. I can't stand to see them treated cruelly." It was true. I didn't want to see an animal suffer. But I sure did like to eat them.

"That's a noble love."

"I'm hoping to get plugged in with a local group. I'm interested in helping with petitions and picketing at events like that ludicrous circus that comes to town."

"I might have some connections for you."

"Do you? I'd love it if you could hook me up." I finished dusting his desk. An invisible weight pressed on my chest each time I realized how he was watching my every move. Maybe Riley was right. Maybe I shouldn't have done this.

"A friend of mine is real involved with stuff like that. Let me talk to her, and I'll get back with you."

I pulled out one of my business cards, freshly made this morning on my computer. I pressed it into his hand. "Here's my number. Let me know."

He stared at it a moment. "Yeah, I'll do that."

I glanced at the clock on the wall behind him. "It looks like it's time for you to go. I didn't get as much done as I'd hoped. Would you like me to stay a little while after you leave?"

He shook his head. "No, I don't want you to do that. I'm not quite that trusting, even with someone with a face as sweet as yours." He looked around. "It does look better. Smells better even."

"Lavender oil. All natural."

"I'll be in touch." He stood and nodded toward my supplies. "Let me help you take those to the van."

"You don't have to do that." I pictured him opening the door and seeing Riley there. That would be no good.

"I don't mind." He pulled the tub from my hands.

I pulled it back, the solution sloshing wildly inside. "Really, it's okay."

He actually had the nerve to try and take them back again. "No really, I insist. My counselor says I need to put other people first more."

My grip didn't loosen. "And my feminist side says why let someone else do what a woman is perfectly capable of doing herself."

He finally raised his hands in the air. He didn't laugh good-naturedly like most people might, proving his social skills still needed some work. "Fine, you win. I've got to run anyway. Can't lose another job."

Diversion, I thought. Diversion is always a good tactic. "Another one? Have you lost more than one?"

"Yeah, lost one just last week as a delivery driver for a bakery on Main St."

"That's too bad."

He shrugged. "Whatever. They were all particular about their deliveries always having to be on time and all. Too serious for their own good."

"Some people."

A grin—one that was supposed to be charming probably—stretched over his ruddy face. "It's been a pleasure, Gabriella."

Against all sensibilities, I shook his hand. "You too, Bruce. Remember, if you know of anyone who needs a cleaner..."

He winked. "I'll give them your information."

I quickly gathered my things and rushed out the front door.

My gut told me that the man was off his rocker. Capable of bombing Harrison Developers? Definitely. Capable of harming my friend? It was a possibility.

It wasn't until I pulled away that Riley popped his head up from the back. "You're pretty convincing, you know. And your phone has excellent speaker capabilities."

"Doesn't it, though? Detecting 101 teaches me that I must try to relate to the person I want information from in order to build trust. You really thought I was convincing?"

"I did. I just wished that you'd opened the curtains."

"I forgot. Sorry. Next time."

He shook his head. "I don't even want to think about that." He climbed into the front seat. "So, what did you find out, detective?"

I shared with him about the manuals and the calendar appointment with S.N. "He's involved in all of this somehow. I'm sure of it."

"Can't you leave the rest of this investigation to the police?"

I looked over my shoulder and gave Riley an incredulous look. "No, why would I do that? No one has more at stake here than I do."

"How about the city of Norfolk? How about James Harrison? How about whomever the next victim is that these people are going to target? The car industry? People who don't recycle? Chemical companies?"

"Okay, okay. I see your point. But I'm not giving up. Not yet." I'd only begun to scratch the surface of this case and giving up was not in my DNA.

CHAPTER 12

After dropping Riley at his car and promising to stay out of trouble, I wandered across the street to The Grounds. I hadn't been in for a week, which was highly unusual for me. I'd been too distracted by everything else going on.

"Gabby. You're back, and the world is right again." Sharon called out across the place. A few customers hung out, but the morning rush was already over. "Love your shirt, by the way."

I looked down at my "Snarky Reply Loading" shirt and grinned. Yeah, this was one of my favorites also.

I crossed the wood floor to the register, absorbing the scent of rich coffee and the sweet earthiness of cinnamon. Latin music playing overhead seemed to mock my mood as I leaned against the granite countertop toward Sharon. "It just doesn't seem right to be here without Sierra."

She paused from wiping down the surfaces. "Still no word on her?"

"No, she appears to have disappeared into thin air."

"If anyone can track her down, it's you."

If only her words were true. "I'm not sure she wants to be tracked down. I think she's hiding for a reason. I just don't know what the reason is."

"You and Riley seem to be putting your heads together for this, don't you? I mean, I knew you two were friends, but lately you seem like more." She offered a glance before beginning a new brew of coffee.

"I'm not Riley's type, Sharon." I frowned. "I'm trying to get out of denial about that fact."

Sharon threw me a look over her shoulder. "I wouldn't be too sure about that. I've seen the way he looks at you."

"You mean, like I'm crazy?"

She smiled. "No, like you're valuable."

"Valuable?" Wow. That was a new one.

She shrugged as she added round scoops of coffee grounds into the percolator. "Yeah, I know it sounds weird, but it's the only word I can think of. He looks at you like some men look at their prized football jersey or their dream car."

I think I might have blushed. I had to process that. Certainly, Sharon was seeing things that weren't actually there. I had to appreciate that she was trying to make me feel better in the midst of everything else that had happened.

"So what's going on with Sierra?"

I filled her in.

Sharon leaned on her elbows across the counter, her full attention on our conversation. "Let me know what I can do to help."

"You can keep an eye on her place when we're not there. Someone's already broken in once." Sharon had a birds-eye view of our apartment building from the coffeehouse.

"Drinks are on the house this morning, Gabby. You just concentrate on finding Sierra." Sharon nodded, giving me her blessing and encouragement as she pushed my drink closer.

I nodded toward the door. "I'm going to get rolling then."

"Gabby, wait one second. Check out these paintings we're featuring." Sharon nodded across the room at the wall on the far side.

I paused a moment, not in the mood to offer any fake admiration for art. But I'd be polite, for Sharon's sake.

"I've been waiting to hear your reaction now for a while. I think of you every time I see those paintings." She rounded the serving area and joined me.

I approached one and paused. My eyes widened at the picture of the ratty house against the darkened sky. "No…"

Sharon appeared at my side, nodding as if she were an art aficionado. "What is it?"

My finger trembled as I pointed at the painting. "That's the house where I grew up."

CHAPTER 13

"You're sure that's your house?" Sharon asked.

"I'm positive. Never been more sure. That's my old house. That's even my old rusty mailbox and the tree that I fell out of in third grade and broke my arm."

"Spooky," Sharon muttered.

I hardly heard her. I moved on to the next picture and tears welled in my eyes at the familiar face. "That's my mom."

"She was beautiful." Sharon's voice sounded soft, compassionate.

I nodded and wiped at a tear. "She was an awesome person. I still miss her. But why would someone...?" I shook my head, trying to absorb all of this.

Dread filled me as I turned to the third painting. My hand covered my mouth when I saw the picture of the boy there. "It's my brother."

Sharon's hand covered my shoulder. "Your brother? I didn't know you had a brother."

"He was kidnapped. I haven't seen him since he was six."

"Gabby, that's terrible. He was like kidnapped for real? Did a family member take him in the midst of a custody dispute or something?"

"No, strangers took him while I was watching him at the park. It tore my family apart. My dad started drinking—even more than he had been. We went on TV and pleaded for the public's help. But nothing. The police never really even had any good leads. My mom died not knowing whatever happened to her son. All these years, all we've had were questions."

Sharon wiped the moisture from under her eye. "I had no idea, Gabby. I'm so sorry."

I reached up and touched the painting of my brother. It so vividly captured the mischief in his eyes. His brown hair looked characteristically messy, so much so that I wanted to reach into the canvas and straighten it. I missed him still to this day and had never forgiven myself for looking away from him, even if it had only been for a moment.

"Why would someone do this?" My voice came out as a whisper.

"I had no idea. I really didn't."

"It's not your fault, Sharon." I moved down the line. Only two more paintings left. What would these be?

I sucked in a breath at the sight of the next one. It was the skeleton of a massive house that had burned to the ground. A lone figure stood in front of it, watching the remains as if they might come to life again.

I knew who that person was. That person was me, and the scene was the first crime I'd ever solved—the death of a senator's wife where I'd nearly been torched after finding key evidence.

The final painting showed a group of friends. None of the faces were clear in this painting, just a blur of paint. But the smiles and the fun were evident as they sat around a table with coffee, in a shop similar to The Grounds. But there, in the background and out of the dark window displaying the street, was the figure of a masked man peering in at its edge. Watching them.

I sucked in a breath.

Just like someone had been watching me.

"Who painted these?" My throat burned as I asked the question.

"A college student. I had no idea, Gabby. I didn't think anything about the paintings except that they seemed to tell some kind of mysterious story."

"Yeah, my story." I glanced at Sharon. "What did this college student look like?"

Sharon shrugged. "Pretty normal. Petite, chestnut brown hair that came to her shoulders. She had a bit of acne and wore black—as in, all black, even down to her flip flops."

"Flip-flops?" I glanced down at my feet to where my toes peeked out beneath my jeans. It didn't matter the temperature. I loved my flip-flops, but not many people around here wore them when the temperature was this cold.

"Do you have her name?"

"I'll get her contact information for you now."

I studied the paintings as Sharon disappeared. Why? Why would someone have done this? And how did they know so much about me?

That eerie feeling pinched my spine again. Someone had been following me and watching me. Now they were sending me another message by picking this spot to display their paintings. They'd sent me cryptic notes, also, which led me to believe that the person behind this was also a killer.

I shivered, wishing for a moment that Riley was here so he could help me make sense of everything. But he had a court case later today. I had to clean another crime scene, and the only way Riley hadn't had a coronary over it was because I'd called Parker and he promised to meet me there to discuss the notes that had been left for me.

Sharon approached with a paper in hand. "Here, I wrote down all the information I have."

"Is this girl supposed to come back any time soon?"

"I told her we'd keep these up for three months. There's a chance I won't hear from her until then."

"Where did she say she'd heard about you?"

"She didn't. She just said she was checking out some local places that were artist friendly and she happened upon The Grounds. I didn't think anything of it. Aside from being a little shy and awkward, she seemed harmless."

I glanced at the paper. "Becca Bowling." Her address wasn't that far from here. I'd be making a pit stop on my way to my job, it looked like. Special Agent Parker could wait on me for a few minutes.

"I gotta run, Sharon. Let me know if this Becca shows up again, okay?"

"You betcha."

I hopped in my van—this time making sure that Henry wasn't in the back—and took off toward the address. It wasn't too far from where I lived, close to a nearby college.

As the facts brewed in my mind, my foot pressed into the accelerator harder than I intended. The van's speed seemed to match my racing thoughts. Why would someone do this? What was going on, and how was I ever going to get any answers?

Finally, I saw the street and turned onto it. Maybe I would get some answers now. Or would that be too easy?

As I searched for the house number—1020—I realized just that. The residence didn't exist. The address was bogus as the street ended at 900.

Another dead end. Literally this time.

When would I ever catch a break?

CHAPTER 14

I sighed and started down the road toward the crime scene I needed to clean up. Another stabbing, and this one had even more blood than the last, so I'd likely be there all day today. I had class this evening at six, so I had to wrap up before then so I could make it. I only had three months until I graduated and nothing was going to stop me. My college degree had been a long time coming and had been stopped by many obstacles. Not this time.

I pulled into an upscale neighborhood, one with brick homes and a massive lake that gave people the right to claim their houses were waterfront property. Not many American-made vehicles were in the driveways, but instead there were Mercedes and Volvos and BMWs. The man who'd been killed—Landon Lancaster –was a landscaper whose designs had apparently won him awards. His designs, however, had not helped his personal life because he'd been married and divorced twice. His sister was the one who'd called me about this job, and she was still struggling to understand how a crime like this could happen. The police were calling this a home invasion gone bad. It seemed as if the home invasion market had really skyrocketed in this area lately, the fact by which would not help me to sleep better at night.

I pulled to a stop in front of a particularly well-kept home. This one had thick white columns across the porch and looked stately. These weren't the kind of homes where I often had to clean up crimes. Wealthy people like this usually reserved their nefarious deeds for the white-collar variety.

Parker's car was already in the driveway. He sat in his sedan, chatting on his phone until he spotted me. Then he stepped out, looking none too happy to see me. It had been like that when we were dating also, so not much had changed—other than the fact that we weren't dating any more.

I pulled my jacket on as I walked across the thick grass toward my fed ex. The weather again today couldn't make up its mind and continued to occasionally pluck down some wet drops of icy moisture. Even though the sun hung high in the sky, little droplets still fell downward.

"Gabby," Parker mumbled.

"Good to see you, too. I need to let you know that something strange is going on, Parker." I filled him in as we walked toward the black and brass front door.

Parker paused at the stoop. "How'd you get mixed up in all of this, Gabby?"

"Not on purpose! This is the one time I can honestly say it's not my fault. I didn't do anything, but some psycho is painting pictures of me and my family and leaving threatening notes for me at various places."

He stared at me a moment before the edges of his mouth pulled up in a … grin? Really? This was amusing him? He nodded toward the door. "Let me check everything out for you inside. I should have sent the local PD out to do it, but I wanted to do you a favor."

"Because you're too good to do menial work like checking out a crime scene for potential criminals?"

The grin slipped. "Yes, that's exactly what I meant, Gabby. Now that I'm a G-man, I'm above all of this." He narrowed his eyes. "Of course I didn't mean that. I just have a lot to do while working this case. I'm new to the FBI and I don't want to blow it."

I held up a hand. "Whatever. Let's just go inside and get this over with."

He unlocked the door, and we stepped out of the cold. I sucked in a breath when I walked inside. What was that oddly-familiar scent? My eyes zeroed in on something on a nearby table. I charged toward it, Parker behind me.

There, stuck between two pictures of Landon Lancaster, was a stick of incense. Just like Sierra's. I leaned closer. No, this was Sierra's. Same brand, same sage scent, same "I love animals" sticker on the bottom. Was this what the person had broken into her apartment to retrieve?

Parker muttered something not-so-nice under his breath.

I looked back at him. "I take it this wasn't here when the scene was released?"

"Deductive reasoning, Ms. Drew." He plucked his phone off his belt. "Let me get the evidence response team in here... again."

CHAPTER 15

Later that night, I lay in bed, throwing an apple up in the air and catching it as I tried to sort out my thoughts.

Housing development burned down. Developer's office bombed. Sierra has bomb-making manual. Her proximity on the evening of the crimes is unaccounted for due to a change in plans. Said manual is then found at the scene of a stabbing. The man stabbed worked for a solar energy company. Sierra's brownies are found at the home of a man who's known for his plasterwork in the area. Then Sierra's incense is found at another stabbing, this time of an award-winning landscaper. Meanwhile, someone has painted pictures of my life and is leaving me cryptic notes.

How did I make sense of all of that? I kept trying to connect all of the dots, but none of them wanted to meet up.

What kind of wannabe detective was I?

I tossed the apple in the air again but missed it coming down. The fruit dropped right into my eye.

"Ouch." I rubbed the spot and sat up in bed. For revenge, I bit a big chunk out of Gala.

That's when I heard the rap on the door.

I pulled a sweatshirt on over my tank top and tiptoed to the door. Who was it now? Did I really want to know? Were the feds back with more bad news? Did Henry desperately need a place to stay?

"Gabby, are you awake? It's Riley." His voice sounded hushed, like a loud whisper.

I unlocked all of my locks—yeah, I had four of them—and cracked the door, confirmed it was Riley, and then stepped aside. "Come in."

His eyes glimmered. "I was hoping you might be awake."

I shrugged, swallowed my last bite of apple, and tossed the fruit into the trashcan. With a thump, it miraculously went inside. "Yeah, I can't sleep."

He squeezed my arm as he slid past me and plopped on my couch. "How was your day?"

I sat across from him, crossed my legs and told him about everything from the paintings to the incense and brownies at the crime scene. I'd been anxious to talk to him all day, but his court cases had apparently gone long, and then I'd been in class.

He leaned back on the couch and blinked several times as I finished. "Wow."

"Yeah, wow is right."

"No leads?"

I shook my head and plucked a piece of lint from my yoga pants. "Nothing. Nada. Zip."

He patted my knee, but instead of withdrawing his hand back to himself, he left it there. I didn't complain. "You'll figure it out, Gabby."

"Why do you sound so sure?"

"Because you always do. You're good at being nosy and getting answers." He shifted his weight and, in doing so, moved his hand back to his lap. I missed it instantly. "By the way, did you talk to the medical examiner anymore about working there?"

"My application is on file, and they sound interested." I shrugged. "You never know. I could be bona fide medical legal death investigator in a few months."

"I'm proud of you, you know. A lot of people in your shoes would have given up already. You stayed strong, and I admire that."

"Thanks, Riley. You've been a great friend throughout it all." Don't blush, Gabby. Don't blush. What was up with me blushing lately?

Riley didn't seem to notice, or, if he did, he didn't make a big deal of it. "What will you do after you graduate? Will you give up the crime scene cleaning?"

I shrugged. "I don't know. I can't imagine myself not doing this. But… I'm not sure. It will all figure itself out."

"There have been a lot of changes over the past year, huh? You became a Christian, your dad is coming to church, and you're almost a graduate. Good things are happening."

I frowned. "Yes, good things."

"Then why are you frowning?"

I pressed myself into the couch, my muscles tensing. "I'm having a hard time with my dad, thinking he's a better person. It was easier when I thought he was scum."

"That's where forgiveness comes in, Gabby."

Forgiveness. That word seemed to echo in my head a lot lately. "I know. I'm working on it. It's easier said than done, however."

"It will come. Just give yourself time. Remember, though, that when you don't forgive someone, you let them have power over you and ultimately just hurt yourself."

I nodded. "You're right. I just have some work to do, still."

Riley's gaze stayed on me until a grin stretched across his face. He pointed to the open newspaper on the table. "You going to see the stage adaption of High School Musical?"

I grabbed the paper to obscure the huge red circle I'd drawn over the ad so I wouldn't forget about the upcoming performance and pulled my head back in disgust. "High School Musical? What kind of self-respecting adult watches High School Musical?"

Riley raised his brow.

"What?"

He shook his head, still grinning. "Nothing."

Why did I have the sneaking suspicion that he knew more than I wanted him to? "Spill it, Rilster."

His brow lifted higher, along with the corner of his mouth. "Rilster? I like that. Maybe I'll keep you guessing so I can hear what comes out of your mouth next."

"I do know how to kill people and clean up afterward so that no one will guess what happened." I waved a finger at him to emphasize my point.

He chuckled and held his hands in the air. "Okay, okay. I admit it. I can hear you singing the songs from High School Musical all the way in my apartment. 'We're All In This Together.'" He did a little musical-like dance move and sang in falsetto.

I scowled and swatted his shoulder.

"What?" he asked in mock innocence.

"You weren't supposed to hear me." I repressed my laugh, secretly grateful for the subject change.

"It's not my fault that your voice sounds amplified, even without a microphone." He stood and started singing, "You Are the Music in Me," grinning each step of the way.

I'd had enough. I tackled him. Yep. Tackled him all the way to the ground.

His eyes widened as he hit the floor, but he quickly composed himself. His startling blue eyes met mine and sparkled like alluring ocean water on a hot day. "That's one mean move you've got there, Ms. St. Claire."

I narrowed my eyes at him, trying to block out our close proximity lest I do something crazy and proclaim my love for him or something. But the musky scent of his aftershave threatened to pull me under. I had to get a grip or I might drown in the moment. I cleared my throat. "I've got more where that came from."

He laughed. "Do you?"

In one motion, he flipped me over so I was the one being pinned. "I have a few moves of my own. I did play football for one lousy year in high school, you know."

"No, I didn't know." I could hardly think about our conversation, though. All I could think about was how close Riley was to me, how I could feel his heartbeat against me, how I could see the startling blue of his eyes.

His smile slipped, and he rolled off of me and onto his side. "Gabby, there is something I've been meaning to talk to you about."

Another secret fiancée? Not again. I braced myself. Before I could offer a sharp retort, his lips covered mine and pure electricity zipped up my spine.

I'd dreamed about this day for a long time, but never thought it would actually happen. And the kiss was even more wonderful in reality than it was in my dreams—tender yet passionate, sweet yet urgent.

He pulled back and my lips still tingled—gloriously tingled.

I cleared my throat and rubbed my hand over my mouth. "That's what you wanted to talk to me about?"

His grin stayed in place, and he leaned closer. "I thought actions might speak louder than words."

"In this case, I'd agree." I propped myself up on an elbow. "But nonetheless, words are still needed. What exactly was that about?"

He sat up and his smile disappeared a moment, replaced with a serious expression. "I can't stop thinking about you, Gabby. Ever since the first time we met, you've grabbed at my heart. I just never thought the time was right—until now."

"It's because I keep on almost getting killed, isn't it? You've realized you don't have that much time because it's me?" There I went again... I just couldn't let a serious moment be, could I? When in doubt, make a joke. I mentally scolded myself.

He laughed and gently tugged one of my hairs behind my ear. "No... I mean, the almost-getting-killed only reinforces what I feel for you, I suppose. But I've just seen you grow so much lately. I've seen how much you really do care about people, how you've risen above the hand you've been dealt and become stronger because of it."

My heart nearly stopped beating as his words flowed over me. I tried to find something to say—the right thing to say—but Riley kept going, so I let him.

"I knew for sure that I had feelings for you when you planned that funeral for the man who had no family."

I remembered the service we had for the man—a man whose house I'd been hired to clean. He'd been dead for several days before anyone missed him. That was life as a modern-day hermit, I supposed. But, with no family, I didn't want him to simply disappear from the earth without so much as a goodbye, so we'd held a wake for him. It had felt good to do something for someone else, even if that person was dead. Everyone deserved a funeral. Everyone. "That was nearly six months ago."

He nodded. "I know. I didn't think you were ready for a relationship then."

And I probably wasn't. I was too confused about too many things—including God. Plus, Parker and I had just broken up, and Chad had pranced into my life.

"I thought you might slap me if I kissed you."

"Slap you? Why would I do that?"

"I just never know what to expect from you. Just one more thing to love about you."

I leaned into him. His arm went around my waist, and we sat there a moment. It felt like pure bliss. I inhaled his scent, something I'd done before today, but I'd felt guilty about—like it wasn't my liberty to take. But now, I felt like I could sit here and absorb every wonderful thing about him with no guilt. Riley was my ... what was he? I didn't want to read more into this than I should.

"What does this mean for us, Riley?"

"I want to give our relationship a chance, Gabby. I think we're going to work well together, but I want to date you—and only you. I want to see where this relationship leads."

"So you're my boyfriend?" I smiled.

A grin cracked over his face. "Yeah, I guess I am."

I stood and began singing, "Start of Something New," being as overly dramatic and cheesy as possible. Riley stood and wrapped his arms around me, effectively cutting me off with a kiss.

And, for once in my life, I didn't argue.

CHAPTER 16

Since I didn't have the chance to stalk—I mean, pay a visit to—Mark Daniels yesterday, doing so was the first thing on my agenda for Tuesday morning.

I dressed respectably in some khakis and a sweater and held my head up high as I strode into the office of Solar Sun Development. I evenly and properly requested to the receptionist that I speak with Mark Daniels. Four minutes and thirty-one seconds later, I was ushered into his office. It almost seemed suspiciously easy.

Mark Daniels wasn't whom I expected. He was well-groomed, in his mid-thirties, and had a million-dollar smile. He had a full head of dark hair and even, kind features that had probably landed him a lot of attention from the ladies.

"Welcome," he said when I stepped into his office. "Please, have a seat." He pointed to the plush leather—or was it pleather?—chair across from his desk. Then he laced his fingers together on his desk and stared at me. "What can I do for you, Ms. St. Claire?"

I'd briefly thought about making up a reason to be there. But instead I decided to dive in with the truth and see where that got me.

"Do you know Sierra Nakamura?"

He blinked, but otherwise remained composed. "Who?"

"Sierra Nakamura."

"The name doesn't sound familiar. Why do you ask?"

"I know about your colleague who died this past weekend in the supposed home invasion."

"Terrible tragedy. Home invasions are just a terrible reality, one I'd rather not think about. Were you a friend?"

I shook my head. "No, I didn't know him. But I do know that you requested some of his books, and I want to know why."

He blinked again and, just for a fraction of a second, his cheek twitched. "I don't know what you're talking about."

"I know the FBI has already talked to you about it."

Finally, he sighed and leaned back in his chair. "You obviously know more than you're letting on." He tilted his head, his eyes suddenly looking weary. "Look, I had suspicions that my *employee* was into some business that he had no business being in. That's why I requested those books. I wanted to get to the bottom of things. He's not around anymore, and I wanted to make sure I didn't have a mess to clean up."

"Were you aware of the bomb-making manual stuck between the pages of the book?"

"No, not until the FBI informed me it was there."

"Any idea what your employee was up to?"

He shook his head. "No, he was passionate about his work to protect the environment, but he wasn't extreme. I don't know why he was reading that material."

Reminded me of Sierra.

"And you're telling me the truth when you say that you don't know Sierra?"

"I've never heard of her."

"Have you been able to uncover any answers?"

He leaned toward me. "Who are you? Why are you asking me these questions?"

"I'm a crime scene cleaner."

"And you're authorized to investigate whatever this is that you're investigating?"

"My best friend is being implicated, and I'm determined to prove her innocence. I'm trying to connect some dots."

He stared at me a moment before offering a curt nod. "I can appreciate that. But I'm not sure how much I can help you. I'm just as interested in getting some answers as you are."

I slid my business card across the desk toward him. "If you discover any of those elusive answers, will you let me know?"

"I will. Would you do the same for me?"

I hesitated. I only shared information if it would benefit the investigation. Would sharing anything with

Mark help me? Being on his side might earn me more information, whereas refusing might keep me locked out. I nodded. "Absolutely."

I said goodbye and felt like dragging my feet as I left the building and climbed into my van, frustrated by another dead end. As I glanced at the front door, I saw someone else enter the building.

Lydia Harrison. Maybe this wasn't a dead end after all.

My internal alarms began wailing. That couldn't be a coincidence. What did Lydia Harrison and Mark Daniels know about each other? I bit the inside of my lip, mulling the thought over. I didn't know. Not yet. But I would.

I sunk down in my seat and waited for Lydia Harrison to emerge.

***

Forty minutes later, Lydia exited the building. She wiped at her eyes, and I wondered if she'd been crying. About what? Wasn't her divorce almost finalized? Was she dating Mark Daniels already? This woman was a major link to these crimes. I just didn't know why.

As she started her Lexus and pulled away from the parking lot, I did the same. I hadn't been schooled in the exact science of tailing someone, but I'd done a pretty good job at learning on my own. Don't stay too close or be too aggressive. Change lanes when possible, but don't let yourself get too far away. If in doubt, ditch the tail and try again later—and when I say doubt, I really mean danger, as in, if someone starts shooting at you or the like. Yeah, I'd been around the block a few times.

Lydia eased onto the interstate and, of course, I did the same. Traffic was moderate so it wasn't hard to remain a respectable and unsuspecting distance behind her. She traveled west from Virginia Beach toward Chesapeake. Finally, she pulled off at an exit and into a ... Waffle City? The greasy spoon hardly seemed like the haunt for a wealthy woman like Lydia.

She glanced around when she exited the car, as if she felt my eyes on her. But she never looked my way. I sunk down in my seat again, praying she wouldn't see me. She seemed satisfied that no one suspicious was around and hurried inside the restaurant. The front of the place was all windows, which afforded me a great view of her meeting... with Broken Arrow.

What was going on? And how was Lydia involved in all of this? After today, I was sure she was involved in this mess somehow. I just had to figure out how. And was it a coincidence that she'd fixated on "winning" Riley at that Bachelor Auction? I didn't believe in coincidences. But what did she want with Riley? Was she the same one who'd sent me cryptic notes? Was she trying to pull Riley and me into this whole mystery?

My cell phone began playing the Pink Panther theme song. I pulled it out and answered. Parker. I frowned.

He skipped any formalities. "Heard anymore from Sierra?"

"No, I haven't. You?" I kept my eyes glued on the restaurant as we spoke.

"I can't share any details of the investigation. Apparently, you're trying to figure those out on your own."

I tapped my fingers against the steering wheel, feeling like I'd had this conversation a million times before. "And you're surprised?"

"No, I'm not."

"What gave me away this time?"

"Mark Daniels told me you'd been by."

So much for sharing any information with that man. I watched as Lydia leaned across the table at Broken Arrow. She slid something toward him. What was it? Broken Arrow looked around before grabbing the paper and slipping it inside his jacket. A bribe maybe? Information? I wanted to see that paper.

"Gabby, are you still there?"

I shook my head, coming out of my stupor. "I'm here."

"If you find out any information, you need to share it with me, Gabby. Understand? This is serious."

Yeah, I'd been told that a million times already—not that I needed to be told. "Got it."

He paused. "Gabby, there's been some other things that have happened."

"Let me guess—you can't tell me what, though. You're just teasing me."

"Actually, some of it will be on the news tonight, so I feel comfortable in giving you a heads up."

I tensed in surprise at the unexpected news. "Okay, shoot."

"James Harrison had a heart attack this morning. It doesn't look like he's going to make it."

CHAPTER 17

I sat up straight, my eyes temporarily leaving Lydia and Broken Arrow. "Heart attack? Heart attack how?"

"The normal way, Gabby. I don't know."

My back loosened some at the anticlimactic news. "Was it really the normal way?"

"We can only assume at this point. I will say that the man has had a lot of stress on him lately. Stress can do crazy things to a body."

I would draw my own conclusions. "Has this whole town gone crazy?"

"We think there's more than one person involved here. We know they're dangerous."

I ran my hand along the edge of my steering wheel, trying to follow my thoughts as easily. "You mean, like a gang?"

"Not necessarily. I just really want you to be careful, though."

"Got it." I hung up, mulling over his words when my phone began playing that familiar tune. What had

Parker forgotten now? "I'm going to start charging you for my time."

"Gabby?"

I straightened again, my heart rate quickening. "Sierra? Where are you? What's going on?"

"Don't trust anyone, Gabby." The phone cackled.

I gripped the phone harder than I intended, so hard that my knuckles actually ached. "Anyone? What do you mean by that? Sierra, I need some answers."

She tried to say something, but I couldn't make it out.

"Where are you, Sierra? I can help."

"No." Garbled words followed.

"But—"

"I have to go. I can't risk my call being traced. Be careful, Gabby. This isn't a game. There are people out there willing to kill in order to keep their secrets."

Before I could say anything else, the line went dead. What was that about? Where was Sierra? How was she involved in this?

Before I could ponder it very long, both Lydia and Broken Arrow stood. They exchanged a handshake before exiting Waffle City. I watched as Broken Arrow walked to his truck, and Lydia to her Lexus. *Who to follow, who to follow?*

I went with my gut and pulled out after the truck. I stayed behind Broken Arrow on the highway for several miles. Where was this man going? Did he sense I was following him? I didn't think so.

Until he turned off the highway onto a two lane road. Here, it would be hard to hide. Did he know that? Did he know I was following him and chose this road on purpose?

I gripped the wheel, hoping I'd made the right decision by following Broken Arrow.

Finally, he turned off the country lane and back onto a four-lane road. A few minutes later, he pulled into a city park. He parked his truck and hurried through the woods toward the lake beyond that. The patch of trees blocked my view. Who was he meeting? What was going on? The answers felt close.

I scrambled from my van, deciding to take my chances. There were several other cars in the parking lot, so I wouldn't be at the park alone with Broken Arrow. And the woods would offer a good cover for me. I just had to see whom he was meeting. I had to know what was going on.

I bypassed the path leading directly to the park and ducked into the woods instead. I stayed far enough away from the trail that I wouldn't be seen. When I got closer to the park, I slowed my steps. I ducked behind a massive oak tree and peered around it, hoping to get a glimpse of Broken Arrow. My flip-flops made it hard to navigate the uneven terrain, but I did the best I could.

Where was he? I craned my neck, trying to spot him. Instead, I saw families with young children bundled in their winter coats, a lone, die-hard fisherman, an underdressed, competitive biker. No Broken Arrow though.

What if he'd decided to take the path around the lake? I hesitated to leave the safety of the park crowd. But if I stayed concealed in the woods, I could still be in the clear. I could discover the answers I sought and then quietly slip away before anyone ever saw me.

I looked in every direction, waiting to see if anyone had spotted me. I didn't see a soul. I had to be careful, though. The woods, though there were some evergreens, were sparse in their winter coats. In the summer, the area was thick with underbrush and vines and greenery. Right now, the trees stood like skeletons.

I swallowed, trying not to think about the possibilities of snakes or other creatures that might be living out here. I guess I'd deal with that when it happened.

I moved down the length of the lake trail, being careful not to step on any branches and make myself known. If a career in forensics didn't work out, maybe I could apply for the CIA. My spy skills were quite impressive today, even if I did say so myself.

I paused behind another large tree as a picnic shelter came into view. Something—or someone—was there. I squinted, trying to get a better look. What was that? A person, hunched over? A trash bag? I couldn't tell.

I sucked in a breath and decided I'd get a little closer. Not too close.

I took my first step when a hand wrapped around my mouth. I tried to scream, but couldn't. Someone pinned my arms and lifted me off my feet.

Maybe I shouldn't think about being a spy after all.

CHAPTER 18

"Why are you following me, Gabby St. Claire?"

I recognized the voice, the cadence of the man's speech. Broken Arrow.

Of course, I couldn't answer him because his hand was over my mouth. That didn't stop me from mumbling into his hand. I could annoy him if nothing else.

"Easy does it, Gabby. I'm going to move my hand, but if you scream, I'll have to take alternative actions. Got it?"

I nodded. Alternate actions? Was that as threatening as he could sound?

Slowly, he lowered his hand from my mouth. His grip around my midsection loosened, and I turned around. I stared up at Broken Arrow, realizing that the man was a good foot taller than me, had muscles the size of machine guns, and could probably snap my neck in one, quick, easy motion.

"What are you doing here, Gabby?" he asked.

"I saw you meeting with Lydia. I'm trying to figure out what's going on."

"Some things are not for you to know, Gabby St. Claire."

He said my full name an awful lot. "There are some things I need to know, Broken Arrow. My friend is in danger."

"I'm afraid you are too."

My throat felt suddenly dry. "Why? What's going on?"

"You have to figure that out. Though I'd prefer that you didn't."

"Are you involved?"

A shadow passed over his eyes. "There are things of which I cannot speak."

"Says who? Who says you can't speak of them?"

"Gabby St. Claire, be glad I found you today instead of someone else. Someone else may have hurt you and left you here for dead. I only warn you."

"But—"

"Go. Go now, Gabby, before we both end up dead."

I stared at him a moment. What did that mean? What was I missing?

I knew one thing. This was more than a case of murder. This was more than a serial killer or a string of robberies. Was it a gang? Drugs? A prostitution ring? Public corruption?

Broken Arrow still stared at me, and I knew I wouldn't get any more information from him. I nodded. "I'm leaving."

"Watch your back. Always. You're going to wish you hadn't gotten involved in this, Gabby St. Claire."

I tromped back through the woods until I found the trail. I went back to my van, feeling like I blew everything. The mystery was only deepening, and I was getting no answers. Sierra could die if the wrong person or people found her, and I was helpless to intervene. I threw my head back into the seat, feeling a headache coming on.

That's when I spotted another piece of paper on my windshield. What now? I grabbed it and unfolded the creases.

As iron sharpens iron, so one man sharpens another. If you play with fire, you're going to get burned. Your efforts are impressive, however. I only hope you're fire—and iron—proof.

CHAPTER 19

I had to find my friend. That was all there was to it. And I had to get the FBI off my speed dial. Enough was enough.

Although being nosy had already gotten me into a heap of trouble today, I decided things couldn't get much worse, so I kept investigating. My next stop was Sierra's place of employment. I would question her coworkers, request to see her desk, eavesdrop. I mean sure, the FBI had probably already done that. But you never knew what you might find that someone else might overlook.

Twenty minutes later, I pulled into the outdated building where her office was housed. Inside, I asked the receptionist if I could speak with the office manager and, a moment later, a chubby, balding man with a fringe of dark hair, a wide nose, and big, deep-set brown eyes emerged.

"I'm Bernard," he said slowly. "What can I do for you?"

"I'm Sierra Nakamura's best friend, Gabby St. Claire."

His face darkened. "I'm saddened to hear about everything that's happened with her. It gives us a bad name. We're a peaceful group, you know."

"I know. And I know Sierra isn't guilty of everything she's been accused of."

"She's bright and intelligent, so I'd hope not." St. Bernard, as I'd already affectionately begun to think of him, shifted his weight. "What can I help you with?"

"I'd like to see her work station."

"What good would that serve?"

"I'm trying to find her, and I thought her work area might give me a clue as to where she'd gone." I resisted the urge to look for dew claws.

"The FBI has already been in here."

"I know. I'm different because I'm her friend."

He remained silent a moment before nodding. "Fine. You've got fifteen minutes. Try not to disrupt everyone, please."

I'd only been to Sierra's office twice before, and mostly when I'd been there, I'd looked for ways to poke fun at the animal-loving freaks. Now, I needed to turn from my ways in order to find out the information I so desperately needed.

St. Bernard pointed to her desk and then tapped at his watch. "Fifteen minutes."

I nodded and plopped in her chair, swiveling around as I did so. Was there something here that would help me find my friend?

I opened her calendar and didn't see anything that set my senses on high alert. I flipped through a few files. I looked in her trashcan. Nothing.

"You're Sierra's best friend, aren't you? That crime-scene cleaner?"

I looked up and saw a girl who looked similar to Sierra, only Nordic. Whereas Sierra had shiny, dark hair that fell to her shoulders, this girl had shiny blonde hair that fell to her chin. Sierra had skin the color of almonds. This girl's skin was pasty white. Sierra wore black, plastic-framed glasses; this girl wore blue.

I extended my hand. "Gabby St. Claire."

The girl grinned. "I'm Helena. Sierra was always talking about you."

"She was?" I propelled the chair back some.

Helena nodded briskly. "We'd always ask her to tell us some more crazy Gabby stories."

Well, I guess that served me right. I'd made fun of them, and they'd made fun of me.

Helena sobered. "I could tell that you two were tight. I'm sorry she's disappeared."

And here I thought the only time Sierra showed any emotion was when it came to animals. Had she really made it clear that we were best friends?

"She's not guilty, you know." How many times would I have to repeat that?

"I know. We all know that." Helena nodded emphatically.

I leaned closer and lowered my voice so that none of her animal-loving coworkers would hear me. "Any idea what happened? Any theories flying around the office?"

Helena looked around a moment and, after her apparent threat assessment was complete, she squatted beside me and spoke just above a whisper. "Sierra didn't seem like herself last week. I wasn't sure what was going on. I tried to ask her once, but all she said was that she'd stumbled onto something that had her disturbed. I assumed it was a puppy mill or one of those horrible fast food restaurant horror stories."

"Logical assumption."

Helena leaned closer. "But I did overhear a conversation she was having on her cell phone while in the bathroom. I wasn't trying to eavesdrop. I really wasn't. But she was in the next stall and didn't know I was there, so what was I going to do?"

"Totally understandable." And a little too much information, for that matter. "What did she say?"

"She said she had to meet someone and that she was trying to find out more information. This was the weird part, though. She said she had the goods they needed."

I leaned back in the chair so hard that it nearly toppled over. The goods? The bomb-making goods?

"One other strange thing that I thought I might mention. She kept complaining last week about this heating vent that's right over her desk," Helena pointed upward to the massive slats above her. "So she moved her work station over to that empty desk in the corner."

"Can you show me where?"

"Sure, follow me."

I stood and wove my way between desks until I reached a secluded little workspace. "Did you tell the FBI any of this?"

She shrugged. "They didn't ask. And I thought it might make her seem guilty. I couldn't do that."

I nodded toward the desk. "Do you think it's okay if I have a minute here?"

"Let me go ask Bernard a question. It will buy you some more time, but make it quick. Bernard is way better at dealing with animals than people. And he hates bad PR. Really hates it."

"Got it." As soon as she walked away I began pulling out drawers and folders. Everything was empty. I dumped the pencil holder, but only found paper clips and three dull number twos. I bit my lip and sat back for a moment. Where else could I look? Was I missing anything? And what in the world were those "goods" that Sierra had mentioned?

I glanced at the desk calendar in front of me. Blank, of course, since this was a spare desk. I lowered my head and looked for any imprints. I squinted when something caught my eye. Could it be?

I pulled out one of those pencils and gently rubbed it over the area where I saw the indentions. Reading those Nancy Drew novels growing up had finally paid off as I'd just used one of the oldest detective tricks in the book.

Before me was an address. I looked up and saw St. Bernard approaching. I quickly ripped off the sheet and shoved it into my pocket. Just as quickly, I stood and offered a polite smile.

"It looks like you're overstaying your welcome here," he growled. "And you did the very two things I precisely asked you not to do."

"I would have thought you'd be happy that I was trying to put some closure to this whole fiasco. Instead, you seem aggravated. Any reason why?"

He scowled. "No. No reason other than you're interrupting our work time, and Sierra has put a stain on our positive reputation. Need I go on?"

I shook my head. "No, I'm leaving. Thanks for your help."

***

The house at 1942 Vermont St. looked like it had been boarded up for years, although I had to say that the majority of the houses in this neighborhood looked abandoned. Most of them, despite their weathered siding and overgrown yards, did not have boarded up windows, however.

This was the part of town everyone warned you not to go into by yourself or at night. It was known for its crime, street gangs, and drugs. How bad could it really be in the middle of the day, though?

More importantly—why would Sierra have come here? Is this place where she'd disappeared? Would I disappear just like her if I went inside that house?

I leaned back in my seat, not quite ready to exit my van, and asked myself the all-important question of: What now?

Why did I even bother asking myself that question? I already knew the answer. If I left the house now, convincing myself not to go any closer, I would only find myself back here in a couple of hours, investigating anyway.

I knew I didn't have any choice. I had to find some answers, whatever the cost.

Of course, if I were dead, what good would I be?

I sighed and climbed from my van. I stuffed my hands deep into the pockets of my bulky winter coat, pulled my stocking cap down farther on my head to ward away the tingles of the lingering flurries, and walked up the driveway.

I decided to start at the most obvious place. The front door. What were the odds that it would either be unlocked or that someone would actually answer? Not good. I'd try anyway before moving to plan B, which just so happened to be a plan I hadn't even considered or begun to develop yet.

The steps to the place were so rickety that I thought I might fall through or a zombie might reach out from beneath the crawl space to grab my ankle.

Zombie? Really, Gabby? Get a grip. What are you going to think when you get inside? That there were ghosts?

Still, I muttered a prayer as I pounded on the door. I waited for a few minutes, noticing a group of young men walking past and checking me out. Of course they were. I was out of place in this neighborhood and they knew it. But just because it was a group of men walking together wearing chains and with their pants hanging halfway down their behinds, didn't mean they were gang members.

So why did my throat feel so dry?

One of them called to me from the sidewalk. I pretended not to hear.

"You looking for some company?" I could hear the voice getting closer, and I shivered. This wasn't good. Wasn't good at all. Even I, with all my dumb courage, knew that gangs were nothing to take lightly.

I had no choice but to turn around and address the man speaking to me. "I'm wondering if anyone lives here."

He raised his brows and laughed. His compadres joined in. "In that place? That's even a dump by my standards, pretty lady. But if you're looking for a place to stay, I think I might be able to help you out. You can come on over to my place." The way he twitched his head to the side and suggestively shrugged as he looked me over made the invitation clear.

"I'm not looking for a place to stay. I'm looking for my best friend, and I heard she might be here."

The glimmer left his eyes. "No one's lived there for months. Prolly longer. Years." He looked over his shoulder at his four friends. "Right boys?"

A round of "yeah," "that's right," "you know it" followed.

My gaze wandered down to the tattoo on his exposed forearm. *The Guardians*. Any hint of moisture left my throat now. The Guardians—a local street gang—were known for their violence. They had people in Norfolk terrified.

I took a step toward the door and away from the group around me. How was I going to get out of this one? I should have known better than to come here alone. I should have called someone first. The FBI? Riley at least.

Lord, help me. I know I'm a knucklehead sometimes. I'm stubborn and headstrong and I don't like to listen to anyone. But just this once? Are you listening?

The gang's spokesperson—I affectionately thought of him as T-Bone because... well, just because it seemed like a good name for the broad man before me—took his first step onto the porch.

This would be a great time for one of those steps to give way. Or for a zombie to reach through the boards and grab someone's ankles.

"I ain't ever seen you around here before."

"That's because I'm not from around here." I held up my hands. "Look, I get it. This is your turf. I shouldn't have come here. I'm leaving." I tried to step down the porch, but T-Bone grabbed my arm.

"Not so fast, Buttercup."

"Buttercup?" Hearing him say buttercup brought an unreasonable amount of hilarity to a totally unhilarious situation. It was the equivalent of me saying fo'shizzle, which I actually had done once. I tamped down any silly impulses to laugh, however.

He swung his head to the side. "You got a problem with that name?"

I shook my head, my impulses immediately sobering as the reality of the situation froze my blood. "No problem."

He nodded to the door, the sunlight reflecting off of his gold tooth. "We can show you the inside of that crib."

Fear shimmied up my spine, skyrocketing into my brain so quickly that my hands began to tremble at the impact. "I'm pretty content to simply go home right now."

"We're going to party. Why don't you join us? You can be my guest of honor."

Every ounce of moisture disappeared from my mouth and throat. How was I going to get out of this situation? Why hadn't I told someone where I was going?

"Me partying with you guys is not a good idea." Not a good idea at all. I had to get out of here.

He stepped closer, and I could smell the alcohol on him. "Why not? Something wrong with me and my bros?"

"Nope." I tried to keep my voice casual as my heart raced into panic mode. I was outnumbered...and they were dangerous. "Nothing at all."

He raised his chin and in that urban vernacular, sneered, "That's what I thought. So why don't you come with us? In fact, we'll move the party right in here. My boys can get inside that place."

"That's not a good idea, boys. Believe me."

"Again, I ask you, why not?"

Would it help or hurt me to mention an affiliation with the police or FBI? Hurt, I decided. To these guys, the authorities were the enemy. I needed to relate to them. I reached deep down inside of myself to do so.

"Because the way to get me on your side is to let me go right now. You want me on your side. Believe me. I'm a good person to know when the going gets tough."

He sneered down at me. "Why would we want you on our side?"

I licked my dry lips. "Because I'm a crime-scene cleaner."

He loosened his grip a moment. "You with the po po?"

"No, the police don't clean crime scenes. The victims' families hire me."

He sneered again. "Why do we want a crime-scene cleaner on our side?"

"Because when you get in trouble and you need to cover up a crime, I'm your lady." Like I'd ever give them tips. I just wanted to get out of here alive.

I had their interest. I could tell by the way T-Bone assessed me before nodding. "Is that right? I think we hit the jackpot boys." He stepped closer. "So give us some tips? How can we 'clean' up after ourselves better?"

My saliva burned down my throat. I stared at each of the leering men around me, and I knew my life was on the line. "Yeah, I've got tips. In fact, I can give you some of my solution. It will clean up any blood evidence around."

"You tripping me?" T-Bone smiled and a row of gold teeth sparkled back.

"No, I ain't tripping you. Why would I do that? I'm just a girl trying to make a living."

"A'ight. A'ight." He nodded, and I could tell that I had him. "You give us some of that solution, and we'll leave you alone."

I pulled my keys out. They tinkered together in my hands. It was no wonder. My hands were trembling out of control. Trying to appear casual, I unlocked the back of my van and pulled out an industrial sized spray bottle, one that I often hooked up to a generator for more effect. "I'll give this to you. All you have to do is turn this on," I reached into my van and flipped on my compressor, "then you turn this nozzle."

The next instance, I sprayed all of them with the solution—right in their eyes. They all groaned and grasped their faces and muttered curses in my direction. I didn't stick around to listen. I darted to the driver's seat, slammed the door—locked it—and pulled away as fast as possible. I cut through the overgrown grass, my tires squealing as I jerked the steering wheel to point my van toward the street.

T-Bone grabbed my side view mirror. His angry face smeared against my window as I hit the accelerator. I didn't care. I gunned it.

Until I spotted a grassy, overgrown ditch.

I swerved the van again, headed back toward the gang. I had to get past them to get to the street. I couldn't risk getting stuck in the ditch.

Uh-oh. The gang wasn't moving. Nor was T-bone letting go.

I closed my eyes and prayed for the best. A life in jail seemed better than releasing myself into the hands of men who were boiling mad at me.

I spun the steering wheel into a hard right and my van bumped onto the driveway. The gang members scattered. My right wheel caught the side of the ditch and the vehicle lurched. T-Bone fell into the grass.

But my van kept going. It blessedly kept going. I jerked onto the street, narrowly missing an oncoming car.

And for the moment, I was safe.

My heart pounded furiously in my ears still.

Was Sierra as lucky?

CHAPTER 20

Wednesday morning was getting me nowhere.

I'd spent a majority of my time doing an Internet search for mouth-breather Clifford Reynolds. I'd finally found someone with his name who worked in zoning and permits for the City of Chesapeake. I'd left a message for him. When that didn't work, I drove down to City Hall. His bulldog of a secretary had insisted he was busy and couldn't see me. I'd waited outside the office for him to emerge for two hours, but never saw him.

As I'd waited, I'd begun to sketch a timeline for Sierra last week.

Thursday—meeting with Bruce.

Friday morning—Sierra argues heatedly with contractor.

Friday at four—left to meet Henry, but never showed up.

Friday at five—development set fire.

Friday evening—Harrison Developers bombed.

Sierra disappears
Saturday morning—climbs through window into her apartment. Why?

Finally, I couldn't wait any longer. My dad and his girlfriend, Teddi, were coming over this afternoon for an early dinner. It had been Riley's idea, and I'd offered the invitation last week, before this whole fiasco with Sierra had started. I'd wanted to cancel, but Riley insisted I should keep this date, that restoring my relationship with my dad was the right thing to do.

And so I hadn't canceled.

And now everyone would be gathering at my house in an hour. Riley's friend had given him a recipe for a shrimp boil, and he'd volunteered to cook. Who was I to turn down a man cooking for me?

As I walked back to my van, I spotted someone familiar leaning against it.

Henry.

How did that man always know where to find me?

I scowled at him as I approached my van, thinking of Henry as a fly that wouldn't go away. He didn't seem to notice. In fact, his face lit up with a smile when he saw me.

I didn't slow down to greet him but went to the door and stuck my key in. "How'd you find me? Are you the one following me?" I called over my shoulder.

He appeared at my side, his smell coming with him. "Someone's following you?"

"Don't sound so innocent." I looked beyond him, wondering how he got here. A maroon sedan perhaps? "Did you give up on your grease-powered car and get an economic one the color of flowers in the autumn instead?"

"What?" He stared at me a moment before shaking his head. "That would be dastardly of me. Of course not. I've been riding my bike lately anyway."

I opened my door before I turned toward him and crossed my arms over my chest. "How'd you find me then?"

"I know you'll find this hard to believe, but I frequent the library across the street. I saw your van pull up—at least, I thought it was your van. When I saw you hop out, I decided I should say hello."

"The library, huh? I suppose checking out books is free, so it makes more sense than buying them."

"Now you're coming around to my way of thinking, Gabby."

"But waiting around for me for two hours? That's strange. You must really want to talk to me."

He shrugged, any playfulness gone. "Maybe."

"Henry, are your friends responsible for this mess?"

His smile disappeared. "My friends? What are you talking about?"

"I know you're way into the environment. Like, crazy into it. Do you know what's going on here? Because so help me if you do and if you've hurt Sierra in some way—"

He held up his hands. "I would never hurt Sierra. She's like a sister to me. I want her to be back here and safe just as much as you do."

"Then give me some answers. Help me to find her." I wanted to shake him until the truth came out, like apples falling from a tree.

His jaw twitched. "I did talk to a mutual friend of ours today."

"And how are you doing all of this without the FBI finding you?"

"I've been avoiding the law since I was 15. I'm pretty good at it."

"I'd say."

"Anyway, I talked to a mutual friend. She told me that Sierra went to talk to someone she works with. You know, another animal rights activist."

"Name?"

"Tree Matthews."

"Tree?" I actually remembered the name. Sierra had mentioned him before. Who could forget a name like Tree? "Is that all you know?"

"It's all I know. I thought you might want to check it out. I was going to sneak over to your apartment tonight to let you know, but I saw you here instead. Coinkidink, huh?"

"Yeah, coinkidink." This man still was not off my radar. There was just something about him that made me ask questions. I wondered, only for a moment, what he would be like without all his craziness. If he were "normal." Probably not a bad looking guy. It was just hard to get past his smell and outlandish ways of doing things.

I wondered again if we'd gone to high school together or something. There was just something about him that seemed familiar, and I couldn't help but feel our paths had crossed at some time or another before Sierra showed up with him.

"Why are you looking at me like that?"

"I'm just trying to figure out if we met before."

He shrugged. "Maybe. It's a small world."

"Where you'd go to high school?"

"Maury."

"Really? Me too." Our paths probably had crossed before. At least that mystery was solved. I opened my van door. "I've gotta run."

"Good seeing you Gabby."

"Yeah, stay out of trouble."

Something about his stare penetrated me. "Yeah, I will."

I couldn't shake the idea that Henry was trying to tell me something more than goodbye when I exited. Was he warning me of impending danger like everyone else seemed to be? Did that look say that he knew more than he let on? Was he some kind of strange stalker? I just didn't know.

***

I should have known something was wrong when Riley walked into my apartment with a bag full of groceries and a trashcan an hour later. I didn't even ask.

Okay, I tried not to ask, but I'm not very good at that. So I did ask, only in an assertive kind of way.

I pointed to the trashcan. "Explain."

Riley laughed and set everything on the countertop of my crowded kitchen. "We're going to use the trashcan as a pot and layer the food inside. It's good. I promise."

I stared at the shiny, silver wastebasket that was the approximate size of a basketball hoop on my counter. "Is the trashcan new?"

He gave me a pointed look. "Of course it's new, Gabby. Who do you think I am?" He began pulling food from the bags, and I half-heartedly joined in the efforts. "This is going to be fun, Gabby. You'll see."

"I think you've been hanging out with Henry too much."

He paused from his sorting for long enough to laugh and turn toward me. "You're funny." He kissed my forehead.

"Just one more thing to love about me... not that you love me or anything."

He chuckled again and pulled me into a gentle hug. He always made me feel so warm and fuzzy, yet grounded and secure. I was pretty sure I did love Riley Thomas, regardless of whether or not the sentiment was mutual. I wondered if it was, though.

Someone pounded up the steps, so I stepped back from Riley. He nodded toward the door. "You ready?"

"Ready as I'll ever be."

I mustered all the energy I could in order to open the door and offer an enthusiastic greeting to my dad and Teddi. My effort must have paid off because they both smiled widely as they stepped inside. "Glad you guys could come," I mumbled as I took their coats.

"Thanks for having us, Gabby. This means a lot." Teddi, who'd always reminded me of a pint-sized former Texas beauty queen with her trim figure and beehive hairdo, handed me a newspaper. "You asked for this?"

I took it from her hands. "I sure did. At Riley's request."

"Well... enjoy."

My dad and Riley decided to do the next best thing to manning a grill. They had "man talk" over a trashcan while cooking our food on the stove. Teddi and I sat in the living room, sipping on peach tea.

Teddi seemed so normal. What could someone normal possibly see in my father? What had she told me last week? She worked at Wal-Mart and had for the past 15 years. She belonged to a book club. And, for some reason, she liked my father.

"It means so much to your father that you invited us today," Teddi whispered.

My heart leapt into my throat. "Does it?"

"He's a good man, Gabby."

I bit my lip. How did I respond to that? I couldn't exactly pour out the grisly details of our floundering relationship, which included alcohol and neglect and self-absorption. But Riley's words echoed in my mind. People change. The thought was so hard to hold onto sometimes.

I wished Sierra was here. Not that she would eat the shrimp or anything cooked with the shrimp, for that matter. But she always made social gatherings more interesting with her save-the-animals stories. She'd been a good friend to me, and I felt a little guilty carrying on like normal right now. The driven part of me wanted to spend every moment investigating. But I knew dead ends when I saw them. I needed some new leads and none were dropped in my lap—not that they should.

The next few minutes were spent with small talk. How long did it take this shrimp boil to cook, I wondered? Because small talk really wasn't an attribute I claimed to have or be good at. Teddi didn't seem to have that problem, though, because she rambled on and on about the weather and church and reality TV shows and a worrisome mole on my dad's back. Too. Much. Information.

Finally, my dad asked Teddi if she'd like to walk to the store with him for some ice. She said yes—and looked exceedingly happy to be spending some time with my dad. To each their own, I guess.

As they walked away, Riley wrapped his arms around me from behind and nuzzled my neck. I drank up the attention. "You okay?"

"I'm trying to be."

"You're doing fine."

"I've only considered putting a laxative in my dad's drink twice. That's good for me."

"Gabby…"

"I wouldn't really do it. But it's fun to think about. Riley, he's never even apologized for anything. He hasn't apologized for being a crappy dad, for allowing himself to live off my goodwill for these years, for asking me to give up my dreams to support his habits. I didn't realize all of that had affected me as much as it had. But it has."

"He may never apologize, Gabby. I hope he does. But even if he doesn't, you still have to forgive him—for your sake if no one else's. By not forgiving him, you're hurting yourself more than you're hurting him."

I didn't say anything. I just processed what Riley said. Or I tried to process it, at least. There still seemed like a major wall stood between me and forgiveness, and I wasn't sure how to get over it.

One inch at a time, I supposed.

***

Thirty minutes later, we all sat down at my kitchen table, where Riley had stretched the newspaper out like a tablecloth. Riley walked over with the trashcan and dumped out the shrimp boil in the middle of the table.

"Dig in!" he urged.

Okay. I was into trying new experiences. And I got that Riley was trying to be authentic with this. I did.

I pulled out some shrimp, potatoes, link sausage, and corn. All of it had been seasoned with spicy Old Bay and some other herbs.

I had to admit that it didn't taste too bad. Maybe having my dad and Teddi over was a good idea after all.

Teddi grinned. "I had no idea when you asked for my newspaper that it was going to be our dinnerware. This is very interesting."

"This is the way I was instructed we had to eat the shrimp in order to be authentic," Riley offered.

"If I'd known this is what you wanted the newspaper for, I wouldn't have pulled it out of my trash."

I stop mid-bite and stared down at the table. Out of the trash? You mean, there had been gross, unsanitary objects touching this newspaper, which now touched my food, which had already been in my mouth? I resisted the urge to gag. Or to grab a bar of soap and start scrubbing my mouth clean.

Riley must have sensed how I bit my tongue, because a steady hand appeared on my back. And it worked. The neurons firing at full speed in my brain slowed slightly, and I took a deep breath. How did I proceed from here?

"Maybe the homeless man downstairs would like to eat." Teddi pointed out the window. I glanced over her shoulder, even though I already knew whom she was talking about. Henry.

Everyone stared at me. They really wanted me to invite Henry up? Really? Finally, I shrugged. "Fine."

Teddi cracked the window open and called down to him. The next thing I knew, Henry stood in my apartment.

I frowned. What would the feds do if they found out Henry was here? Arrest him? Arrest me?

What would Jesus do?

With that thought, I offered a smile and extended my hand to invite Henry to the table. Baby steps. That's what I was taking.

Henry looked totally at ease as he glanced around my place. His eyes stopped at the food piled on a dirty newspaper on my kitchen table and the trash can on the stove. "That's my kind of food—cooked in a trash can."

"A clean trash can," I added. Never mind the newspaper.

My dad was staring at him, so I realized I should probably introduce everyone.

"Dad, this is—"

"Tim," my dad muttered. He rose to his feet, looking a bit dumbfounded and wide-eyed.

Tim? Was my dad losing his mind?

My father walked toward Henry, his arms outstretched. What had gotten into my father? Had he traded alcohol for drugs?

I had to intervene. I stepped in front of my dad and shook my head. "No, this is Henry, Dad. He's Sierra's friend." Also known as "The Smell." A total weirdo with bad body odor.

My father didn't seem to hear me. He stepped around me, grabbed Henry and pulled him into his arms.

"I knew you'd come home one day," my dad muttered, his voice hoarse. "I knew you would."

What was going on? My mouth gaped open, and I wondered if I should call a psychologist or act as referee before Henry pulled back and slugged my father for his weird behavior.

My dad stepped back and turned toward me. The tears streaming down his face caused my heart to lurch. "Gabby, it's your brother. He's come home. He's come home."

CHAPTER 21

I blinked. "My brother? Dad..."

I looked at Henry. Maybe he looked a little bit like Tim, but he wasn't Tim. He couldn't be. Tim was gone. And Henry was... well, he was weird.

But Henry just stood there staring at us. Tears streamed down his cheeks also, leaving little rivulets in the dirt.

"Henry?" I questioned, waiting to hear his denial. Why wasn't Henry denying this and setting my father straight? Why was he crying?

He locked gazes with me, and I knew my father's words were true.

"Tim?" I whispered. I stepped backward and clutched something—it just happened to be Riley's arm was there—to balance myself.

He nodded.

I shook my head, the skeptic in me rising to the surface. "No, I can't believe this. It can't be true. This is... it's some kind of set up or something."

"Pompadour Tim, rah rah rah, here comes a bull so rah, rah, run," Henry said.

It was a rhyme I'd made up about my brother once, and it had stuck. We'd sit in Tim's room and make up silly rhymes for hours. We'd both be giggling so hard by the end that our sides hurt. The memory squeezed my heart.

Next thing I knew, I sank to my knees, weeping. No, this couldn't be my little brother. He couldn't have been in my life for this long without me ever knowing. Siblings could sense each other...

Riley put his arms around me, but there were no words at that moment. Just emotions. Strong emotions that collided inside me.

My dad hugged Henry—Tim. Tim held onto him also.

"Maybe we should all sit down and talk," Riley muttered.

I nodded. Yes, I needed some answers.

We shuffled into the living room. The silence in the room was thick. No one seemed to know what to say or do or where to start. Finally, I drew in a deep breath and attempted to pull myself together. Truth and doubt collided inside me. One minute I believed that Henry was my brother; the next I knew this was a mean-hearted trick.

I had to bring out the investigator in me and get to the truth of the matter. I rubbed my sweaty hands on my jeans and swallowed, my throat suddenly dry.

"Did you know that I was your sister this whole time?"

He nodded, his emotions restrained as he sat across from me. Henry no longer looked like a fanatical freak. Something about the way he sat reminded me of a lost little boy. I knew he wasn't the prodigal son because he hadn't left on his own accord, but he was the lost son who'd come home.

"Why didn't you tell me? Why wait until today?"

"I actually came over to the apartment to meet you a couple of months ago, but I chickened out. In the process, I met Sierra, and I realized that by getting to know her, I could get to know you." He looked down at his hands. "I've had a lot of hurts in my life. I didn't want to be rejected by my sister also."

"How about dad? Why not go to him?"

Tim looked at our father. "The same reasons." He squeezed the skin between his eyes as if fighting tears. "Look, I know it probably doesn't make sense. I had all of these crazy expectations of what our reunion would be like. Then fear set in, and I began to wonder how you'd both accept me. With open arms? With skepticism? Had you moved on with your lives and forgotten about me?"

"We'd never forget about you, Tim. Never." My dad reached forward and grabbed his hand.

I wanted to say the same thing, but the words stuck in my throat. Instead, I asked, "What happened, Tim? After you were taken at the park that day, what happened?" My voice sounded shaky and unsure and very much not like my voice.

"You mean after those two men snatched me?"

I nodded, tension digging deep into my back as I braced myself for what I might hear. I had so many fears about what had happened to Tim, so many nightmares...

Tim wiped one of the tears rolling down his cheeks with the back of his hand. "They took me to a nice couple. They lived in Northern Virginia. I guess they'd desperately wanted kids but when they couldn't have their own, they decided to adopt. Only they couldn't afford to adopt. So they went with the next option. They kidnapped me."

My throat burned, and I closed my eyes, unable to face my brother. "I'm sorry. I'm so sorry."

"It wasn't all that bad. After awhile, I kind of forgot about my old life. Living with them seemed to be the norm. They told me that you guys died in a fire. I believed them for a long time, just like I believed that they'd legitimately adopted me."

"So they were nice to you?" My voice cracked with emotion. I'd had nightmares about him being hurt at the hands of someone merciless.

He nodded. "They were a little shady with other people, but they never treated me poorly."

My heart calmed for a second. Good. He hadn't been tortured or abused, which had always been my nightmare for all of these years.

Thank you, Jesus.

"Three years ago, they both died in a car accident. That's when I decided to do some research for myself. I didn't come up with anything until a couple of months ago. That's when I saw the article about Gabby and something clicked inside me. I kept digging and eventually found a newspaper article detailing my kidnapping. I realized what had happened."

I realized at that moment just how little I knew about this man. When he was just Henry, I just dismissed him as a weirdo. But now there was so much I wanted to know. "Where are you living down here, Tim?"

He shrugged. "Here and there. With different friends. I got laid off from my job, you know."

"Is that why you became a freegan? Out of necessity?"

He cracked a smile. "You're really hung up on that, aren't you? No, I'm a freegan because I really do believe in that way of life. It started for me in high school, just for fun. Dumpster diving and stuff. It just progressed from there. We didn't have much when I was growing up, so I learned to appreciate things. It's a lesson most people in America could learn."

"I looked for you every day," my dad muttered. My dad wept again. I'm not sure I've ever seen my dad cry like that. Usually, he just drank away his troubles.

I turned my head sharply toward him. My dad did? All I'd seen him do was drink. When had he searched for Tim?

"I did Internet searches, hoping I'd find some more information. When I didn't, I turned to the bottle to numb the pain."

My heart beat at double time. That's why my father had begun drinking like a fish? Guilt pounded with each heartbeat. Perhaps I just shouldn't have judged him so easily.

My dad stood, still touching Tim's shoulder as if afraid he might disappear again. "Stay with me. I don't have much but what I have is yours."

Who was this man? What happened to my dad, the one who only thought about himself?

Tim nodded solemnly. "The police are looking for me."

"I don't care. You're my son. You have a place at my house."

Tim nodded again. "Okay then. I could use a warm place to sleep."

My dad put his arm around Tim's shoulders. "Let's go then. We all need some time to process this great news. And you, my boy, need to settle into your new home. I'm going to clear out the spare bedroom for you, and you're welcome to stay as long as you need. I don't care about those cops looking for you."

They stepped toward the door. I couldn't let them go. Not yet. "Tim..."

They paused and looked back at me.

I cleared my throat. "I'm sorry," I muttered.

He nodded. "I know."

With that, they left.

***

Riley looked at me from across the couch. After several moments of silence stretched by, he finally asked, "Are you okay?"

I'd hardly heard the silence as my thoughts absorbed me. "I'm in shock."

"Do you think that's really your brother?"

I nodded. "Yeah, that's him. I don't know why I didn't see it earlier. I thought he looked familiar, but…"

"It's been a long time."

"Yes, it has."

Riley squeezed my hand. "What can I do for you?"

I shrugged, wishing I had an answer. "I'm just processing everything still."

"It will take time."

"How could I not have seen it, Riley? He's my brother."

"People change. He was just a boy when he was taken. And now his looks are concealed behind that beard and those bulky clothes he wears. Don't beat yourself up over this. I thought you might be happy. Are you happy?"

I wiped at a tear that pricked my eye. "I am happy. I'm in shock. I'm a lot of things."

"How about we grab a bite to eat? Especially since the shrimp boil didn't go over that well, not with the dirty newspaper and all of that."

I actually cracked a smile at that. "That sounds good."

We walked across the street to The Grounds. The paintings still glared at me when I walked inside, feeling like stabs to the heart. Riley put on brakes when he saw them. "Wow," he muttered.

"I know."

He touched the painting of Tim. "This is creepy, Gabby."

"You don't have to tell me."

Sharon appeared behind us. "I haven't seen Becca since I found out these paintings were about your life, Gabby. I tried to call the number she left, but it was bogus."

"So was the address."

"Gabby," Sharon muttered, clutching my arm.

"What is it?"

She pointed at the window. "There! There she is!"

I stepped toward the window, at the young woman standing there peering inside. She spotted me and took off in a sprint.

CHAPTER 22

I took off after the girl. "Stop!"

She didn't slow. She'd gotten a good head start. My leg muscles burned as I tried to catch the petite woman, who didn't look much older than a college student.

Riley darted in front of me. Rush hour might have been over, but traffic was still thick. The girl darted in the middle of an intersection, narrowly missing oncoming cars. I dodged a few myself and nearly broke one of my legs in the process. I didn't even care. I just wanted to reach that girl and find out who she was.

Riley reached the other side of the road just as the girl took a hard right into an alley

Get her, Riley, I silently urged.

I gasped in deep breaths, trying desperately to catch up, wishing my legs were longer and that I was in better shape. Neither was true, though.

I rounded the corner into an alley. My foot caught on some cracked concrete, and I nearly toppled but caught myself. So close, so close.

Finally, I reached the end of the alley and stopped abruptly. Riley stood there, hands on hips, staring at the parking lot in front of us.

"Where did she go?"

He shook his head. "I don't know. I lost her."

"You take the left, I'll take the right." I didn't wait for him to respond. I darted to the right. No sooner had I done so, did a maroon sedan squeal out. Before I could reach it, the car pulled onto the street and to safety.

"Did you get the license plate?"

I shook my head. "Mud covered the numbers." Just two weeks ago the temperatures here had been in the sixties and it had been raining. Maybe the mud—frozen now—was left over from that temperamental weather shift.

"I don't get it. Who is that girl, and what does she want with you?"

I shook my head again. "I have no idea. This just keeps getting stranger and stranger."

And something else was bugging me also.

Why did the girl look familiar?

***

I'd talked Riley into watching High School Musical with me that evening. And now, only halfway into the show, his head tilted back on my couch and his body didn't move.

He was asleep.

Meanwhile, I couldn't stop thinking. If only I could turn my brain off sometimes. But I couldn't.

I thought about Tim. I thought about that dreadful day he'd been taken. My whole world had been shattered. So had my mom and dad's. We'd never exactly been a normal family, but, after that day, we'd gone downhill quickly.

I'd known it was my fault. I should have been keeping a better eye on Tim. I shouldn't have ever turned away. But I had. And then he was gone.

Days and weeks passed, and there was no word on him. There were no leads. It was like he disappeared into thin air.

Slowly, our lives had returned to a new normal.

But it never felt complete. Never.

Halfway into college, my mom found out she had cancer. I dropped out of school so I could take care of her. Meanwhile, my dad drowned his sorrows with his new best friend, Jack Daniels.

It was strange because I'd dreamed for so long about what it would be like to have Tim back. And this scenario was never a part of my dreams. I thought I'd be elated. Instead, I still felt guilty.

I mean, had my dad really searched for Tim every day? All I'd seen him do was drink.

Perhaps I should do what I did best. Whenever worries overwhelmed me, I just poured myself into being nosey—yes, I poured myself into other people's problems.

And there were plenty of other people's problems to distract me. Facing their reality seemed better than facing my own.

I slipped out from underneath Riley's arm, pausing just one moment to watch him. Now that I thought about it, he kind of reminded me of Zac Efron from High School Musical. They both had the same hair—a little too long—the same blue eyes, the same awesome smile.

How was I ever so lucky that Riley had actually wanted to date me?

Again, I needed to stop thinking about myself and focus on other people. Isn't that what the Bible said to do? It probably wasn't meant quite that way, but still.

I found one of my little spiral bound notebooks. Call me old school, but I still liked to spell things out using pen and paper sometimes.

I needed to make a list of all of my suspects. Maybe writing everything down would help to sort out this crazy mess.

First suspect: Crazy Stalker-Painter...code name: Becca Bowling. Who was she? I had no idea. What was her motive? Again, I had no idea. But she was there, in my life, shadowing me and painting pictures depicting my history. That made her a suspect in my book.

Second suspect: Lydia Harrison. She would have the most to gain by her husband dying. But she'd have nothing to gain by bombing his building, unless he had some kind of insurance policy that would guarantee them more money.

Third suspect: Mark Daniels. What was his connection with Lydia? Was someone paying him off? Was that reason to murder?

Fourth suspect: Clifford Reynolds. He'd definitely acted suspicious at the Go Green meeting, and he seemed to be avoiding me like life avoided the Grim Reaper.

Fifth, and perhaps mostly likely, suspect: Bruce Watkins. He marched to the beat of his own drummer, to use a cliché. And he was fanatical about the environment. He'd possibly written the how-to manuals for ecoterrorists everywhere. Seemed a good suspect to me.

Final suspect: Broken Arrow. He was definitely up to something. But what? What did he know? Was his Native American tribe bent on revenge?

And who was that person that Henry—I mean, Tim—had mentioned to me? Sierra's friend, Tree? I'd be paying him a visit tomorrow.

I guess I could cross off Henry—Tim? How long would it take me to get used to that?—off my list of suspects. But that still left me with a lot of people to wade through.

I looked at the list and sighed again. I don't think I'd ever had so many suspects, or so few leads. There'd always been at least one front-runner in my mind. Looking at this set of people, no one jumped out. Was there someone I was missing?

And where was Sierra in all of this? I closed the notebook. Maybe tomorrow I'd get some answers. For now, I'd go back to staring at Riley and marveling at the fact he was my boyfriend.

I ever so softly traced his jaw with the backside of my fingers. He was one in a million, the man of my dreams.

So why did I feel inadequate? He'd never made me feel inadequate.

I'd been in enough bad relationships to know a good relationship when I saw one. What Riley and I had was good.

So why did fear linger in the back of my mind?

"Are you trying to seduce me?" Riley popped an eye open and grinned.

I slapped his arm playfully. "You know me so well."

His arms reached for me and pulled me toward him. He tucked my head under his chin. "Do I even want to know what you're thinking?"

"I'm just awestruck that we're together."

"Awestruck? Wow. I like that word. But you've got to know that I'm the lucky one."

I pulled back and looked him in the eyes. "Why are you lucky?"

He straightened some. "Because you're spunky, you're caring, you're gorgeous. You don't take things at face value, but you search for the truth yourself. You don't let anything stop you from getting what you want—in a good way, not a run all over people way." He squeezed my hand. "You're my Gabby."

My face warmed at his sincerity. I tucked my head back under his chin, content to be "his Gabby."

***

Tree Matthews agreed to meet with me for lunch the next day. I pulled into a parking garage in downtown Norfolk and then hurried across traffic until I reached a popular restaurant located on the Elizabeth River. In the evenings, it transformed into a bar that beckoned those into the nightlife scene. But right now, the place was just a restaurant full of business men and women, taking their lunch breaks.

I spotted Tree in the corner sipping on some water. He was just as I remembered. Tall and thin with sandy brown hair. In fact, his frame kind of reminded me of a barren tree in the winter. Stick thin and all limbs.

He nodded when he saw me, but didn't even attempt a smile. "Gabby."

I slid into the booth across from him. "Tree. Thanks for meeting me."

"Any word on Sierra?"

I shook my head. I wouldn't even mention those phone calls she'd made to me. I didn't know if I could trust him yet, and I didn't want to offer any more information than necessary. "No, I have no idea where she is or what happened." That was the truth.

"Why did you need to meet with me?"

"Rumor has it that you were one of the last people who saw her."

He shrugged. "I don't know when she disappeared, so I don't know if that's true or not."

The waitress came, but I waved her away, not wanting to waste any time. Instead, I leaned across the table. "Look, it's like this. I can go to the FBI with that tidbit and they can question you themselves. I'm giving you the chance right now to set the record straight. I know you saw Sierra before she disappeared. Were you the last person?" I shrugged purposefully. "I don't know.

That's what I'm trying to find out. So why don't you tell me where you were last Friday?"

He looked in the distance and drew in a tight breath. He'd always seemed a bit brittle and uptight, but even more so today. "I did see her on Friday. She came by my place."

"Why?"

He ran his hand over the condensation on his glass. "She wanted to pick up some papers from me."

"Papers that told her how to build bombs and use them for ecoterrorism purposes?"

Just barely, and just for a millisecond, I saw his eyebrows flicker in surprise. "Yes, I did give her those papers, but not on Friday."

"Why in the world would you give her those papers? She's not the bomb building type."

His gaze flickered up to me. "You're right. She's not. She wanted to get the information out of my hands so I didn't do anything stupid."

"So you were thinking about bombing something? Harrison Developers, perhaps?"

He shook his head. His gaze looked burdened...or guilty. "It's not like that."

"Tell me what it's like then."

His nostrils flared again, and he remained silent a second. He pushed back in the booth and, for a moment, I thought he might flee. Instead, he sighed. "It's complicated, Gabby."

"That's what everyone keeps telling me. Make it uncomplicated."

"She didn't want me to do something I'd regret. She came over to talk me out of it."

"Did it work?"

He paused again before nodding. "It did. I saw the error of my ways."

"Why do I feel like there's more to this story?"

His gaze shifted again. The action made him seem untrustworthy. "She left after giving me a verbal lashing. I haven't seen her since then."

"Do you have any idea where she went after she left your place?"

"No." His gaze shifted again.

"I don't believe you."

"What do you want me to do? Lie to you? I don't know."

"There's something you're not telling me."

"You're grasping at straws. I've told you everything I know."

"Don't you even care that your friend is in danger?"

He tapped the table and stared at me. "I do care. I don't want her to get hurt."

"So tell me more."

He stared at me another moment, and I thought he was going to tell me something that would blow my investigation out of the water. I stared back, waiting, trying not to break the moment. He opened his mouth, but then shook his head. "That's all I know. That's it." He stood up and tossed some money on the table. "Take care, Gabby."

I leaned back into the booth and closed my eyes. Really? I'd have more luck trying to infiltrate the mob than I was having trying to break this case.

My cell phone rang, breaking me out of my raging thoughts. I saw the number listed as the Norfolk Police Department. Interesting. Why were they calling me?

With a lead in the case? Like I'd be that lucky. But still, a girl could dream. I popped the phone to my ear. "Gabby St. Claire."

"Gabby, it's your dad." His voice sounded strange. Low, mellow...craggy with emotion.

My alerts instantly went to red. "What's going on, Dad?"

"Gabby, I need you to come down to the police station."

I straightened in the booth, feeling as rigid as Tree had looked. "Are you okay? What happened?"

"I need you to bail me out."

I froze, my thoughts screeching to a halt. "Bail you out? Dad, what's going on?"

"I was arrested for drunk driving."

CHAPTER 23

I glared at my father from across the table in the police precinct. I shouldn't have paid his bail. I should have let him rot in jail. So why didn't I? Why was I here, making life too easy for him again?

"Let's go." I started toward the door, not bothering to check if he was following me.

Unfortunately, he was. Outside, he climbed into my van. We sat there in silence for several minutes before I finally found some words.

"What happened? I thought you'd turned over a new leaf?"

He looked terrible with his red-rimmed eyes and unshaven face. His wrinkles even seemed deeper today. "I thought I did too. I don't know what happened. Teddi and I got into a big fight. I did what I do best. I started drinking, hoping to drown out my troubles."

I tapped my finger on the steering wheel, trying to rein in some patience. No luck. "Did it work?"

My dad openly cried again. I'd never seen him cry before this week, and now I'd seen him weep twice. I didn't have any tissues, so I handed him a fast food napkin, the best I had at the moment. He blotted his eyes and blew his nose with enough force to wake an army. "I shouldn't have done it. Old habits are just so easy to fall back into."

My compassion was running low today. "You said you were past this." I started my van and pulled onto the street, my patience also depleted apparently.

"I thought I was past it."

"You could have killed someone." Didn't he know how serious drunk driving was? I knew he did.

"I know."

"You're going to have your license taken away from you, and I'm not going to drive you around everywhere, Dad. I'm done with this." I sliced my hand through the air. "You're a grown man. I'm sorry for all the bad things that have happened to you in life, but do you know what? Bad things have happened to me too. I lost my mother. My brother was kidnapped. I had an alcoholic for a father. Do you think those things were easy? Do you think I wanted to drop out of college? Did you think I wanted to give my freeloading father money to pay his bills because he claimed he couldn't work himself?"

My dad started to say something, but I forged ahead. I jammed my finger into my chest with enough force that I nearly flinched. "Why did I do that? I did it because I felt guilty. I felt like it was my fault you were like this. If I had just kept an eye on Tim that day, you wouldn't have turned to alcohol. I thought that you were my fault."

His wrinkles on his face seemed to ripple with pain as he grimaced. "I'm sorry, Gabby. I've been a terrible father."

"You're right. You have been. And then you said you turned over this new leaf, that you were a new person. Your son is back in your life even. You have no excuses." I pulled up to a red light, fuming. I could feel the steam coming out of my ears, and I knew I should stop myself. But I couldn't. I'd bottled these things up inside me for years. Maybe this wasn't the way I should express them, but it might be my only shot.

My dad opened his door and stepped out onto the street, between the cars at the light.

"What are you doing?"

"I'm sorry, Gabby. I won't mess up your life anymore." His voice crackled as he slammed the door and walked away, dodging traffic.

I lowered my head onto the steering wheel. I'd really screwed that one up, hadn't I? Dad was trying to do better, and I'd raked him over the coals.

I closed my eyes, my head pounding.

Should I follow him? Chase him down and apologize?

The car behind me pressed on their horn, so I had no choice but to turn—away from my dad. Maybe it was best that way.

***

"You sure you're okay, Gabby? You're not acting like yourself."

I nodded, still staring off into space as I sat across from Riley at The Grounds. I hadn't even touched my latte yet, and me with a cold latte was never a good sign. Riley had known me long enough to know that.

"Yeah, I'm okay." But my voice sounded listless, even to my own ears.

He reached across the table until his fingers touched mine. Those lovely blue eyes of his met mine. "Give your dad some time. Give yourself some time. And then talk again. You guys can work this out."

At the mention of my dad, all happy thoughts vanished. "He got drunk and went driving around town, Riley. He could have killed someone. He could have killed himself. He tells everyone that he's changed, but he hasn't."

"Sometimes change takes time, Gabby. What he did was horrible. I agree with you, and I don't have any tolerance for drunk driving. More so, I'm sorry he hurt you. I know you've been trying to repair your relationship for a long time now."

I straightened, not wanting to talk about this anymore. I had to figure some things out and wrestle with my own thoughts for awhile before anything would make sense.

Instead, I looked beyond Riley. I looked at those paintings that depicted my life. Sharon had offered to take them down, but I told her not to. I still held onto the hope that maybe I'd be able to corner the artist if she stopped by again.

I had so much to process.

My thoughts drifted to Sierra again. Where was my friend right now? It wasn't the same hanging out here without her. I needed to hear her crazy stories. I needed to tell her my crazy stories so she could tell her crazy friends. I wanted her to be here laughing with me about whatever misunderstanding it was that had stirred up this whole mess.

Would that be how this all ended? Would we ever be able to laugh about this situation? Or would it end in tragedy?

My cell phone rang—again. Who was it this time with bad news? I saw Parker's number on my caller ID. My stomach sank. "What is it?"

"Someone else has been murdered, Gabby."

"And you're calling to tell me. That's a first."

"You haven't been here to clean up because the scene hasn't been released. There's a picture of Sierra here, though. I thought you'd want to know."

"What do you mean a picture of Sierra?"

"Someone stuck it on the bookshelf between pictures of the family."

"What kind of picture is it?"

"Gabby, I don't know how to tell you this, but it's a picture of her with a bullet between her eyes."

CHAPTER 24

The room felt like it was spinning. "I want to see it."

"You can't see it. It's evidence. Besides, you shouldn't see it."

"Is it real? Is the photo real?" It couldn't be. This couldn't be true.

"We'll send it to our lab for them to look at it. It's hard to say."

"Who died this time?" Which crime scene was this at?

"I can't release that information. The family hasn't been told yet. As soon as the information is public, I'll let you know."

A sob escaped as my phone fell to the floor. I closed my eyes. Pinched the bridge of my nose.

"What is it?" Riley, who'd been staring at me, eyebrows scrunched, now slid his chair across the floor until he was beside me. "Your dad?"

I shook my head. "Sierra. They found a picture of her. Dead. She's dead."

Riley pulled me into his arms. "I'm so sorry, Gabby."

"This is my fault. I should have helped her. I should have tracked down the bad guys faster. She begged for my help every time she called, but I failed her."

His piercing gaze met mine. "That's ridiculous. You're not guilty here, Gabby. Whoever is playing this terrible game is."

No, I wouldn't relinquish—my guilt or my responsibility—that easily. "I shouldn't have been having shrimp boils and rejoicing that my brother is home again. I shouldn't have even been going to class or bailing out my dad. I should have been spending every moment looking for my friend."

He shook his head, probably the way he did in court when he argued before a jury. "You did everything you could. You followed every lead. You've been worrying yourself sick. Gabby, you've got to listen to me. This isn't your fault. Do you understand that?"

I barely heard him. "I'm going to figure out who did this. I will find them..."

"I don't like this, Gabby. I don't know what's going on here, but I don't like it. I think you should step back from this investigation."

Step back from this investigation. Those words pulled me from my daze and ignited something in me. "Nothing can keep me away now. Nothing." I wiped a tear that flowed down my cheek. "I hate this. I really hate this."

Riley cupped my cheek with his hand. "I'm so sorry, Gabby."

He held me for a moment. I tried to digest everything, but I couldn't. I needed some space for a moment.

I pulled back and grabbed a napkin to wipe under my eyes. "Riley, would you go get some ice cream?"

"Ice cream?"

I nodded. "Chocolate ice cream. I just need to process things, and ice cream always helps. I know the request seems odd, but..."

He nodded, seeming to understand. "Don't explain. Do you want to go with me?"

I shook my head. "I'll wait here."

"I'll run to the market up the street and when I get back we'll go back up to your place and try to sort this out. Okay? There's nothing you can do right now, so we might as well talk and clear our heads."

Ice cream. Talking through things with Riley. I could handle those two things.

Most of all, I could handle a few minutes alone so I could figure out my next plan of action. Who should I track down first about this? Lydia maybe? Broken Arrow?

I nodded. "It's a plan."

***

I tried to wait at The Grounds, but I really just wanted a moment alone and I wasn't getting that here among the chatter of patrons and strands of acoustic love songs. Instead, I crossed the street, trying to ignore the frigid wind that crept through my clothing and chilled me to the bone. I'd told Sharon to pass on the message to Riley that I'd headed back to my place.

My head pounded when I walked up to the apartment building. How could this have happened? Could it be true? Could Sierra really be dead?

Could things be any more of a mess? And, to top everything off, I'd missed my class tonight. I couldn't miss any more. I had to graduate or I'd let myself down—again. I wasn't sure my ego could survive another disappointment like that.

At least I was alive to even contemplate these things.

I nearly felt too exhausted to even lift my key and shove it into the lock. Somehow, I managed. Inside, the stairway was dark. Had the light burned out again? Something had to be wrong with the socket. I needed to tell our landlord about it, because I was tired of changing that light bulb myself.

I stopped in front of Sierra's door and felt more tears prick my eyes. She wasn't dead. I refused to believe that it was true. She'd emerge from her apartment again one day with a plate of acorn brownies in her hands. Or she'd be wearing her tiger costume that she liked to don when protesting the circus. Sierra… well, she'd made me feel normal with her outlandish ways and that was quite an accomplishment in itself.

I took a step toward the stairs when I heard a creak. I paused. Or did I hear a creak? This place was old and full of odd sounds.

I tried to ignore that tension that pinched my back muscles, tried to ration that I was paranoid.

Just as my hand gripped the railing, a figure flew out from behind the staircase. His fist collided with my face, the force of the punch knocking me into the wall before I slid down onto the floor. My world began spinning, and I tried to right it. But before I could, another punch connected with my jaw.

Everything blurred around me as pain screamed down every inch of my body.

A man. Dressed in black. Ski mask. I tried to observe and soak everything in. I never got very far, though. His fist rammed into my stomach, knocking the wind out of me.

Fight back, Gabby. Fight back.

But I couldn't even stand up. How could I fight back?

This man was going to kill me, wasn't he?

Lord, help me.

The man jerked me to my feet and threw me back into the wall. Before I could even scream, he jerked me toward him, spun me around and shoved me back against the wall again. He pressed into me, pinning my arms at my side.

I could feel his breath on my neck and the very feel of it caused sickly sensations to pool in my stomach.

I needed to fight back. But I couldn't move. The parts of my body that didn't ache felt frozen. Tears rushed to my eyes as fear caused trembles to overtake me.

"Listen closely, Ms. St. Claire."

I said nothing, so he rammed me into the wall again. My forehead slammed into the wood causing flashes to blink in my vision. My shoulder collided with the wall also and a screeching pain ripped down my arm.

"Are you listening?"

I nodded.

He pressed himself into me harder, and that sickly feeling roiled in my gut again.

"I said, are you listening?"

"Yes." My voice sounded strained. I hated myself for sounding so weak.

"Leave it alone."

"Leave what alone?"

"Whatever it is that you're doing. Your investigation. Drop it."

"Why?"

I could feel his lips on my ear. "Because if you don't, I'll kill you next time. This is just a warning. Got it?" He grabbed my hair and pulled back so far that my neck felt like it could break. A whimper escaped me.

"Yes, I've got it."

"I'm going to make sure you don't forget."

He slammed my head into the wall again, and everything went black.

CHAPTER 25

"Gabby? Gabby, can you hear me?"

Someone shook my shoulder. I wanted to scream for them to stop, to explain the pain that seeped into every cell of my body. But I couldn't. Instead, I wept.

"Gabby, it's going to be okay. The ambulance is on its way."

Who said that? Where was I? What had happened?

It all flashed back in my mind. Sierra was dead. I'd been beaten up. And, apparently, if I decided to follow this investigation, death would continue to follow me.

I opened my eyes and saw Riley's blurry face peering at me.

"I shouldn't have left you alone," he muttered. "I should have known better."

I wanted to tell him that he shouldn't feel guilty, just like he'd told me that I shouldn't feel guilty only moments ago. But my lips wouldn't move. Blood washed down into my throat. My entire face ached and felt swollen. My ribs felt like a thousand pounds rested atop them. My shoulder felt like it had been moved to a new location.

Yeah, someone had done a number on me. Didn't they know that the more they tried to stop me, the more determined I would become?

"Gabby, stay with me."

Blackness closed in on me, though. I reached for the light, tried to stay lucid. But it was no use. I slipped back into the darkness around me.

***

When I opened my eyes again, I was surrounded by bright light. I waited to hear the heavenly angels singing their choruses or to see some clouds float by. Instead, I heard beeping. I felt my body aching. No, this wasn't heaven after all.

It was the hospital.

My gaze traveled down, and there was Riley. His chair was pulled up to my bed. His hair was tousled and his eyes closed as he rested his head on my hand. How long had he been here? How long had I been here?

I tried to sit up, but my neck hurt. My head hurt. Heck, my whole body hurt. Instead, I let my gaze travel the length of my body. A bandage of some sort was wrapped around my mid-section, as well as my shoulder. A neck brace prevented my chin from bobbing downward. I couldn't be certain, but I was pretty sure that bandages circled around my head also.

I had to be a sight.

Riley lifted his head. His sleepy eyes blinked at me a moment before he straightened and leaned toward me. "Gabby, you're awake."

"I feel like I'd be better off dead." My lips even ached when they moved. Not a good sign.

Riley's eyes glimmered with concern as he stroked my hand. "Don't say that. I was afraid you were dead there for awhile."

My throat was dry, but I didn't ask for water. There were more important things to ask at the moment. "How long have I been here?"

"Since last night." He glanced at the clock beside my bed. "Fourteen hours or so."

"Give me a damage report."

"Bruised rib, your shoulder was popped out of place—separated I believe is the correct term—concussion, and lots of bruises and cuts." His eyes softened. "What happened, Gabby?"

Everything flashed back, each memory hitting me like a blow to the stomach. I closed my eyes. "There was someone waiting inside our apartment building for me. He told me to stop investigating or else this was just the start of it."

He dipped his head. "I should have stayed with you."

"I should have stayed at the coffeehouse like I said."

He didn't seem to hear me. "With everything that's happened, I should have known."

I squeezed his hand. "Riley, you can't be with me every minute. I'm a big girl. I don't want my boyfriend babysitting me all the time."

"You could have been killed. I wouldn't be able to live with myself if you were." His eyes said it all. He felt guilty, worried, burdened.

I patted his hand. I wished I could offer more, but the motion was all I could muster at the moment. "But I wasn't."

"Not this time. What about next time? You've got to stay out of this, Gabby."

"Riley—" Someone burst into the room, effectively cutting me off.

For the first time in my life, I was happy to see Parker. He charged into the room before Riley and I could continue that conversation. I knew it wouldn't go well when we revisited the topic. And I just didn't feel up to arguing at the moment.

***

The next several hours were spent giving reports, being checked on by doctors and nurses, and delighting in my pain medicine.

Riley stayed with me the whole time. The way he walked made it look like he wore a coat lined with iron weights. He was worried about me, and I could appreciate his concern. If I'd found Riley unconscious, I'd be the same way. I just wished I could wipe away those worries—but I couldn't.

"Why are you looking at me like that?" Riley paced over to my bed and leaned toward me, his eyes serious, his forehead wrinkled.

"I'm sorry, Riley."

He sat in the chair at my bedside. "Why are you sorry, Gabby?" He looked honestly confused—was it simply because I was apologizing, which was a miracle in itself?

"You probably wish I was an accountant, cleaning up people's financial messes, don't you?"

He stroked my hand. "I want you to be you, Gabby. I just wish that didn't mean you were in danger."

"I guess I'm not going to be making it to class tonight, huh? So much for graduating this semester." Disappointment pressed on me.

"Talk to your professors. I'll bet they'll let you make it up."

Maybe. Just maybe, I supposed.

I pushed my head back into the lumpy hospital pillow and closed my eyes. A thought had been swirling in my head since I regained consciousness. "Riley, if Sierra is dead, why is someone coming after me?"

He shrugged. "Maybe they think you know something."

"Or maybe Sierra isn't dead..."

Riley's eyes looked misty. "I hope that's true, Gabby."

My heart pounded with enough intensity that everyone within a mile could hear it probably. "But you don't think it is."

"I'm praying it is."

My throat burned. My eyes watered. And that was on top of my swollen, bruised face, my achy shoulder, and my tender ribs. I had to change the subject before my pain—both physical and emotional—pulled me under. "So, did you schedule that date with Lydia yet?"

He shook his head, his face still lined with tension. "No."

"Her divorce should be final now."

"Gabby…" He opened his mouth and closed it again.

"What? What is it?"

"She's disappeared, Gabby."

I tried to sit up, but my ribs ripped with pain. "What do you mean?"

He shook his head, but the action looked heavy. "She's gone. No one knows what happened to her."

I closed my eyes, but Riley nudged my chin up.

"Hey, let's move on to happier subjects."

"Like what?"

"Like the fact that you were quick enough on your feet to call 911 before you passed out."

I stared at him, waiting for him to crack a grin and show he was joking. "I didn't call 911."

"Sure you did. The phone was in your hands. Your call record showed 911."

I shook my head. "But I didn't call."

He stared at me with those intense blues. "Then who did?"

"I have no idea."

CHAPTER 26

The next morning, I felt both better and worse—kind of like after a stomach virus when you're thankful because you know the worst is over, but you still feel depleted and rotten.

Tim sat across from me. I couldn't be certain, but it almost appeared that he'd shaven and even taken a bath. Could it be?

But there was even a greater "could it be" that I'd asked myself lately. Could it really be that God had brought my brother back into my life?

I glanced over at Riley. "Would you give us a few minutes?"

He nodded toward the door, but his motions were slow, as if he didn't want to go. "I'll just be outside."

After he left, I turned to my brother. My eyes filled with tears. The events of the past week had caused my emotions to break. The protective walls around me seemed as battered and weak as my body at the moment. "I'm sorry."

He squinted. "About what?"

Where did I start? "About everything. About not watching you more closely when you were little. About not making more of an effort to talk to you once you came back into my life."

He bit the side of his lip for a moment, studying me. "Why haven't you made more of an effort?"

I shrugged—at least, I tried to shrug. My body hurt too much to carry it to completion. "Why would you want to talk to me?"

"Because you're my big sister."

"I've been horrible to you."

"You have?"

"I nicknamed you The Smell." I couldn't look at him as I admitted it.

He chuckled. "You've always nicknamed people, Gabby. Remember we'd sit out on the deck and nickname our neighbors? That one woman who smoked all the time? You called her Chimney."

I smiled, picturing the woman perfectly. "You remember that?"

"Of course. You're bad with names, so you assign objects to remember people by."

Wow. Not a lot of people got that about me. I was impressed.

He drew his eyebrows together. "But really… The Smell?"

A smile cracked my face. "It's the dumpster diving."

He nodded. "I get it." His eyes got misty as he stared at me. "You remind me of mom, you know."

My heart lurched. My mom was a great woman. I still missed her to this day. I wished she'd had the opportunity to be happy, to see Tim again. "You think?"

"Absolutely. You look just like her. Deceitfully angelic." He grinned.

I swatted him. "Not nice."

He held up his hands in mock surrender. "If your brother can't say that, then who can?"

My smile slipped. "Nearly every day since you were kidnapped, I've dreamed about how life would have been different if I'd been watching you more closely that day at the park. Maybe you wouldn't feel the need to dumpster dive now. Life would have turned out different for you."

He shrugged. "I didn't turn out all bad. And dumpster diving is cool. I don't do it because I'm poor. I do it because of the environment. We're such a wasteful society." He sobered. "Besides, life wasn't always that easy for you growing up, Gabby. Even before I disappeared, I remember how dad couldn't hold down a job and how he liked to drink. I'm sure when I disappeared that only escalated. Dad's always used alcohol as a crutch."

"You still seem to love him."

"Of course I do. He's my dad."

I shook my head. "He got worse after mom died, Tim. He called me every week begging for money. He lost our house because he couldn't make the payments and had to move into the trailer where he lives now. It's been bad."

"You've been a good daughter helping him out like that."

"I was mean to him."

"He's seemed truly sorry since you had that talk with him. Maybe it was just what he needed to hear."

"I was rude."

"You've been good to him, Gabby. I think this was the first step to healing your relationship."

I laughed as I wiped the moisture from my cheeks—again. "Awfully wise words from someone who's been gone for two decades."

"What can I say? You got the looks; I got the brains." His smile slipped. "He wants to come see you, you know, but he's afraid you'll turn him away."

I rubbed my fingers against my blanket. "Maybe that's for the best."

We caught up for the next thirty minutes, talking about everything from school to Sierra to other childhood memories. Finally, Riley stuck his head in the door. "I'm going to run get a bite to eat. Will you be okay while I'm gone?"

I held up my arm, which was attached to an IV still. "I'm not going anywhere."

"You'll keep an eye on her?" Riley looked at Tim.

"I'd be honored."

As soon as Riley left and after I'd counted to ten for good measure, I turned to Tim. "I want to take a walk."

"But you just told Riley—"

"I know, I know. I don't want him to worry about me. Poor guy has probably lost ten years off of his life since he met me. " I pointed to my face to bring home the point that being around me could be stressful. "I just need to breathe."

"Where do you want to walk?"

"You'll see. Just help me get in the wheelchair."

It took several minutes to get situated, but finally I settled in my new transportation. As Tim wheeled me past a mirror, my hand clutched the wheel, and I jerked to a stop. I stared at my reflection. Wow. I looked bad with a capital B. I hardly recognized myself. No wonder Riley was freaking out so much.

My lip was busted, my left eye bruised and the entire right side of my face swollen. The bandage around my head did nothing for my hair, nor did the wrap around my neck.

"Someone did a number on you, Sis."

"I'd say." Chills raced through me as I remembered the attack.

"You're lucky you're still alive."

"Tim, do you know anything about the National Federation for a Cleaner Earth?"

He began pushing me out of the room. "Yeah, I know about them. What do you want to know?"

"Who's involved?"

"That, I couldn't tell you. I've seen their literature. I've been on their website. I've heard whispers about them at my freegan meetings."

"You have freegan meetings?" I tried to look back at him, but my neck wouldn't turn that far.

"Of course."

I shook my head, trying to get my focus back. "You're not affiliated with them, are you?"

"Of course not. They're some serious dudes. They're bent on revenge. Think that's the best way to get their message across. Why?"

"I wonder if they're behind this whole fiasco."

"I wouldn't put it past them."

Why did my brother seem so normal all of the sudden? Just last week, I'd thought he was the strangest person on the planet. Now he seemed like someone I wanted to have coffee with and give a wedgie to.

"Where are we going, by the way? Anywhere in particular?"

"Room 132."

"Who's there?"

"James Harrison."

***

Tim knocked on James's door, and a tired "come in" sounded from the other side. We gave each other a quick glance before pushing the door open, and Tim wheeled me inside. Thankfully, no one was there except James.

He looked thinner and frailer than I remembered him. His bony face was even more pronounced and paler than usual. His already-thin hair even looked like it had thinned more. I guess a life-threatening heart attack and subsequent surgeries could do that to a person.

"Who are you?" he demanded.

Tim nudged me closer. "I'm Gabby."

"Why are you here?" His voice held an edge of authority, even in his weak state.

"I have a few questions for you."

"I'm not in the mood for questions. Besides, I've told the police everything I know. I certainly don't want to rehash anything with…" He sneered at me. "With you."

"You don't even know who I am."

"You're that crime-scene cleaner. You spilled punch on me at a benefit last year."

I blinked in surprise. "You remember that?"

"Yes. What I don't know is why you're here to ask me questions."

"My friend is being accused of bombing your office building."

His sneer deepened. "And?"

"She didn't do it. And now you've had a supposed heart attack. I'm just trying to figure out what's going on here."

"I most assuredly had a heart attack. Ask my doctors."

"I think someone poisoned you. They thought you would die and a heart attack wouldn't cast any suspicion on them. The police would think it happened naturally."

"Those are some crazy theories you have. No merit to them at all. You're just trying to create things."

Was I? "I don't believe in coincidences. Someone's trying to make you pay. I just have to figure out why. And I have to figure out why my friend is being framed for it."

"Listen to me. Mind your own business. Keep your silly theories to yourself. You'll regret it otherwise."

Things began clicking in my mind. The housing development. The bomb at his office. The victims—a solar energy guy, a plaster man and a landscaper. All men who could have worked for James.

I wheeled myself closer. "You're behind everything that's happened, aren't you?"

"Don't be ridiculous. I'm in the hospital."

"Everything happened before your heart attack. What are you trying to cover up?"

"You don't know what you're talking about."

"What did you do to my friend Sierra?"

"Sierra? That nut job?"

"She's not a nut job."

"She was about to have a coronary over that housing development."

"You were going to harm delicate wetlands where precious creatures critical to our ecosystem lived. What did you do? Pay off people in order to build there?"

His face reddened. "You don't know what you're talking about. And if you're smart, you'll stay out of it."

"Don't make him have another heart attack, Gabby," Tim whispered.

A nurse bustled in, her hands on her hips and a scowl on her face. "Who are you? Didn't you read the sign out front? No visitors. He's supposed to be resting."

I'd said what I needed to say and found out what I intended. Something was going on. His reaction only proved that.

"Let's go." I looked back at the frail, angry man behind me. "Rest well, Mr. Harrison."

Tim pushed me from the room. No sooner had I stepped out did I see a figure in the distance. My stalker. She saw me too, and her face froze. In a split second, she took off.

I looked back at Tim—or tried to, at least. Finally, I shouted, "After her!"

***

Tim ran down the hallway, pushing my wheelchair so fast that my IV bag flapped in the wind. We flew past nurses, a lunch cart and a few horrified visitors—horrified probably because I looked like the living dead more than anything else. My neck ached at the speed, but I ignored the pain.

Why was my stalker here? What was she doing?

We rounded the corner just as she disappeared into the stairway. Rats. There was no way I was getting this wheelchair there.

But I could send Tim after her.

I opened my mouth to tell him, when Riley stepped into sight. His expression—rigid and unapproving—said it all. "What are you doing?"

I pointed to the stairway. "My stalker. She was here."

"Why aren't you resting in your room like you're supposed to be? Do you not realize how serious your injuries are?" Riley looked at my brother. "And you? You're supposed to be watching her, not helping her get into trouble."

"She's very convincing," Tim mumbled.

Riley grabbed the handles of the wheelchair and pushed me back toward my room. "But my stalker…"

"I'm more concerned about you right now, Gabby. Once I get you back to your room, I'll call security."

I didn't argue. Whatever medicine it was that they'd given me earlier was beginning to take effect, and I couldn't fight it anymore. I needed to lie down before I fell asleep here in the wheelchair.

But I felt more certain now than ever that James Harrison was involved in this. Now I had to figure out why.

CHAPTER 27

Riley was acting more skittish around me than a father with a newborn baby. After they'd released me from the hospital this afternoon, he'd carefully helped me to his car and then, once at the apartment, up the steps to my home, acting as if I might break if I accidentally banged into anything. He'd carefully lowered me onto my couch inside.

And now he stared at me, as if absolutely unsure what to do.

I stood, which caused him to freak out and reach for me. "What are you doing?"

"Standing."

"Why?"

"Because I'm going to take a shower."

He opened his mouth, but shut it again. What would he say to that one? There was nothing he could do to help me, and that's exactly what I wanted. I needed to be alone for a moment and what better place than the shower.

"I'll be fine. I just want to clean up a little."

"I can see if Sharon can come over."

I shook my head. "Really. I'll be fine. Just give me a few minutes."

I hobbled into the bathroom and locked the door. I stared at my face for a moment while leaning on the sink for support. The swelling had gone down some. They'd taken the bandage off my head, so I didn't look quite as crazy. My hair was matted, though and frizzy like electricity had zapped it.

A shower was just what I needed, I'd decided. On more than one level.

The bruises on my body, now that I had a good look at them, made me wince. That man could have killed me. But he hadn't. Why not? Why had he kept me alive?

I started the spray and waited until it was good and hot before stepping under the water. Washing my hair with one arm was going to be challenging, but I could do it.

My thoughts turned to Sierra as I let the water wash over me. Was she really dead? Or was she alive, and someone wanted me to think she was dead? And if she was alive, just where was she, and how would I ever find her?

What did James Harrison know? What had Sierra known that could possibly have gotten her killed?

What about my stalker? How was she involved? Security hadn't been able to find her, and I wasn't surprised. The girl seemed to be able to walk through walls.

I still had so many questions, and so few answers. I felt certain I was inching closer to the truth, though. I'd get there eventually, and I'd find the evidence that would nail whoever was behind all of this.

I turned the water off, towel dried, put some lotion on, and combed my hair. At least I felt halfway decent. Finally, I stepped out, the steam from the bathroom following me. Riley sat on the couch looking contemplative. He stood when he saw me.

"You have a strange look in your eyes," I told him as I approached.

"You should sit down."

"Why?" My guards instantly went up.

"Parker just called."

"Okay...?"

He gripped the sides of my arms. Compassion shone from his eyes. "The forensic team thinks that the photo of Sierra is real."

The room began spinning around me.

***

Riley slept on my couch that night while I slept in my room. Normally, this would have been totally off limits for Riley because of what people might say. But I guess he feared for my safety so much that he was willing to take the risk. And really, if anyone looked at me with my cuts and bruises, would they really think something funny was going on? I was in no state to entertain any kind of ideas of romance or the like.

I did feel better the next morning—other than having a heavy heart, at least. Riley was already up and making coffee and scrambling eggs when I walked into the kitchen. I'd just spent thirty minutes trying to figure out how to dress myself in jeans and a T-shirt and already felt exhausted.

"Morning," he smiled.

I had to admit that I kind of liked having him here in my kitchen. I could get used to something like this. I sat down at my dinette. "Morning."

"How are you feeling?" He set a plate of food in front of me, as well as my biggest mug full of coffee.

"Better now." I dug into my food, happy visions of being able to do this with Riley for the rest of my life floating in my head.

Riley slid into the seat across from me. "Doctor's orders that you need to take it easy for a few days. I know that's hard for you."

"Hard for me" was probably the understatement of the year. I'd checked my messages last night and had three calls to clean crime scenes. No way would I be able to do those with my arm in a sling. I needed to call Chad and tell him to get home.

Riley and I chitchatted as we ate, steering away from any stressful subjects. Today was Sunday, church day. I convinced Riley to go to the service late and leave early so I wouldn't have to answer any questions. Mostly though, I didn't want to talk to my dad. I managed to successfully do that. I was grateful that Riley was so understanding. After church, we headed back to my apartment. I felt like I needed a nap... or at least some more pain medicine.

But just as I'd settled on the couch, a knock sounded in the building, loud enough that it had probably come from across the hall. Riley walked across the room and peered out the peephole. When he turned around, I couldn't be sure, but it nearly looked like terror in his eyes.

My guard instantly went up. Who was it? The bad guy returning to finish what he started? An angry mob trying to find Tim because he'd gone through their trash? Annoying FBI agents demanding I tell them things I didn't know? "What is it?"

Riley licked his lips. "It's my parents."

CHAPTER 28

"Your parents? They're here?" I rushed to my feet and pointed at the floor. "As in here, here?" I tucked a hair behind my ear, the pain in my face pulsating even more intensely at the thought of meeting Riley's parents for the first time.

"Yeah, they're outside my apartment door."

I frantically searched for excuses not to meet them and settled on, "Pretend you're not home."

"I can't do that," he whispered, reaching for the doorknob.

I lunged across the room and grabbed his hand before pointing at my face. "I can't meet them like this!"

"Gabby, they'll understand that you don't normally look like this."

"Riley—"

He cut me off with a soft kiss, which did the job quite nicely. "Gabby, stop worrying. You're beautiful."

I bit my lip. What did I want Riley to do? Did I honestly want him to avoid his parents simply because I looked terrible? My brain didn't seem to be functioning properly at the moment. I took a deep breath and lifted a prayer for wisdom. My racing heart slowed for a moment, until I finally nodded. "Okay."

His gaze lingered on me another moment before he opened the door.

I'd dreamed of this moment when I'd finally meet his parents for a long time. I'd wear my best clothing. I'd get my hair done that day, maybe even get a manicure. Heck, I'd lose ten pounds and even buy some new furniture for my place.

Had I done any of those things?

No.

I had a swollen face, a busted lip, and a black eye. My ribs were wrapped with a bandage. And my apartment? I looked behind me. Let's just say it had seen better days. Houses surviving tornados looked better than my place did at the moment.

I did my best to plaster on a smile as Riley greeted his parents with hugs. I studied them for a moment. His mom was just what I'd expected. She was thin and tall with deep brown hair cut to her chin. Her every movement and word seemed to drip confidence and affluence. Riley's dad looked just like Riley, only older.

Riley stepped back and extended his arm to me. His eyes sparkled when he looked at me, so much so that I forgot for a moment just how terrible I looked. "And this is Gabby."

The grins on their faces slipped. And I wasn't imagining things or being paranoid here. Their smiles literally slipped so fast they put water rides to shame.

Finally, his mother seemed to return to her proper etiquette. She smiled again and extended her hand. "So nice to meet you, Gabby. We've heard a lot about you."

I started to reach for her hand, but my shoulder stopped me. Instead, I waved and pointed to my injury. "Nice to meet you also."

Riley's dad stood behind her. He winked, calming my anxious thoughts for a moment. "Gabby. It's a pleasure."

Riley kept an arm at my waist. "What are you doing here? I had no idea you were coming."

"We wanted to surprise you. We're on our way to Raleigh for one of your dad's conferences. We took a little detour and decided to see your place." His mother's gaze roamed my place instead. My terribly messy, out-of-date place. My cheeks burned.

Then I realized my manners. "Can I get you a drink?" What did I have? Uh… nothing but cold coffee, at the moment. "Maybe some water?"

Mrs. Thomas shook her head. "Oh, no. We don't want to be a bother." She looked at Riley. "I was hoping you might grab a bite to eat with us. Gabby, too, of course."

Did she mean it? Or was she just being polite?

Riley turned toward me. "Do you feel up to it?"

Not particularly. I'd actually wanted to jump on the Internet and continue my investigation. I wanted to do whatever I could until my energy level returned to me. But instead of saying that, I said, "Sure. That would be great. I would just need to freshen up a bit."

I'd look through my closet. No, I wouldn't find any clothes from Nordstrom's. But maybe I had something from Target that would work?

"Wonderful. Riley, how about if we wait over in your apartment? We don't want to impose here." Riley's mom blinked, a smile stretched her face. She was the perfect picture of polite society and manners.

What was I doing here? I bit back my self-doubt.

Riley nodded toward his place. "I'll be across the hall. You just come over whenever you're ready, okay?"

I nodded, hoping that a satellite orbiting the earth might choose this very moment to fall from the sky and land on me. Yeah, that sounded like a better option than trying to impress Riley's family right now.

I sighed and went to find my Target best.

***

"So, Gabby, Riley tells us that you're going to school to be a forensic investigator?" Riley's mom daintily put a bite of her shrimp scampi onto her fork, running her knife across the bundle until it was neat and suitable to eat.

The whole restaurant had me nervous with its white linen tablecloths, sparkling crystal and a real—yes, real as in *live*—string ensemble in the corner. I found myself longing for Applebee's at the moment.

Just don't spill your water, Gabby. Or drop your fork. Or choke on anything.

Lord, help me. I couldn't remember the last time I felt like this much of a mess.

I wiped my mouth. No water had drizzled out of my swollen lips and onto my crisp black trousers—yet.

"Yes, I'm almost done. Just another month or so and I'll be official."

"What a fascinating career choice." Riley's dad nodded, seeming incredibly sincere with the sentiment. So much that, for a moment, my nerves settled.

"I love science, so why not combine that with helping to see justice served."

"Noble calling." He actually sounded like he meant it. I bit back my surprise.

Riley's mom set down her water and focused on me a moment. My nerves returned—stronger than before. "Riley tells us that you've made quite a name for yourself around town as a... a crime-scene cleaner?"

I couldn't be certain, but I almost thought that Riley's mom wanted to curl her lips down in disgust at the thought.

I nodded. "It sounds morbid, but it's really not. Don't get me wrong—it's not a career choice for the squeamish. But someone has to do the job. And there's more to it than simply cleaning up after crimes. I like being able to connect with families, being able to make their lives a little easier, being able to piece together what happened."

Riley's hand covered mine. "She has a knack for picking up clues that other people have missed. She's going to do great as a forensic investigator."

I wondered for a moment if Riley would accept me if I decided to remain a crime-scene cleaner. Was this relationship only in progress because Riley saw an end in sight? Because I'd be getting a respectable career soon enough?

I pushed the thought aside.

Since everyone was too polite to ask about my face, I decided to approach the subject. I pointed to my obviously battered features. "Sometimes I can get in over my head."

Riley's mom blinked rapidly. "You mean, that happened because you were cleaning a crime scene?"

"It would depend on how you define 'because.'"

Riley swallowed so hard his Adam's apple bounced up and back. "There are some shady things surrounding a job she did. Someone didn't like her asking questions. She's decided to let the police handle it from here on out, though."

I had? Had I said that? If so, it had been in one of my drug-induced moments.

"Have they found the person who did this to you?" Riley's dad leaned closer, his face etched with concern.

I shook my head. "No, not yet. They will, though. Just give them some time." *Or give me some time and I'll do the job myself.*

Riley's dad nodded, his eyes sparkling. "I always said, if in doubt, look at what a person's thrown away. I guess you would say if in doubt, clean!"

I smiled but inside something clicked. *Look at what a person's thrown away.* The person who was setting up Sierra was bound to have left some evidence, even in this digital age. Someone had built a bomb. There would be wires and chemicals. Certainly the FBI had already gone through computers and trashcans. But had they gone through the right person's information?

CHAPTER 29

Two long hours later, Riley's parents departed, and Riley and I sat on my couch decompressing from the whirlwind visit. At least, I was decompressing.

"I think they really liked you, Gabby." Riley leaned back into the couch. His fingers played with the hair at my neck.

I cleared my throat, resisting the urge to spill what I *really* thought. "They were nice." And in a totally different league than me. Why did I ever think I could fit in with Riley's family? We were from two different worlds.

"They're great parents. I can really see you fitting in."

I blinked, trying not to show my surprise. "Really?"

He nodded. "Of course." He shrugged. "I mean, I know they can be a little intimidating sometimes, but you're never one to let people intimidate you. That's why you're such a great fit."

"Oh, of course. Right. People never intimidate me." I resisted the urge to roll my eyes.

Riley's eyes got a far off look until finally worry settled there. "I have a court case up in Richmond tomorrow, Gabby."

"Okay..." Where was he going with this?

"I wish I could rearrange things, but I can't."

"Why would you want to rearrange things?"

His hand went to my knee. "Until someone is arrested, I don't want to leave you alone."

Sweet gesture. It really was, but... "I'm a big girl, Riley. I'll be okay."

His voice took on a strained tone. "You almost died, Gabby."

"Minor detail."

"This is serious, Gabby. Bigger than anything else you've investigated."

"How do you know that?" I straightened. It was the second time he'd alluded to the fact that he knew something he couldn't tell me.

"Gabby, there are some things that legally I'm not allowed to mention."

"Legally? You mean you're representing someone involved in this fiasco? Who?"

He looked away, his jaw set. "I can't say."

"Riley..."

"I would if I could. But I can't. I just know this is serious. Really serious."

My heart squeezed. "I know." It was so serious that my friend may have died because of it. That wasn't something I could easily forget.

Someone else rapped at the door. This time, I knew who it was. I'd called Chad earlier and he'd promised to come home right away.

He took one look at me and shook his head. "You look terrible."

I scowled. "Way to make my day brighter."

"You should have called earlier."

Riley held out his hand, and Chad shook it. "Good to see you, Chad. Thanks for coming back early."

"Thanks for keeping an eye on Gabby. It's a hard job."

Riley grinned. "I can't deny that."

Over some coffee, I began filling Chad in. I didn't get very far before his eyes widened and he stood.

"Sierra? Sierra's missing? You should have called me right away."

What was I missing here? "You were skiing. Besides, what could you do?"

"I could have helped you with this whole mess."

"I didn't realize you liked snooping as much as me."

"Sierra's our friend. I would do anything to help out."

I nodded slowly, thoughtfully. "Okay. I don't know what to say. I'm sorry? I thought I should give you space and let you do your thing. You're a free spirit, and I didn't want to drive you away."

"So, what are you doing next?"

I opened my mouth, but Riley beat me to answering. "She's not doing anything. She's recovering."

Chad locked gazes with me. "He's right. I don't want two of my friends to end up dead. You should take it easy."

I didn't feel up to arguing. Actually, I really just wanted to sleep. That pain medication knocked me out.

Chad stood. "I'll go return those calls and take care of business. You don't worry about anything, Gabby."

I nodded, my eyes beginning to sag. As soon as he left, I laid down, unable to fight sleep any longer.

***

The next morning, Riley and I stood face to face at the door of my apartment. He pulled me close, and we practically touched foreheads as he spoke. His fingers locked behind my neck as his thumb caressed my jaw line. "Promise me you'll stay out of trouble, Gabby."

I nodded. "I promise. I realize that I'm in over my head."

"Why don't you come with me on this trip?"

I shook my head. "No, I'm not up for sitting in court all day. I'll be fine here. I'll stay out of trouble."

Riley's gaze searched mine until finally he nodded, satisfied. He kissed my forehead. "I wish I could take you somewhere away from all of this so you'd be safe. The Bahamas maybe? Even Detroit sounds better right now than being here."

"The Bahamas do sound tempting. But Detroit? Really? In the winter? Not so much."

He smiled. "I'll be back tonight, okay? You'll take it easy while I'm gone, right?"

"Right-o."

He gave me a sweet kiss goodbye and then tucked me in on the couch before leaving. I listened as he closed the door and stomped down the steps. As soon as the front door of the apartment building closed, I threw off my blanket and walked to my kitchen window. I saw Riley climb into his car and, a moment later, he pulled away.

I'd appreciated Riley's concern for me over the past couple of days, but I was beginning to feel suffocated. Whatever Sierra had found herself in the middle of, it was serious. I had a feeling I'd just scratched the surface of this investigation. I'd figure out who did this to Sierra and see justice served.

I picked up my phone and dialed Henry—I mean, my brother's—cell phone number. He answered on the first ring. "Hey big sis. What's going on?"

"Tim, are you interested in dumpster diving?"

***

"So where are we going dumpster diving?"

I drove with both hands on the steering wheel, ignoring the pain pulsating through my shoulder. I wasn't sure how much dumpster diving I was going to be able to do. I felt like walking in a straight line for five steps without bending over in pain was a huge accomplishment.

"There's a man. His name keeps popping up in the investigation, and I think he had something to do with Sierra's disappearance. He knows more than he's letting on, at least."

"Name?"

"He goes by Broken Arrow. His real name is Wayne Wood."

"He's an Indian?"

"Native American, little bro. Indian isn't politically correct."

"Whatever."

"Why do you ask?"

"I saw Sierra talking to this Indian guy the week before she disappeared. They were whispering outside of her work. As soon I approached, the man left. Sierra looked all flustered."

"You could have mentioned that, oh, I don't know, last week sometime."

"I didn't think it was important. Sierra was always acting kind of suspicious."

This only confirmed my thoughts that Broken Arrow was involved in this. What had he done to my friend? Was he the one who'd set up the crime scenes to make it look like Sierra was involved? Had he actually been the killer knocking off people all over town? Perhaps he was not only concerned with the land where the housing development was being built because of the burial ground; perhaps he was concerned also because he was an environmentalist. What if he'd drawn Sierra in only to make her look guilty, because he knew she'd make a good scapegoat?

It was one theory. More than I'd had before.

I pulled up outside of his apartment building—one of many similar two-story structures that stood side by side in a long row off of the parking lot. I found a space marked "visitor" and pulled in.

Tim stared at the buildings in front of us. "How'd you find out where this guy lives?"

"Easy enough. I did an Internet search. What can't you find on the Internet nowadays?" I turned the van off and opened my door, ready to get to business.

Tim joined me as I hurried through the parking lot. "And why are you focusing on this guy?"

"Because he's hiding something, and he knows more than he lets on." Quite possibly, he was guilty. Certainly he was smart enough to shred his papers, so I didn't expect to find anything incriminating there. What I wanted to search for was evidence that he'd been at those crime scenes. Maybe some ground-up acorns? A doctored picture of Sierra with a bullet through her forehead? Crumpled up copies of the clues that were being left on my van? I had no idea. I just knew I had to start somewhere. Why not here?

I stopped by a dumpster next to Broken Arrow's apartment. "Show me how it's done, little bro."

Tim hopped up on the dumpster like he'd done it a million times before—probably because he had. "Here goes."

He jumped into the trash bags inside. I could smell the scent of decay and rot scatter around me. Wow. How could anyone do this?

Something inside the dumpster clattered against the metal sides. I shushed Tim and looked around to see if anyone had noticed. No one was in sight—yet. "We've got to keep it down. Isn't this illegal?"

"Not if they don't catch you."

I crossed my arms. "Nice."

"What am I looking for?"

"Something of Broken Arrow's."

"And I'll know what that is how?"

I shrugged. "I'm not sure yet."

He held up one bag. "Does he have a baby? This one has diapers."

"No, no baby."

He jerked another bag up. "This person is married, lives with a woman or actually is a woman."

I squinted at the bag. "How do you know?"

He stared at the bag. "Let's see. There's some hair dye, some fancy shampoo, and yogurt. No self respecting guy eats yogurt."

"Points taken. No, I don't think he's married or living with anyone."

He disappeared again and reappeared with a pair of shoes. "Hold these. I think they're my size."

He tossed the shoes into my hands, and I fumbled with them like some people would have fumbled with a dead rodent. Who knew where these shoes had been? Or what they'd been lying in? "Really, Tim?"

"Really. There's nothing wrong with those sneakers."

Why argue? I put the shoes down beside me. "Just don't pull up any food and say you're going to eat it."

His head popped up for long enough to give some commentary. "People throw away a lot of food that's perfectly good."

I held up a hand. "That's fine. I don't want to hear about it, though."

He dove back into the trash and emerged with another "treasure." "This one must be the family with the baby. Talcum powder."

He started to toss the bag over his shoulder when I stopped him. "Wait. Sierra uses talcum powder. She said it's better for the environment or something."

"It is. Talcum powder—"

"Tell me later. Please. Right now, toss me that bag."

As I caught it, something wet drizzled down my arm. Disgusting. I pushed aside those thoughts and pulled the bag open.

Let's see what was inside this one. A plastic carton that had contained organic spinach. A package of soybean "hot dogs." My heart sped up. Could she have been here? Or was this just someone else who was a conscientious eater?

Something shined at the bottom of the bag. I reached down and pulled it up.

It was Sierra's name tag.

My heart thudded. Sierra had been here. What had Broken Arrow done to her? And why?

"What is it, Gabby?"

I held up the plastic-covered tag. "She's been here."

"Hey! What are you kids doing down there?" A man stood at the entranceway of the alley. Based on his speech and slight frame, he wasn't Broken Arrow.

Tim hopped out of the dumpster in one fluid motion and grabbed my hand. "Come on. Let's run!"

We took off down the alley, heading away from the man. We kept running until we could no longer hear the man's yells. My lungs burned. My shoulder throbbed. And my head felt like it might explode.

I'd say I might have overdone it today.

But I had evidence. Sierra's nametag burned in my hands.

We circled the block and made it back to my van. After we'd safely pulled away, my heart slowed slightly. I tried to process the new information.

Tim, who reeked of garbage, looked like this was all in a day's work for him. He didn't breathe hard or look a bit flustered—maybe he even looked invigorated. "So Gabby, what next? Are you going to call the FBI?"

I shook my head. My eyes remained glued to the road as I feared the pain coursing through my body might distract me from driving. "I can't tell the FBI. If I'm wrong, then I'll be like the boy who cried wolf. They'll never listen to me again. I have to be absolutely sure."

"But you've got evidence."

"I have evidence that Sierra's been here. I need more."

"Well, until you figure out your next step, do you think we could go back to that dumpster?"

"Why?"

"So I can get those shoes I found?"

I hoped my scowl was answer enough for him. Brothers...

I smiled. It felt good to think that. Brothers.

My brother was back.

CHAPTER 30

That night, guilt pounded at me—at my temples, at my heart, at my conscience.

I'd missed another class, and let myself down by doing so. I'd been blaming my dad all of these years that I'd never graduated, but maybe I should point a finger at myself.

But more importantly, I'd broken a promise to Riley.

I had to come to terms with the fact that I wasn't relationship material. Like my dad, I was destined to screw up anything good that came my way. Why did I ever think a relationship between Riley and me would be successful anyway?

I was still pondering the thought when I heard a car door slam outside. I rushed to the window and saw Riley walking toward the door. I was going to have to own up to what I'd done.

And I wasn't sure what the outcome of all of this would be. I wanted to crawl in bed and pretend not to be home. Except then Riley would get worried and call the police probably.

I opened the door to greet Riley before he even made it up the stairway. But I couldn't even smile. From the way he tilted his head and squinted, Riley could tell something was wrong.

"What's going on?" He stepped into my apartment and deposited his briefcase by the front door.

I decided to cut the chitchat. "I think Broken Arrow is involved in Sierra's disappearance."

He crossed his arms. "Why would you think that?"

"Because Tim and I found her name tag in his trash."

His expression would best be described as somber. "What do you mean you 'found her nametag in his trash'?"

At the moment, I would rather actually go dumpster diving than own up to what I'd done. But Riley stared at me, rightfully angry. There was no hiding the truth. I told him what we'd done.

His hands went to his hips, and his voice sounded low—disappointed. "You probably couldn't wait until I left so you could sneak behind my back and keep investigating, could you?"

"I'm your girlfriend, not your servant. You don't control me." Where did that come from?

Riley let out an exasperated breath. He reached for me, but I stepped back. Finally, his hand dropped to his side.

"I'm not trying to control you, Gabby. I'm just pointing out that you promised me you wouldn't do this. You promised me you'd stay out of it."

My soul felt like it was shrinking. "I couldn't ignore what happened to Sierra, Riley. I couldn't sit back and do nothing."

"There are dangerous men out there, Gabby. More dangerous than any you've encountered before because they'll stop at nothing to accomplish what they want to accomplish."

"What do you know that you're not telling me, Riley? You keep hinting at it, but not telling me anything!"

He looked away. "I can't say."

"Is it something that would help me to find Sierra? At least, to clear her?"

His jaw flexed. "It's attorney-client privilege. I can't share."

"You might know something that could save my friend's life and you can't share it? You've got to be kidding me!"

"What do you want me to do, Gabby? Be disbarred? I'm between a rock and a hard place."

I crossed my arms and scowled. "I don't even know what to say to that."

Riley pinched the skin between his eyes and leaned back against the kitchen counter. Awkward silence stretched between us. In between fighting my anger, I fought the tears that wanted to show themselves.

Finally, Riley raised his head. "What are we doing, Gabby? Why is this conversation turning into a fight?"

Tears stung at my eyes as the truth that had been haunting me the past couple of days replayed itself in my mind. Finally, I raised my head and forced my chin out. "Maybe people can't change, Riley. Maybe I'm just like my dad after all."

"That's not true, Gabby." His voice sounded low, even, and I wanted to believe him. But I couldn't.

"We're from two different worlds, Riley. Your family could be on the Real Housewives of Washington D.C. and mine could be on Jersey Shore. The two don't mix."

Riley's eyes softened, his head tilted, and he reached for me. "We're not that different. Don't do this, Gabby."

I stepped back before his hands rested too long at my shoulders. "Do what?"

"I hope you're not going where I think you're going."

I turned my back toward him and paced toward the door, knowing if I looked into those gorgeous blue eyes that I would break. "You're going to want me to be a reserved little girlfriend who goes to your little hoity-toity functions with you and never makes waves."

"I just want you to be you."

But did he? Did he really? "You don't want me to investigate this case."

"Because I care about you! Because I know what kind of danger you're in!"

I twirled around and saw that he'd followed me into the living room. "Is that really why, Riley? Or is it because I make you look bad?"

He winced. "Gabby, you know that's not true."

I wiped at a tear streaming down my face. "You should go now." I pointed toward the door.

His eyes were watery now, also. "I'm not ready to give up on us. Please don't do this."

I didn't answer. I turned and stomped to my bedroom, slamming the door and locking it. A moment later, I heard Riley leave. I shoved my face into the pillow and wept.

CHAPTER 31

The next morning, I felt depleted after a night of crying. I didn't feel like I was ever going to run out of tears lately. I wasn't quite sure what to do with this new emotional Gabby.

I drug myself out of bed and tried not to listen for any sounds of Riley across the hall. I was so used to doing just that, though. My heart panged at the thought.

I knew I'd just ruined something great. But our break up was inevitable.

But if it was inevitable, why did I feel so terrible? Why did my every thought and heartbeat cause my entire body to ache?

I began a pot of coffee and looked at the clock on my microwave. I blinked at the blurry blue numbers there. 11:30. Really?

I stuck a cup in the microwave, waited for the time to be up, and then sat down at my dinette. I didn't even take a sip. Instead, I wiped my tears with my sleeves.

I had to do something to get my mind off Riley. I had to focus on Sierra. Even though the FBI thought that photo they'd found was authentic, I still held on to the hope that she was alive. After all, wouldn't I feel it down in my soul if my friend were dead? And if she were dead, I needed to know who did it. I needed to make sure they were behind bars.

The phone rang, pulling me out of my misery. I didn't recognize the number, which probably meant it was someone calling looking for a cleaner.

"I'm trying to reach Gabby St. Claire." A crisp feminine voice came through the line.

Chad was going to be busy for the next couple of days working on his own, which meant we wouldn't be able to accommodate any new clients time-wise. "I'm a bit out of commission at the moment, so if you're looking for someone to clean up after a crime…"

"This is Glenda Perkins from the Medical Examiner's office."

I sat up straight, my earlier despair momentarily gone. I ran a hand through my hair as if Dr. Perkins could see me. "This is Gabby. Sorry about that."

"I was hoping you could come in for an interview tomorrow."

"An interview? Yes. Of course. Absolutely."

She chuckled. "Great. Does 3:30 work?"

"I'll be there."

Wow, I'd actually gotten an interview. I hung up and leaned back in awe.

My phone rang again. Who now? Bruce's number popped up. I nearly didn't answer. But I did. I tried to lighten my voice as I said hello.

"Gabriella. It's Bruce. You cleaned my house last Monday."

"And I did such a good job that you want to hire me?"

He chuckled. "Not quite."

"Your friends want to hire me?"

"I was actually calling to see if you wanted to get coffee sometime."

My throat went dry. "Coffee?" Would this be my chance to find out more information about Sierra and what had happened to her? Until there was a body, I wouldn't accept that she was dead. I was a need-proof kind of girl. Besides, coffee would be safe. It would be out in public with lots of escape routes and witnesses. "Sure, that sounds nice."

"I was hoping you'd say that. How about tonight? Around seven?"

I'd rather have my teeth pulled than actually go on a date with the man. But I shoved those thoughts to the side for the greater good. "Only if I can pick the place."

"I suppose I could let you do that." Just the way he said that gave me the creeps. Socials skills he had not, which just added to the image I had of him as a crazy lone wolf taking on the evil world.

Despite that, we agreed to meet at The Grounds. It was the place where I'd feel the safest. Also a place where I was most likely to be discovered. But I'd take my chances.

I glanced at my watch. Eight hours until game time. I expelled the breath I held.

Sierra. I had to think about Sierra.

Because if I thought about Riley, I was going to break.

***

Butterflies seemed too nice a term to describe what was going on in my stomach. It felt more like bats floundering around in my innards or maybe even vultures clumsily circling around my gut and maybe even a few more organs. I wasn't sure. I squirmed in my chair one more time.

Sharon walked over. "Are you sure you're okay?"

I nodded. "I'll be fine. Just remember my signal that I need help."

"Right. You'll stand up and yell fire. I should get the hint."

Perfect. That's what I intended. Desperate times called for desperate measures.

She paused and raised a pierced eyebrow at me. "Does Riley know you're doing this?"

Those bats in my stomach began nose-diving at everything in sight. "No, I didn't tell him. Besides, we…we broke up."

Her mouth drooped open, her black lipstick forming something close to a typeset "O." "Broke up? Why?"

I shrugged, not really wanting to talk about it. Every time I did, my heart squeezed with what I could only describe as anguish. "I don't know why I ever thought we'd work out anyway."

"You're perfect together. A lot of men would feel really threatened by your strong personality. Riley is confident enough to handle you, yet to let you be yourself." Sharon stared at me, wrinkles forming at the corners of her eyes. "We need to talk later."

Her words started to do a number on my heart when someone walked into the coffeehouse. I quickly straightened, putting those thoughts aside. "Later," I whispered.

Sharon went back to work wiping down the tables. I noticed she stayed close, probably because she realized what a dumb idea this was. I even acknowledged that. But I wasn't going to back down.

Bruce must have dressed up for me because his jeans actually looked clean and his shirt only had one stain. He smiled when he saw me, though the action didn't look quite natural. Did it ever with Bruce? He was one odd bird, and coming from me that meant a lot.

"Good to see you, Gabriella." He pulled a potted plant from behind his back. "For you. I usually don't believe in giving gifts—the gesture seems so superficial and inauthentic—but since you cleaned my house, I thought I would bring this to you."

"It's..." I stared at the skinny plant with large, green, puppet-like leaves on top...leaves with little fang-like points surrounding them. "Is that a Venus flytrap?"

He nodded. "Yep. It sure is. Aren't they the coolest?"

I had to admit that the little plant was pretty cool, even if the thought behind it seemed a little twisted and morbid. Who gave someone a Venus flytrap on the first date?

Sharon cleared her throat, eyeing the plant before turning that sharp gaze on me. "Can I take your orders?"

Hm… she'd never taken orders at the table before. Nonetheless, I complied, as did Bruce. After she left, awkward silence fell. Normally I went into acting mode pretty easily, but at the moment, my heart just panged. I missed Riley. I wanted to be sitting across from him right now and not Bruce.

Would my relationship with Riley ever be the same? I doubted it. We'd given romance a shot, and it hadn't worked out. I just had to accept that fact and move on.

Bruce pointed to my eye, twirling his finger in little circles, and frowned. "Everything okay? You look like you've been through the ringer."

He sure knew how to butter someone up with sweet words. "Just had a little accident. I'll be fine."

He leaned forward, his eyes serious. "I'm glad you agreed to meet for coffee, Gabriella. I have to say that I was really impressed with you when we spoke at my place. You showed a great depth of knowledge and concern for our environment. I liked that."

"Thanks. I try. I mean, we've only got one chance to take care of our planet, right?"

"Absolutely." He leaned back and shifted his weight. "I wanted to talk to you about a special project I'm working on."

And here I thought he'd wanted to sweet talk me with his flattery. I swallowed, my saliva burning my throat. "Oh really? What is it?"

He observed me a moment, his eyes as piercing as a knife glimmering in the moonlight. "I can't tell you that yet."

A shiver ran down my spine. "Why not? You brought it up."

"I'm not sure if I can trust you." He tapped the table with his fingers.

"Then why are you here? Why are you talking to me?"

"I'm trying to figure out if I can trust you. That's why." He continued tapping with enough frequency that I wanted to slam my hand over his to stop the noise. I resisted.

Sharon brought our drinks, and I welcomed the interruption. I wrapped my fingers around my latte, wondering if I should have gotten something stronger.

As soon as she left, I leaned toward Bruce. "So, what is it? You want to boycott something? Form picket lines? Write a newspaper editorial?"

He took a long sip of coffee. The strands from angry girl music wafted through the place as I waited for him to finish his coffee and his thought. Finally, he shook his head. "No, I've tried all of those things, and they didn't work."

My heart skipped a beat. "Are you talking about something..." I rubbed the side of the warm ceramic mug. "Illegal?"

He blanched, baring his teeth with the action. "No, not illegal. Just something that would make a statement."

Tread carefully, Gabby. I tried to keep my voice even. "You mean like setting that housing development on fire? The one that was built on the wetlands in Chesapeake?"

His lips twisted in a frown. "No, someone beat me to that. I wish I could take credit."

"That would have been illegal, Bruce. People died."

"Yes, that was the tragic part. Someone should have planned much more carefully. It was sloppy work."

"Any idea who did it?"

He shrugged. "Rumor's going around that it was an amateur. I don't believe the person being accused is guilty, though."

"You mean that animal rights activist? I saw her picture on the news."

His mood seemed very somber as he nodded. "Yeah, her name is Sierra."

"You know her?"

"We've met. She was too smart to do something like that, though."

I drew in a shaky breath. "How about that office building that was bombed? Do you think that was connected?"

"It could have been. I don't know, really. No one I know has taken credit for it. I think something else is going on. Something bigger."

"Something bigger than ecoterrorism?"

He scowled. "I hate that word."

"Isn't that what it is?"

"There shouldn't be anything 'terroristic' about trying to save the earth."

I remembered my cover and nodded. "You're right. I've just been watching the news too much. All of their language is stuck in my head right now." I took a sip of my drink. "Have you talked to your friend Sierra lately?"

"Yeah, I saw her last week. She showed up at my place."

I nearly choked on my latte. "Really? I thought she was wanted by the police."

"Yeah, she is. The FBI, actually."

"Why'd she stop by your place?"

He twisted his head. "You're not a narc or something are you?"

I snorted. "A narc? Really?"

"You're asking a lot of questions."

I leaned back, trying to look uninterested. "Sorry. Sometimes I'm too curious for my own good. My mom used to always say I should be a reporter because I ask so many questions."

"I get that." He nodded, as if appeased by my explanation. "No, she just stopped by to say she was not guilty. Then she asked about another mutual friend of ours."

"She must think your friend is the guilty one."

"Perhaps. I haven't talked to him in a few days either. He dropped off the radar, so maybe he is guilty."

"Is he a friend from your environmental group?"

"Nah. He worked with Sierra at Paws and Fur Balls. Get this. His name is Tree. Isn't that the best name for someone who's a tree hugger?"

My throat burned. Tree. Tree was involved in all of this?

"Why was she looking for him?"

"She wasn't. She wanted to look through his stuff."

His stuff? "So why did she go to see you?"

"Tree used to be my roommate."

Bells began dinging in my head. "I didn't know you had a roommate."

"He moved out a couple of weeks ago."

"Is his stuff still there?"

He shook his head. "Nah. I gave it to Goodwill."

Did Sierra think Tree was guilty, that he'd followed through with his nefarious plan? Was that why she wanted to see his belongings?

He leaned closer. "Why do you sound so interested?"

I shrugged, realizing I had let on too much probably. "Other people just fascinate me. That's all. I got carried away, I guess."

He studied me another moment before leaning back in his chair and nodding. "I'll tell you what. You can come with me tonight. This can be a little initiation to see if you're ready to join ranks with me and some of my friends."

All the moisture left my throat. "Really? You would let me do that now."

He nodded. "Yeah, I will." He glanced at his watch. "I still have another hour and a half. Until then, let's talk about something else. Tell me about that kitty litter."

***

I locked the door to the coffeehouse bathroom and pulled my cell phone from my purse. My head swirled from my medication. I shouldn't have taken it; should have traded clear thinking for a little discomfort. Even with this new development, which would have normally been an adrenaline surge, my energy felt depleted. Still, I would see this through till completion.

I leaned against the graffiti-lined stall and dialed Parker's number.

"Parker, I'm with Bruce Watkins right now," I whispered.

"The eco-terrorist?"

"Yeah, him. I think he's going to do something to one of the contractors who worked on that development on the Elizabeth River."

"Why do you think that?"

"Because he invited me to help him."

Parker muttered something not so nice under his breath. "You can't go with him, Gabby."

"This could be our chance to get the evidence we need to frame this guy and finally find Sierra."

"Gabby…"

I shook my head. "Don't say it, Parker. She's alive, and I'm going to find her."

He remained silent a moment. "You're in over your head."

"I'm already in over my head, so I might as well learn to swim."

"Let me put a wire on you."

"There's no time. He's waiting in his car for me."

"At least take Riley with you."

My throat burned. "I can't. But Parker, try to be there to catch this guy red-handed, okay?"

"I don't even know where 'there' is."

I didn't know what to tell him. "Leave your cell phone on mute. I'll leave my phone on so you can hear everything. You'll figure out where we're going."

I slipped the phone in my pocket, waited a minute to make sure Parker had actually muted his phone, and hurried out, not wanting to spend any more time in here lest Bruce become suspicious.

I took a deep breath and, as I stepped out of the bathroom, I felt like I was stepping right into a death trap.

CHAPTER 32

Despite the cold, I was sweating as I rode with Bruce into the night. This had to be my worst idea ever. The idea was so knuckle-headed that I felt guilty even asking God to protect me through it.

Bruce rattled on and on about global warming, carbon emissions and the overpopulation of the earth. I barely heard him. Instead, I soaked in everything we passed. I tried to offer commentary so Parker could get a clue.

"Oh, William's Barbeque Barn. Best barbeque around, I've been told."

"There's that seafood restaurant I like to eat at, The Marina."

"Look, you can ride a monster truck there! How cool is that?"

We headed toward Chesapeake, then through Chesapeake toward North Carolina. He pulled off the bypass and drove into wooded farmland. The road narrowed, surrounded by trees and a murky looking creek.

His eyes seemed beady and snake-like as we slithered into the night. "I've got everything we need in the back."

I sucked in a deep breath, trying to remain cool. "What exactly is everything?"

He smiled. "You'll see."

I really didn't want to add "felon" to the list of words to describe me. Especially not before my interview with the medical examiner.

Finally, he pulled off the road and down a dusty lane. A half a mile later, he parked in the woods. He quickly got out, and I followed suit. The sounds of nature surrounded me and just then I realized how secluded we were. He could kill me here, and no one would find me for days. Nausea churned in my gut. Worst. Idea. Ever.

He pulled a bag out of the trunk. I tried to ascertain what was inside. I supposed it could be a bomb or some gasoline to start a fire. But I didn't think it was.

Just what was Bruce planning? And had Parker figured out where we were headed yet? Had he put an all-points bulletin out on Bruce's car and had law enforcement officers been tracking him? Maybe he put a trace on my cell phone? Something? Anything?

We began trudging through the woods. My head pounded. My eyelids felt heavy. And, even with the pain medication, my ribs ached.

Tree branches slapped me in the face. Roots tried to trip me. Water soaked the leg of my jeans.

Finally, he stopped at the edge of a nearby clearing. In the distance, I could see lights twinkling. It was a house. Who was inside? A man with a family? Little kids who'd already been tucked into bed? No way would I let Bruce hurt someone with me here to stop him. No way. But I had to plan my moves carefully.

Please, Parker, find us. Fast.

He dropped the bag and grinned at me. "We're going to leave him a message that he and his family won't ever forget."

"How'd you even get this guy's address?"

"Tree left the information."

"How did Tree get it?"

"His uncle owns Harrison Developers."

I paused. "His uncle is James Harrison?"

Bruce nodded, looking a little annoyed. "Yeah, but he hates the guy. He wants to see him destroyed."

I tried to absorb that information.

Bruce handed me something. "Take this."

"A hammer? What's this for?" Awful images danced in my head.

"You'll see." He nodded toward the house. "Come on."

He took off and I had no choice but to follow him. My heart lurched when I saw a swing set in the backyard. This man did have children. I wasn't going to let Bruce hurt them, even if it meant my own well-being.

Bruce squatted behind a car in the driveway. I tried to do the same, but my ribs ached. My face throbbed. The cold bit me down to the bone.

He unzipped the black bag at his feet. I braced myself for whatever was inside. He reached into the folds and emerged with… a stake? Did he think this man was a vampire or something?

"The picture fell off," he mumbled. He reached into the bag again. "Take this one instead."

"Picture?" I looked down at the object in my hands. A picture of a dead sea turtle? "What…?"

"These are the animals that are being killed because these people are destroying our wetlands."

Pictures? This whole thing had been about putting pictures of dead animals in this contractor's yard?

I might have laughed if I didn't feel so awful.

Before I could react, lights flooded us. Men surrounded the car. And, out of a bullhorn, I heard, "This is the FBI. Put your hands in the air."

CHAPTER 33

The next morning, I stared at my computer, trying to figure out where to go next with my investigation. I couldn't even think of anything to do an Internet search on. In my frustration, I nearly wanted to throw my computer out the window.

That would do no good. I could barely lift the beast, especially not with my arm still sore. I'd taken off the sling, but my appendage still ached. It didn't help that I didn't take my pain medicine this morning. I wanted to be able to think clearly, though. And I wanted to be able to drive, especially since my interview was today.

The events of last night replayed in my head. Bruce had simply been going to do the equivalent of an environmentalist forking or toilet papering of a yard.

Bruce may be crazy, but he wasn't our guy.

And based on the way he'd sputtered out insults at me, he wouldn't be calling me again anytime soon. I wouldn't be shedding any tears over that one.

More than anything, I wanted to race across the hall, pound on Riley's door and tell him about everything that had happened. He'd always been my confidante. Not talking to him was killing me. But this was for the best, I reminded myself. My world and Riley's world would never merge, no matter what Sharon or anyone else thought.

My cell phone rang and brought me out of my misery. "Trauma Care," I answered.

"I'm trying to reach Gabby St. Claire." The male on the other end spoke quickly, like he was hurried.

"This is she. What can I help you with?"

"I was hoping we could talk." The man breathed heavily on the other end. Was he trying to scare me? Or was he nervous?

"Who is the second person in this 'we' equation?"

"My name is Clifford Reynolds."

I sat up straight. "Clifford. You called back."

"Sorry it took so long. I... I was hesitant."

"Why?"

"Lots of reasons."

"Why do you want to talk to me now?"

"Because I can't talk to the police. I'm hoping you can help me, though. I'm in a boatload of trouble."

I wanted to tell him he should get a lawyer. But instead, I agreed to meet him. I'd get whatever information I could from him first. Then I'd advise him.

"Can you come to my office down at City Hall?"

"I'll be there in thirty minutes. Does that work?"

"I'll see you then."

***

I stared at Clifford, who was still by all accounts a mouth breather. I pushed that thought aside as I stared at him from across his desk. The man wasn't trying to scare me as I'd wondered earlier. This man was scared.

"What can I do for you, Clifford?"

He squirmed in his leather chair. His eyes looked everywhere around his tidy office until his gaze finally met mine. "I think I'm going to die tonight."

Woe. This was big. "Why would you think that?"

He wrung his hands together on top of his desk calendar. "Here's the deal, Gabby. I don't want to die and the person behind my death to get away with it. I have to say that these people are dangerous, though. They'll stop at nothing to get what they want."

These people? The ecoterrorists?

"Okay, I'm a big girl. I've beat death a couple of times already."

He stared at me, his brown eyes dull. I could tell this conversation was hard for him. Finally, he blurted, "I've done some bad things."

I crossed my fingers on my lap, trying to gather my patience. Was this man to be taken seriously? Or would this be another let down, like the one from last night? "Why don't you tell me what you've done and let me be the judge of that?"

His lips pulled into a tight line, and I could tell that whatever he wanted to say was heavy on his mind. He did a half-swirl in his chair, until the window behind him illuminated his profile. After a moment, he turned back to me. "I'm in charge of permits for the city. I give my stamp of approval whenever someone wants to build something—anything from a shed to a housing development."

I nodded, getting a better idea of where he was going. "Okay…"

"The area where Harrison Developers wanted to build in Chesapeake should have been off-limits. That land has been preserved for years. It's important that we keep our wetlands intact. They help to filter the water that goes into our rivers and, from there, the bay and the ocean."

"I understand that."

"I'm not proud of this, but I was offered 10K if I granted the permit for them to build there. Harrison Developers was going to make millions on the development. So I found a loophole, and I pushed the permit through."

"Wow. Did you say ten thousand? That's a lot of cash."

He nodded and wiped his forehead where beads of sweat had formed. "I know. It was dangled in front of me. I've had some financial troubles, so it looked like an easy way out."

"Who bribed you, Clifford?"

"James Harrison."

"But James Harrison wouldn't burn his own development nor would he bomb his own office building."

"I can't help you there.

"Why do you think you'll die?"

"They've been blackmailing me since then. Now they want to buy me off to assign them other permits that they want. They say if I don't go along with their scheme that they'll expose me."

"There's a difference between being exposed and being killed."

"I told them I was going to talk. They said if I did, they would kill me." He shook his head. "I don't have a family. But I have to do the right thing. So when I tell my boss today, I fully expect repercussions—not just from the city, but from Harrison Developers."

"But James Harrison is in the hospital. How has he communicated all of this with you?"

"He hasn't. His ex-wife has."

"Lydia? Lydia is in on this?

Clifford nodded. "Yeah, she's in on it. Big time."

***

I spent the next hour sitting in my van outside of City Hall debating about what to do...and trying to recharge my energy.

Should I share what Clifford told me with someone? Or should I continue to investigate his claims myself?

My body ached, and I couldn't imagine driving all over town today for this investigation.

I stared at my bottle of pain relievers on the seat beside me, desperately wanting to take one. I picked up the bottle and shook it like a maraca.

No, deal with the pain, Gabby. Think clearly.

Clifford was going to die. I had to tell Parker. After last night, he probably wouldn't take me seriously. But I had to talk to him.

Just as I dialed his number, I saw four police cars pull up to City Hall. What was going on?

"Gabby? Is that you?"

I watched carefully as numerous officers rushed inside, nearly forgetting about Parker in the process.

"It's me."

"Where are you now?"

I told him about my conversation with Clifford.

"Thanks for the information. I'll look into it. By the way, there's an update I need to tell you about, Gabby. I can say that you helped us reach this conclusion, thanks to some information you found out."

"Okay. What is it?"

"We arrested James Harrison last night."

"James? Did he burn down his own development?"

"No, he hasn't owned up to that. But he did admit to having one of his men beat you up. He's guilty of public corruption, racketeering, bribery and a whole list of other charges. We've had our eye on him awhile. Best of all, we found bricks of cocaine in some of his antique cars. He was going to make millions off of that."

"But he's already a millionaire."

"For some people, money is like a drug. You can never have enough. He craved money and power. He had men to do his work for him and, in the process, he made a lot of enemies. Enemies who may have hated him enough to burn down that development or bomb his office."

Someone talked to Parker in the background. "Hold on, Gabby."

I waited, absorbing that new information. Wow. Was all of this really over? If it was, then where was Sierra?

Parker came back on the line. "What about Sierra, Parker?"

"He claims his innocence there, Gabby. We're still questioning him, though. Listen, Gabby, one of my guys just came in and told me something you should know."

"What's that?"

"Clifford Reynolds just shot himself in his office."

CHAPTER 34

When I pulled back up to my apartment, I saw Pastor Shaggy waiting at my doorstep. I couldn't ignore the anxiety I felt at seeing him. Would he tell me that I'd made a mistake by becoming a Christian, that I was a terrible witness to the name of Jesus?

He stood as I approached. "Hey, Gabby. I hope you don't mind me stopping by."

"I'm...honored?"

He smiled. "I was hoping I could just have a few minutes of your time."

I contemplated saying no, but I'd already gotten myself in enough trouble, and I didn't want to add any more to the list. "Sure, how about we go up to my place? Is that okay?"

"Absolutely."

We sat across the coffee table from each other. I rubbed my hands on my jeans, noticing they were sweaty. What was this meeting about? Would he ask me to leave the church he pastored, condemn me for all of my failures?

He leaned toward me with his elbows on his knees. In that scraggy voice of his, he began. "I hope I'm not out of line here."

Starting with that sentence was usually the first sign that you were, indeed, out of line. I kept my mouth shut, though. "Don't beat around the bush. I'm a big girl." I didn't feel like a big girl at the moment, though.

"Gabby, I've known you for awhile now. What is it? Six months or so?"

"That's right."

"I've made an observation that I'm going to share with you. I want to tell you this because I worry if you don't get past this, that you're never going to be able to live life to the fullest."

I swallowed, my throat achy with emotion. What was he going to say? That the church wasn't for perfect people, but I'd gone above and beyond and therefore, needed to leave? I wouldn't blame him if he said that.

"Gabby, you've got to learn to forgive."

I blinked. "Forgive?"

"Yes. You have to forgive your dad for all the mistakes he's made in the past, and you've got to forgive yourself for all of your mistakes in the past."

"I don't know what you're talking about." The truth nudged the edge of my reason, though. I just didn't want it to come any closer.

"I know you're bitter about your father and the way he treated you for all those years. He's a changed man, though, Gabby. Sure, he's going to make some mistakes.

We all do. But I've sat down with him. I think his sorrow is real. He wants to be a better man. He wants a relationship with you."

I tried to let that truth settle over me, but couldn't. "He hurt me. How can I treat him with respect after the way he's lived?"

"That's what forgiveness is about, Gabby."

"I'll think about it."

He shifted. "More importantly, you have to forgive yourself."

"For what?" What part of my past was he referring to specifically? Because there were lots of areas where I'd screwed up.

"You have to forgive yourself for what happened to your brother. It wasn't your fault."

"I was watching him."

"You were a child."

"It was my fault."

"Even if it was—and it wasn't—he's back now. He's forgiven everyone involved in the situation. You have to let it go."

"I can't," I whispered. "I should have done more."

"You can't save the world, Gabby."

I wiped my eye. "I couldn't even save my best friend."

"You did everything you could. You almost got yourself killed in the process."

"I should have done more."

He shifted again, and I braced myself for whatever he had to say. "Gabby, do you know why your dad drank for all of those years? He drank to try and soften his guilt over your brother. That's what can happen when you don't forgive yourself. More importantly, Gabby, when you don't forgive others or forgive yourself, you can't fully experience the redemption that Jesus offers us."

I said nothing as I tried to process those words.

"Jesus died to take away that guilt. He died to give us new life. If you continue to carry around these burdens, you're going to ruin every relationship you ever attempt."

I sniffled. "You've been talking to Riley."

"He's heartbroken, Gabby. He's really worried about you and this obsession you have for finding out who killed Sierra."

"I don't like it when people tell me what to do. I don't. I know it's wrong, but it's just how I am."

"Riley isn't trying to tell you what to do. He's trying to protect you because he loves you."

I blinked. "Loves me? Did he tell you that?"

"He doesn't have to. I can see it in his eyes, and I can hear it in the way he talks about you." He clasped his hands in front of him. "Will you at least think about what we talked about?"

I nodded. "I'll think about it."

Pastor Shaggy left and I curled up on the couch in thought. Where did I even begin? Why did I have to acknowledge that there was truth in his words? I didn't want to admit it. I wanted Pastor Shaggy to be wrong. But if I kept on the path I was on, I was going to continue in a downward spiral. I was going to end up like my dad. Maybe alcohol wouldn't be my drug of choice, but would anger? Anxiety? Loneliness?

Lord, I can screw up anything you give me. I seem to have a talent for that. Please, forgive me for not trusting you, for constantly trying to take things into my own hands. Help me to be a better person. Help me to let go of the vices I hold on to and learn to forgive others who have wronged me also.

***

My soul felt empty—or was it renewed?—as I drug myself from my apartment. I guess the best way to describe my feelings were as depleted. Did one have to be brought down to size before they could grow, though?

I had an interview to get to. Afterward, I was going to meet Chad at a job. I wouldn't be able to help him, but at least I'd have someone to chat with.

As I stepped outside, a figure rounded the back of my van. My senses went on full alert. Had my attacker returned to finish the job?

I blinked. It was my stalker. I braced myself, ready to chase her.

But she didn't run. She stepped out and held up her hands. I remembered where I'd seen her. She was there on the night Harrison Developers had been bombed. She'd been holding a camera. Was she the same one who'd followed me that evening also?

I stepped closer. "Who are you?"

"My name is Megan."

"Why are you following me?"

She swallowed somberly. "Because I... because I want to be just like you."

"Just like me? Why in the world would you want to be just like me?"

"I read the story on you in the paper. You're just so smart and pretty and you have so many adventures."

"Listen, you don't want to be like me. Go and get yourself a college degree and get a normal job. I don't want to burst your bubble, but what I do is nothing to write home to mom about. I clean up blood and guts...and, every once in a while, kitty poo. That's it."

The girl swallowed. She couldn't be more than a teenager. Was she in high school still?

Her eyes shifted uncertainly. "I don't agree."

"You painted those pictures?" I pointed across the street toward The Grounds.

She nodded. "I did. I researched you. Everything's on the Internet now, you know. I read about your brother. I saw your mom's obituary. I thought you would like the paintings." She shuffled her feet. "I guess I was wrong."

"I might have if they hadn't been so creepy."

Her hazel eyes seemed to plead with me. "I wanted you to like me, Gabby."

What did I say to that? Part of my heart panged with compassion; the other part urged caution. "You've freaked me out. You're the person following me."

"I'm one of them."

I arched an eyebrow. Had I heard that correctly? "One of them?"

"Yes, there's been another man following you." She nodded so hard that her glasses bobbed down to the end of her nose.

"How do you know?"

"I've seen him. Here's the thing…I'm one of those people who no one notices. I'm a wallflower. I look ordinary. Nobody ever sees me." Tears filled her eyes.

I ignored the urge I had to give the girl a good hug. Blasted. Why did I have to feel compassion toward this girl who'd been making my life miserable? Why did she have to be near tears?

"Who is he?"

Before she answered, Tim, Teddi and my dad appeared from across the street. What were they doing here? Didn't anyone believe in calling before they came anymore?

"Why are you coming out now and actually talking to me, Megan?" I rushed. I wanted to finish this conversation before everyone arrived.

The girl's face looked even whiter than it did earlier. "Because I know something I think you need to know."

"What could you possibly know?"

"That your friend Sierra is still alive."

CHAPTER 35

My heart leapt into my throat. "Sierra's alive? How do you know that?"

"Like I said, no one notices me. I'm practically invisible. She started to approach you on the evening you were beat up. She fled, though. I think she saw something—or someone—that spooked her."

"Were you the one who called an ambulance?"

Megan nodded. "I couldn't sit back and do nothing."

I could seriously hug this wonderful, creepy little leech right now. "Where is Sierra?"

She shrugged. "I can show you."

Warning alarms sounded in my head. "How do I know this isn't a set up?"

"You have to trust me." She raised her chin defiantly.

I made a quick decision and nodded toward my van. "Okay. Let's go then. I'm driving."

"Where do you think you're going?" My dad put his hands on his hips.

"None of your business. I have something urgent to attend to." Forgiveness, I reminded myself. I was doing an awful job at it so far.

He shook his head. "I don't think it's wise that you go anywhere alone right now. Riley said you won't let him go with you."

"Great, now Riley's talking to you?" Who would he talk to next? My seventh grade science teacher who tried to have me expelled? My landlord? Dr. Phil?

"He's worried." Teddi wrung her hands together.

"So I've heard." I hopped in the van. "Sorry, everyone. I've got to run."

The back door opened, and Tim climbed in. "We're coming with you."

"Really? I don't have time to waste here, people. I've got to get moving." Could I find Sierra and still make it to my interview with the Medical Examiner's Office?

"Then we're coming with you." Teddi climbed in and then my father.

Megan slid into the front seat.

Really? I needed to take four people with me on this mission?

As luck would have it, Chad's Vanagon pulled up at that moment. I sighed. I'd overcome obstacles before. I'd overcome my friends and family right now.

"Hey, hey, hey!" Chad's surfer-like tones were enough to make anyone feel more laidback. "What's going on?"

I scowled. "You were supposed to meet me at the crime scene."

"I got a message saying to meet you here."

"From who?"

"Your father."

I craned my neck around. "Dad?"

"We decided to schedule an intervention."

"An intervention for what?" I nearly screeched.

"You and Riley. You're throwing away something good, Gabby." Teddi's sweet voice did nothing to calm the anger that flared through me.

"Chad—everyone—I don't have time for this. I've got to go get Sierra."

Tim leaned between the two front seats. "Sierra? What about her?"

"I think I know where she is… thanks to Megan."

The back door opened again, and Chad joined the gaggle. "We'll just do the intervention on the way then."

"I don't have time to argue. Everybody hold on because I'm out of here."

I backed the van out—probably a little too hard. I glanced in the back of my commercial van and saw four people sitting on the sides of the van, between my equipment and suddenly felt more like someone smuggling immigrants from Mexico than a crime scene cleaner.

This had the makings of a terrible sitcom…or a beautiful tragedy, depending on how you looked at it.

"Where do I go?"

Megan pointed in the proper direction. "Emeryville Wildlife Rescue."

"The Wildlife Rescue? That's where Sierra's been?"

Megan nodded. "She's been hiding out in the stalls with the animals for the past few days. Before that, she was with that Indian guy."

"Native American," I corrected.

"Whatever."

"You said someone else was following me also?"

She nodded. "I don't know who he is. He always wears a ball cap and keeps it low, along with a big coat and sunglasses. I couldn't give a description if my life depended on it."

"Nothing else?"

She shrugged. "He left you those notes. He seemed…casual, like sneaking around and scaring people didn't faze him."

I tried to process that, but came up with nothing.

"Gabby, about your relationship with Riley…" my dad started.

I shook my head. "This is not the time for an intervention. Can we save that for after I save my best friend's life?"

My van bumped down the road, and, at the moment, I didn't even feel bad for my passengers in the back, whose bums probably ached. Served them right for trying to interfere.

The irony of the moment hit me. I was going to rescue my best friend whom I'd thought was dead, all the while toting along my father, his girlfriend, my kidnapped brother who'd come home, my business partner and my stalker. Was God trying to teach me something through this? Because if I weren't so anxious to find Sierra, I might laugh hysterically at the picture I'm sure we all formed.

    We headed out to the rural area of Virginia Beach. My breath came in short spurts as I drove. All I could think about was Sierra, not the bickering people in my backseat who chatted about the weather and the van needing new shocks or how I should use vinegar to clean instead of my chemicals.

    Could I even trust this crazy girl sitting beside me? What if she was leading me to a death trap, and I was taking everyone I care about with me? Everyone but Riley.

    My heart panged every time I thought about him. Had I made the biggest mistake of my life by breaking up with him? Probably. Was it too late to fix it? Possibly.

    I glanced in my rearview mirror and saw my dad talking on his phone—a Smartphone. How did he afford that? He could barely afford to pay his rent. And more importantly, whom was he talking to right now?

    Finally, we pulled down a narrow, mostly gravel lane that was surrounded by swampland on either side. The wildlife refuge. I knew Sierra was friends with the woman who ran it. And it was out here in the middle of nowhere—well, nowhere for Virginia Beach, at least. Was this why Sierra's phone connection with me always sounded so broken?

    As I pulled up, I didn't see any cars around. How had Sierra gotten here? Where had she hidden her car?

    I put the van in park and turned around to look at my passengers. "I want all of you to stay here. Got it?"

My tone must have been harsh because they all grew silent and nodded.

I looked at Megan. "You get in the back with everyone else, just in case anything funny happens. Chad," I tossed him my keys, "take these just in case."

He held up his phone. "I already have 911 on speed dial."

"You're a good man. And you've known me way too long already."

I got out just in time to see another car pull up. I blinked in surprise when the car parked, and someone stepped out.

"Riley?" My heart pounded in my throat. I'd missed him and mourned for what could have been ever since we'd broken up.

His blue eyes soaked me in as he approached with his hands shoved into his pockets. There was still a heaviness about him, one that I wanted to erase. I guess that breaking up hadn't done that trick. "Your dad called and asked me to meet you here."

"You can't be here."

He nodded toward the distance. "I'm coming with you."

"I can handle this myself."

He stepped closer, close enough that every inch of my skin seemed to sizzle with electricity. "No, you can't. You have no idea what's out there."

His nearness made my heart pang. "My best friend hopefully."

"Please, let me come with you."

Why argue? "Okay. Just don't tell me what to do."

"I won't as long as you don't get yourself in any hair brained situations."

"Hair brained situations? Is that what you—"

"Kids, kids. Don't you have a mission to accomplish here? You're losing sight of your goal." My dad, for once in his life, the voice of reason and wisdom.

"Fine." I resisted the urge to cross my arms and stick out my chin in pure stubbornness. "Let's go."

As I ran toward the barn in the back, I glanced around, making sure no one was watching me. All I saw was the wood-edged property surrounding the refuge. Nothing that would set off any alarms in my head.

But every once in a while, I remembered the feeling of my attacker's fist as it connected with my face, my ribs, my limbs, and I nearly lost courage. But when I remembered Sierra, I kept going. Riley was beside me.

He'd always been beside me, hadn't he? Through all of my "hair-brained" adventures, he'd been there.

But there were more important things at stake right now than our relationship.

I tugged at the barn door, but nothing happened.

"Here, let me." Riley's muscles were quite an impressive display as he pulled the barn door open, revealing the musty, dark interior. With the door open, the smell of animals drifted outward. But it was strangely quiet. Where were the barks and squawks and brays?

Riley looked at me and I was pretty sure his thoughts mirrored my own. What was going on here? Was this a trap? Should I have gotten that gun I'd briefly considered purchasing?

I took a step back as I imagined being ambushed the moment I stepped foot inside the confined space before me. *Be strong and courageous.* Perhaps this wasn't what the Bible meant by that?

Riley took a step forward instead. "Sierra? Are you there?"

Silence stretched.

I stepped closer. "Sierra, it's Gabby. Please, I know you're here."

Again, not even crickets responded.

"Do you want to call the police? The FBI?"

"They'll arrest my friend."

"Better arrested than dead."

"They already think she's dead."

"It's your call, Gabby."

My throat burned. "Thank you." *Please don't let me get anyone killed during "my call."* I took another step inside, chills racing up my already frozen skin.

Sunlight filtered into the space through the door and cracks in the wood. The result looked hazy, creepy. Something didn't feel right, I just didn't know what. But I couldn't leave without answers.

A beam cut through the darkness. I glanced over and saw that Riley had a flashlight. He walked over to the first stall and peered inside. "It's empty. No animals, no Sierra, no nothing."

We went through the remaining stalls and found the same. There was no evidence that Sierra had ever been here. Had Megan set me up? Had she sent me here on a wild goose chase? What if she wasn't stalking me because she admired me, but if she had an ulterior purpose? Maybe that purpose was to advance the bad guy's agenda?

"The only place we haven't checked is the loft." Riley pointed upward with his flashlight. "Should we try it?"

"I don't think that will be necessary."

I twirled around at the familiar voice. Broken Arrow. He had a gun, and it was aimed at us.

I bit my lip. Here we go again.

CHAPTER 36

"I told you to leave it alone, Gabby St. Claire." Broken Arrow's tone was all business and annoyance.

Riley stepped between me and the gun. "Let's talk about this. I'm sure we can work something out here without someone getting hurt." He used his best negotiating skills. Would they work?

Broken Arrow's jaw flexed, and his gaze remained steely. "You don't understand."

From behind Broken Arrow, I saw Chad approaching with a broom, my dad with some aerosol spray cleaner, Teddi with a hammer, and Megan with… her camera?

"I wouldn't do that if I were you," Broken Arrow muttered over his shoulder. "One person makes a move on me, and I could take your friend down. Valiant effort, though."

My menagerie of companions lowered their "weapons." Great. I should have taught them sleuthing 101 before I left the van, I guess. Broken Arrow was totally outnumbered. Couldn't they see that? Didn't they have any type of plan before they tip-toed from the van?

I glanced over at my little "shadow." "A camera, Megan? Really?"

She shrugged. "I was going to document everything so the police could know to look for The Rock when we all died."

The Rock? Maybe Broken Arrow did resemble him slightly. I had to give her kudos for at least thinking of that.

Broken Arrow sighed. "Look, everyone just put the weapons down and let's talk. There's something you all need to understand."

"What did you do with Sierra?" I blurted.

"I didn't do anything with Sierra. She was here, but now she's gone."

"So Megan was telling the truth..."

"I would never lie to you, Gabby." Her voice was just so earnest. I wasn't used to having people look up to me.

My gaze remained on Broken Arrow. "Do you know what happened to her?"

"We're still trying to piece it together."

"Define 'we're,'" Riley said.

Broken Arrow looked behind him. "I'd be happy to explain some more. This is more complicated than it seems, and I need everyone to take a step back for a moment. And I need the homeless guy to drop his screwdriver."

Tim scowled. "I'm not homeless." But he dropped his screwdriver anyway.

Broken Arrow finally lowered his gun and glared at me. "You've almost ruined a very important investigation several times, Gabby St. Claire."

"What are you talking about?"

He flipped a badge out. "I'm DEA and deep under cover. Sierra has been one of my informants, but she got in over her head. The threat on her life became so great that she went into hiding under my protection."

My mouth dropped open. "Does the FBI know about this?"

"They do now. Interdepartmental communication is something we still need to work on. But we've been busting our behinds for months. We're close to getting the evidence we need if you don't screw it all up."

"You're giving me a lot of power. I haven't done anything. I haven't gotten any answers. I can't even find my friend."

"You've been poking in the right places. Nearly got me killed that day at the park."

I sliced my hands through the air. "You know, that's all fine and dandy, and I'm sorry. But I really just want to find my friend."

"So do we. She was here this morning, and now she's disappeared. We don't know what happened."

"Just what was she informing you on?"

"That's classified. I can't give you information on current investigations. In fact, I've probably told you too much already."

A car rumbled up the lane. "You have backups coming?" I asked.

"No, everyone down!" Broken Arrow shouted.

Just as we hit the ground, a spray of bullets littered the area around us.

CHAPTER 37

The ammunition kept coming and coming. The smell of acid filled the air. Wood splintered. Riley covered me, protecting me from anything that might rain down on me. I could feel his heartbeat against my back, feel his strong arms sheltering me.

Riley would give up his life for me, I realized. How many people could I say that about? So what if we were from two different worlds? Did that really matter when you loved someone? It didn't seem to for Riley; I was the only one who seemed to care.

Wheels spun on gravel. Dirt sprayed the air. And then silence.

The shooters, just as quickly as they'd come, had left.

This didn't make sense, though. James had been arrested. Sure, he probably still had men out there to do his dirty work. But how had he advised them from jail?

As soon as the dust cleared, I looked up. Was everyone okay? Had anyone been hurt? I prayed they hadn't.

One by one, everyone stood and dusted off their clothes.

"Anyone hurt?" Broken Arrow asked.

Everyone mumbled that they were okay. Thank God.

"Who was that?" I brushed some dust from my slacks, trying not to bend over in pain.

"Good question." His gaze zeroed in on me like a laser. "We need to talk."

Riley stepped up behind me. I could feel his protective gaze on me.

I nodded toward him. "You remember Riley?"

"Your male secretary?" Broken Arrow's eyes twinkled, but only for a moment.

I shrugged. "Yeah, that one."

"Can you and I talk? In private? Better yet, I'll drive you back to your apartment. You're not looking well."

I wasn't feeling well either. "I guess."

Chad volunteered to drive everyone home. I offered Riley a slight wave that hopefully communicated my desire for us to talk later. Then I followed Broken Arrow to his car. He cranked the engine, and we started silently down the road.

"You should have stayed out of this like I asked you to, Gabby," Broken Arrow said quietly.

I stared at the man beside me, watching his guarded expression. "You think I'm dense, don't you?"

"No, I don't think you're dense. Sometimes I think you're too smart for your own good. Combine that with being hard-headed and having a personal stake in this case, and I think you're a bad person to have involved."

I bit my lip in thought. Were his words true? And even if they were, would I really be able to stay away? "Do you know where Sierra is?"

He shook his head. "Not anymore. I'm trying to locate her."

"What exactly is going on here? I know James Harrison has been arrested. I know Bruce Watkins has been cleared."

"James Harrison is involved with a huge crime ring."

"Crime ring? I'm so confused here. I thought James Harrison was simply bribing people so he could get his way and make lots of money. I'm still unsure how Sierra is tied in with this?"

"Have you heard of the Gottis?"

I nodded, remembering the well-known—and dangerous—crime family.

"James Harrison and his crew make the Gottis seem like the Brady Bunch. It's more than bribing people in power. They're also smuggling drugs, involved in prostitution rings, extortion, racketeering, public corruption. You name it, they're involved with it."

"And Sierra?"

"She's alive. But she's disappeared. I don't know where she went."

"Why was she working for you?"

"James Harrison's nephew is someone named Tree Matthews."

"I've met Tree."

Broken Arrow scowled. "She was trying to get some inside information for us. We thought Tree might know something."

"So this was never about his ties to ecoterrorism?"

Broken Arrow shook his head.

"So why did you hire Sierra of all people?"

"When I met Sierra, I knew she'd be perfect to get me some inside information. And she was. But in the process, she became a target. I've been keeping her hidden in protection until the past six days. That's when she disappeared and apparently has been trying to track down some answers on her own."

"Sounds like Sierra." Sounded like me.

"Gabby, if one of James Harrison's men finds Sierra before I do, they'll kill her."

His words hit my heart and froze it. I was hanging on to getting a happy ending. But what if things didn't work out that way?

"Did his men kill all of the people at those crime scenes?"

"They claim they didn't."

I shook my head, confused. This was bigger than anything I'd imagined. But was the worst of it behind us?

CHAPTER 38

Thanks to some crazy driving on Broken Arrow's part, we beat Chad and the rest of the gang back to my apartment. Broken Arrow checked out my place for me before he left.

As I sat there by myself, some random factoid nagged at my subconscious. What was it? There was something I was missing. I was sure of it.

All of the clues and facts of the case twirled around in my brain. The wildlife refuge. The antique cars. Tree Matthews. Lydia Harrison. Helena from Paws and Fur Balls.

The house I'd attempted to visit before the Guardian gang had shown up. I'd never investigated that property any further.

Out of curiosity, I called the tax assessors office for the City of Norfolk. I told them the address of that property and requested the owner's name. Five minutes later, thanks to public record codes, I had the information I needed.

I stared at the name I'd just jotted on some scrap paper.

I had a feeling I knew exactly where Sierra was.

***

I stepped into the hallway and pounded on Riley's door. I'd heard him come in while I was on the phone, so I knew he was back.

His eyes widened when he answered, but I didn't give him a chance to say anything. Instead, I grabbed his neck and pulled him toward me, planting a firm kiss on his lips. His hands seemed to instinctively wrap around my waist.

I wanted to enjoy the moment, to make it last longer. But I had other things I had to do at the moment. So I stepped back, instantly missing Riley's closeness.

"What was that for?" Riley asked.

"It's because I love you. I do. I know I have a weird way of showing it. And I know I have a lot of faults that I'm constantly trying to work through. But I had to tell you."

"Gabby, what are you doing?" He said it so quietly that I could hardly answer.

"I have to do something. I'm not sure how it's going to turn out."

He stepped out and closed the door behind you. "I can't let you go alone."

"I can't let you go with me."

"Why not?"

"Because what if you get killed and it's my fault?"

"Gabby, that's the exact way I feel about you when you go off investigating these cases. I can't stand the thought of something happening to you because... because I love you, too."

My heart softened. "You do? Even after I broke up with you and accused you of those ugly things?"

He nodded. "Yeah, even after that. That's what love is, isn't it? Loving the good and the bad?"

I nodded, tears rushing to my eyes—again. I wiped my eyes with my shirtsleeves and pulled myself together. "Can I have your keys now?"

He started toward the stairs. "Nope. You get me with the keys or nothing. What will it be?"

"Are you sure, Riley? I'm really not sure how this is going to turn out."

"I'm sure. But you have called the authorities, haven't you?"

"I'm going to call them on the way." I grabbed his hand. "Let's go."

I filled him in on what I knew after I called Parker and Broken Arrow. They both, of course, told me to stay put. They had to know that I would never do that, though. Not when my friend's life was at stake.

"This is a bad neighborhood, Gabby."

"I know." I remembered last time I was here. I hoped the gang didn't show up again. Please don't let them show up again. Let them be... in school? At work? I had a feeling those guys were at neither of those places, nor had they been for a long time.

We sat in Riley's car for a few minutes. I tried to wait for someone else to arrive. But what if Sierra was lying inside the building, suffering and hurt? What if she needed me?

I made a quick decision. I put my hand on the door and unlatched it.

"What are you doing?"

"I can't wait, Riley. I have to see if Sierra needs my help."

"I'm going with you."

Instead of going to the front door, as I'd done last time, I went around back. The back door was nailed shut. How had Sierra gotten inside?

"How about down there?" Riley pointed to a window at the bottom of the split-level home. The wood covering the orifice had been pulled back.

"It's worth a shot."

"So is this where your friend is hiding?" The voice wasn't Riley's. I looked up and saw Mark Daniels standing there, a gun in his hands. Three other men stepped from around the house—one of them was Tree.

What was this? Gabby against the Gottis?

"I knew you'd lead us to her eventually," Mark said. "It was just a matter of time."

"I don't know what you're talking about."

Mark sneered. "You think your friend is here. We're going to find out after we have some fun with you."

I appealed to the younger of the two. "Tree? You're involved with this too? What is this—save the environment but destroy people? That's messed up."

He lowered his gaze a moment. "It's complicated, Gabby."

"I thought you were Sierra's friend."

"Sierra knows too much. She has too much information."

"Information that will bring down your crime ring?"

Tree's nostrils flared. "She was collecting evidence against me to turn in to the feds. That's not cool."

"I agree. It's not cool. But is killing her or me going to do any good?" I locked gazes with him. "You're the one who wrote those manuals for the National Federation for a Cleaner Earth with Bruce Watkins, aren't you? The 'T' was for 'Tree,' and you used Bruce's last name."

His glare said it all.

Mark Daniels pointed his gun toward the window. "Why don't we go inside and talk?"

"I'd rather not. I say we talk out here." Riley edged his shoulder in front of mine. He did care about me. I knew he did.

I had to keep talking until the feds got here.

Where *were* they? I'd called them. They should be here by now. For once in my life, I'd tried to play it safe and playing it safe was getting me to nowhere right now.

"So, this is all about a fight between you and your half-brother?" Jacob and Esau had nothing on those two.

Mark sneered. "You don't know anything."

"I know your dad died and left everything to James. But you rose above that, Mark. You're successful. Why go through all of this? Revenge?"

"Partly. James didn't deserve everything, but he was the favorite son, I suppose. I wanted to expose him and bring him down."

"Were you the one who left those notes for me?"

His sneer turned into a smirk. "I like playing head games with people."

"You're good at it. But destroy your brother's business? Really? Let me guess. You got a huge government grant for your 'green' solar energy work. But you squandered it, and now you have nothing. Meanwhile, your half-brother is one of the richest men in the area."

"You think you're so smart."

"You killed those men to make your brother look guilty. You wanted to destroy him." This man was a psychopath, I realized. A cold-blooded killer without conscience. I shivered at the thought. I hadn't met too many people that I actually thought were evil. But Mark Daniels, by all accounts, was destined to be a case study.

Voices mumbled from around the corner. Were the feds here? Why were they being so noisy? Didn't they learn better than this up at Quantico?

I looked over my shoulder and my stomach sank. The Guardians. They were back, and they had vengeance in their eyes.

CHAPTER 39

"I was hoping you'd come back, Buttercup," the ringleader called out. Hatred glimmered in his eyes.

I took a step back—but a step back meant a step toward the mob. Choices, choices. "Yep, here I am."

"Gabby, you have a street gang mad at you too? What's next—the Mafia? A drug cartel? Al Qaeda? Is there anyone else you can possibly upset?"

"The possibilities are endless, I suppose."

"You sprayed me and my boys with that cleaning solution of yours." The leader stepped closer, close enough that I could count his gold teeth. "We didn't like that." He called over his shoulder, "Did we boys?"

A round of "Nah, that was just wrong," "she was out of line," "my eyes still be hurting" followed.

"What's going on here?" Mark Daniels asked behind me. He sounded annoyed and testy—probably not a good combination.

I shrugged as a quick—but unlikely—plan formed in my mind. I looked at the leader of The Guardians. I had no other plan at the moment, so why not? "If you mess with me, you mess with my boys back here."

The leader's gaze flickered over my shoulder. "These are your boys?"

"Yep, and they're armed and loaded. I wouldn't mess with them."

"Your boys?" Mark Daniels coughed, looking bewildered for a moment.

I kept going before too much time settled, and people could think too much.

"We got guns, too. Right boys?" On cue, the Guardians pulled out their weapons.

Rats. The only bad part of my plan was that Riley and I were now in the middle of this potential gun battle.

The Guardians took the first shot at Mark Daniels and his crew. Mark Daniels didn't hesitate before firing back. His bullet chipped the brick corner of the house, sending debris flying. Men on both sides scrambled, not quite mirroring an old west showdown.

I grabbed Riley's hand. I dodged T-bone, who had a new object of fury. Riley and I ran toward the side of the house, desperate for shelter as more shots pierced the air. Shouts ensued behind us. Gunpowder tinged my nostrils.

As we rounded the corner, Broken Arrow's sedan jerked to a stop. He rushed from his car, gun drawn.

I could hardly breathe. "What took so long?"

"Accident on the interstate." He paused only a moment. "What's going on?"

"Gun battle. Mark Daniels. The Guardians."

He looked dumbfounded. "You really have a knack for trouble, don't you?"

"So I've been told."

He nodded toward his car. "Get inside and stay there. Backup is on the way."

He disappeared into the fray.

And Riley and I sat in his car like sitting ducks. These windshields would be no match for a bullet if the bad guys came this way. And there were a lot of bad guys out there, so the possibility was good that one of them might end up here.

Or that Broken Arrow might end up dead.

Or that I might never find Sierra. Was she inside the house? Was she okay?

"Don't even think about it, Gabby."

I swung my head toward Riley. "Think about what?"

"Sneaking inside the house. You should just stay put."

I nodded. I couldn't even argue his point, not when I considered what was going on in the backyard.

Out of the corner of my eye, I saw movement in the distance. I jerked my head toward the commotion. Mark Daniels stepped from the side of the house.

His gaze found me, as did his gun.

Just as I sucked in a breath, Riley threw himself over me. Glass exploded around us. Crystal pellets rained all over the car's interior.

My heart stammered in double-time, and the hairs on the back of my neck stood up straight. Would Mark find us? Would he reach the car and finish us off? Did I dare peek and see what was happening?

I didn't have a choice. Riley remained over me. It was just as well—fear seemed to paralyze me.

Just then, another car rumbled up the gravel driveway.

Good. Backup was here. Back up was finally here.

***

An hour later, everyone was either arrested or in an ambulance or both. Riley and I still hung out in Broken Arrow's car. I continued to pick pieces of the broken windshield from my hair. But we were alive and relatively unharmed.

I hoped I could say the same for Sierra.

"Gabby?" Riley turned toward me and cupped my face with his palm.

My heart raced. "Yes?"

"I'm sorry if I acted like a jerk. I didn't mean to smother you. I was just worried—"

"Don't apologize. I'm sorry that I'm so selfish. I didn't want to listen to anyone, and I could have gotten you killed."

His lips covered mine. I missed those kisses. I'd missed Riley, and I never wanted to lose him again. And I was going to tell him that—

Before I could, someone rapped at the window. I looked over and saw Lydia standing there, staring at Riley. I gave my boyfriend a pointed look. "What's going on?"

Riley opened the door—since the car wasn't running, he couldn't put down the window. He greeted her with a certain familiarity that got my hackles up. "It looks like it's all over, Lydia."

I squinted in confusion, trying to put some puzzle pieces that had seemingly appeared out of thin air together. "All over? What does that mean, Riley?"

He turned back to me and grabbed my hand. "Lydia traded our auction date in for a legal consultation with me. She was an informant also."

I blinked in surprise. Clifford had said she was in on the bribery. Was she simply a part of this mess as a cover? Understanding slowly spread over me. "So you knew some of this?"

He nodded. "I did but I couldn't say anything because of confidentiality. That's why I wanted you to stay out of it. I knew what you were up against."

Lydia peered into the car, looking as polished and beautiful as ever. "I told Riley because it was the only way I could figure out to keep you away. I knew that if Riley knew what was going on, he'd do everything he could to make you stay out of it."

I tilted my head, my processor whirling at full speed. "Why did you want to keep me away? You don't even know me."

Her expression remained unchanged. "No, but I remember what it was like to be young and to have dreams. I didn't want to see those taken from you."

"That's ... kind of you." And unlikely...

She looked over us at the slew of police officers and feds swarming the area. "Well done, Gabby. You brought down the mob and a gang in one fell swoop."

Had I? Bringing them down had never even been my goal. I'd simply wanted to find my friend.

I looked beyond Lydia. Neither Broken Arrow nor Parker would let me go inside the house and look for Sierra. They were inside now, combing the place for evidence. Had they found my friend? Was she really alive? Or had someone else gotten to her first?

Please, Lord, help her to be okay.

I wished all of my prayers weren't quite so selfish, but that didn't change the fact that I desperately wanted my friend to be safe. I hoped that God understood.

I blinked when I saw someone coming around the corner from the backyard. Was it really Sierra? Yes, it was. I knew it was.

I popped the door open and sprinted across the grass. Sierra took off in a sprint also and, when we reached each other, I threw my arms around my friend.

"Sierra. You're alive!" I stepped back and looked at her. She had a cut across her forehead, and she looked dirty and disheveled. But she was alive. There were no bullet holes in her forehead or any of the other terrible scenarios I'd conjured up in my mind.

Thank you, Lord. Thank you, thank you, thank you.

Sierra wiped her eyes, and I thought I saw a tear there. It was the first time I think I'd ever seen my friend cry. "I knew you'd find me, Gabby. I knew if anyone could do it, you could."

Riley appeared behind me and also gave Sierra a hug. "Good to see you."

"You better believe it. I've been on one wild ride." She looked at me. "How'd you know I was here?"

"I saw where you'd written down this address at your office. Then I did a search on the property and found out it was owned by your friend Helena."

She shook her head. "I didn't write down this address."

"Your friend must have written it down, knowing that I'd find it then. Either that or you have an angel looking out for you."

Sierra nodded. "Helena. She seemed to sense that something was going on. She said I could come here if I needed to."

I put my arm around her. "We have a lot to catch up on."

"That we do."

Her gaze bounced from Riley to me for a moment until she wagged her eyebrows.

"I should have nearly gotten myself killed a long time ago. Who knew that was what it would take to get the two of you together?"

I didn't know what to say to that because Riley and I still needed to talk. To really talk. Instead, I said, "Are you okay?"

"Now I am."

"Not really." Both Sierra and I jerked our heads up at the sound of the familiar voice. Lydia stood in front of us, a gun protruding from her jacket. I looked around. Every other law enforcement officer was busy arresting people and filing reports. No one had noticed what was going on here. Not good...

CHAPTER 40

"Lydia? You said you were a good guy." I couldn't keep the incredulous tone from my voice.

Nor could Riley. "No, Lydia... not this."

She smirked. "What can I say? I guess I'm a dirty informant. We worked hard to get the empire that we have, and now I'm poised to lose it all, thanks to you and your friend."

Riley tried to step forward, but Lydia shoved her gun toward him, and he stopped. He shook his head. "Lydia, don't do this. You're only going to make things worse for yourself."

The smirk left her face, the look replaced with vengeance. "I've lost everything as it is. I'm going to have to go into witness protection. They're going to try and kill me once they find out I was a snitch."

"Witness protection isn't that bad. It's a fresh start." It was the only argument I could think of at the time, as lame as it was.

"Easy for you to say. I might as well spend the rest of my life behind bars."

I glanced behind her and saw someone in the shadows. Could it be? I averted my eyes, not wanting to draw attention to the person who could possibly get us out of this mess.

"You need to think through this, Lydia," Riley said. "Right now, you're going to have the esteem of the community for your help in bringing this operation down. Don't do something stupid."

She sneered. "The esteem of the community has gotten me nowhere. Now it's time for some revenge. At least this way I get to keep my self-respect and stand up for my family. If you're going to go out, go out in style. That's my motto."

Megan charged toward us, a guttural sound escaping her. Just as Lydia turned around, Megan pulled out... a spray bottle? She began dousing Lydia in the face with the solution. Lydia bent over in surprise—and pain. It gave Riley the chance to wrestle the gun from her hands—and for the cops in the area to take notice and step in to help.

Parker came over and slapped some handcuffs on her, while Broken Arrow just shook his head. "Big mistake, Lydia," he said. "Big mistake. I should have known I couldn't trust you. You were feeding information to your family all the while, weren't you?"

She spit at me. "I never should have gotten involved in all this."

Parker began pulling her away. "It's a little late to be realizing that now."

I turned to Megan, who still held the spray bottle in her shaky hands.

My stalker saves the day. Only in my life.

"Spray solution?" I asked.

She shrugged. "I saw you use it that day with the Guardians."

"You saw that, too?" Who was this girl? The invisible woman? Was there anything she missed?

She nodded. "I see everything."

I supposed that I would choose to be flattered rather than freaked out, since the girl had just saved our lives. "Thank you, Megan. I owe you. We all owe you."

"No, Gabby, I owe you. After watching you, I'm not afraid to step out of the shadows anymore."

Thank goodness because the girl was a little freaky hiding out around every corner. "You can do it, Megan. Take control of your own life and chase your dreams."

My heart sank. My dreams had gone out the window. I'd missed so many classes now that I wasn't sure if I would graduate. I'd missed my job interview with the medical examiner's office. But there was always crime scene cleaning, right?

I looked around me at Riley and Sierra. My friend was safe. That was worth more than anything else.

People first. How could I ever regret that?

EPILOGUE

Two Months Later

I'd dreamed about this moment for a long time. The president of my college made his pronouncement. I grabbed my graduation cap and threw it in the air. I had a title to add after my name—one I was proud of. I was a college graduate. Finally.

I looked out in the audience and saw that everyone I cared about was here to support me. My dad, Teddi and Tim. Sierra and Chad. Yes, Sierra and Chad. I was just as shocked as anyone that they'd started dating over the past month. But when I looked at them together, they fit—they made sense. And I was so happy for them. Sharon, Pastor Shaggy, my upstairs neighbor Mrs. Mystery, and radio talk show host Bill McCormick had come. Riley's parents had driven down. Megan was there—because I'd invited her, not because she'd been shadowing me—at least not that I was aware of. Even Parker attended with his very pregnant fiancée.

Of course, most importantly, Riley was there.

I smiled at him and gave a little wave. He returned the gesture with a grin and wave of his own.

As soon as we were dismissed, I found everyone, and we all exchanged hugs and squeals. It was May, and the weather was perfect. Not too hot and not too cold. Yes, the weather could be temperamental in Virginia. But, today, that had worked out in my favor.

Parker extended his hand. "I heard you start next month with the Medical Examiner's Office. Congratulations, Gabby. You deserve this."

I couldn't stop smiling. "Thanks, Parker. I appreciate that. Especially coming from you. And I appreciate you putting in a good word for me, especially since I missed the interview and everything."

He shrugged. "I know I've given you a hard time, but you've got a knack for this stuff, Gabby. And you missed the interview because you were tracking down bad guys. How could I fault you for that?" He shrugged. "I mean, I could fault you for that since you weren't an official part of the investigation, but—"

I held up my hands. "I get it. And thank you."

Chad clapped my back in a chummy hug. "Good job, Gabby. We're still going to work together, though, right? You can't stop cleaning crime scenes."

"Uh, yes she can," Sierra said. "She's earned it."

I shrugged. "I don't know. I've been doing it so long that I'm really going to miss being the cleaner. Maybe I will have to make guest appearances sometimes or step in when you need help."

Riley appeared on my other side. "I'm hoping you might be occupied with other things."

"Like what? My new job?"

Riley lowered down to one knee. "I was actually hoping that you would marry me, and we could get busy planning a wedding."

I stared at the ring in his hands. He couldn't be serious. But he was!

I gently took the ring from his hands and examined the beautiful princess-cut diamond that sparkled at me.

"It's real, Gabby."

Rats. He knew me too well. Of course the ring was real. Riley was real. Our relationship was real. Everything just seemed too good to be true sometimes.

"Will you marry me, Gabby St. Claire?"

Tears actually popped to my eyes. I'd dreamed about this moment for so long, but never thought it would actually happen. "Yes, I'd be honored, Riley Thomas. I'd be honored."

Everyone exchanged hugs all around.

As I pulled away, my phone rang.

"I'm looking for someone to clean a crime scene."

I stepped away from my family and friends. "A crime scene, you said?" I bit my lip. Just one more case couldn't hurt, could it? "Sure, I can help you out."

###

Dear Reader,

Thank you so much for reading **Organized Grime**. I truly hope you've enjoyed following the adventures of Gabby and her zany friends. Even as the creator of this series, Gabby continues to surprise me with her antics and choices.

Organized Grime is followed by **Dirty Deeds. Dirty Deeds** follows Gabby and Riley as they travel to a fancy mountain resort to meet Riley's law school friends. Needless to say, Gabby feels a tad out of place. When one of Riley's friends goes missing, Gabby can't resist getting involved.
Book 5 in the series is **The Scum of All Fears**. An old foe comes back into the picture and wreaks havoc in Gabby and Riley's life. The fight of their lives continues in **To Love, Honor, and Perish**.

Taking place at the same time as **Dirty Deeds** is the new novel about Sierra Nakamura, **Pounced**. Sierra finds a mystery of her own while Gabby and Riley are out of town, and of course her investigation involves animals! But Sierra not only finds trouble . . . could she find love as well?

Again dear reader, thank you so much for helping Gabby and her friends come alive. Stay tuned for more books about Gabby as she searches for the perfect job, as she explores faith, and as she tries to figure out life.

Many blessings to you,
Christy Barritt
www.christybarritt.com

P.S. Please feel free to sign up for my infrequent newsletter. I send it approximately once a quarter, and it includes updates on my new and future releases. The link can be found on my website, at the bottom of the homepage:
www.christybarritt.com.

Want more of Gabby? Then check out Dirty Deeds!

If you enjoyed this book, you may also enjoy these Squeaky Clean Mysteries:

Hazardous Duty (Book 1)
On her way to completing a degree in forensic science, Gabby St. Claire drops out of school and starts her own crime-scene cleaning business. When a routine cleaning job uncovers a murder weapon the police overlooked, she realizes that the wrong person is in jail. But the owner of the weapon is a powerful foe . . . and willing to do anything to keep Gabby quiet. With the help of her new neighbor, Riley Thomas, a man whose life and faith fascinate her, Gabby seeks to find the killer before another murder occurs.

Suspicious Minds (Book 2)
In this smart and suspenseful sequel to *Hazardous Duty*, crime-scene cleaner Gabby St. Claire finds herself stuck doing mold remediation to pay the bills. Her first day on the job, she uncovers a surprise in the crawlspace of a dilapidated home: Elvis, dead as a doornail and still wearing his blue-suede shoes. How could she possibly keep her nose out of a case like this?

It Came Upon a Midnight Crime (Book 2.5, a Novella)
Someone is intent on destroying the true meaning of Christmas—at least, destroying anything that hints of it. All around crime-scene cleaner Gabby St. Claire's hometown, anything pointing to Jesus as "the reason for the season" is being sabotaged. The crimes become more twisted as dismembered body parts are found at the vandalisms. Someone is determined to destroy Christmas . . . but Gabby is just as determined to find the Grinch and let peace on earth and goodwill prevail.

Organized Grime (Book 3)
Gabby St. Claire knows her best friend, Sierra, isn't guilty of killing three people in what appears to be an eco-terrorist

attack. But Sierra has disappeared, her only contact a frantic phone call to Gabby proclaiming she's being hunted. Gabby is determined to prove her friend is innocent and to keep Sierra alive. While trying to track down the real perpetrator, Gabby notices a disturbing trend at the crime scenes she's cleaning, one that ties random crimes together—and points to Sierra as the guilty party. Just what has her friend gotten herself involved in?

Dirty Deeds (Book 4)
"Promise me one thing. No snooping. Just for one week." Gabby St. Claire knows that her fiancé's request is a simple one she should be able to honor. After all, Riley's law school reunion and attorneys' conference at a posh resort is a chance for them to get away from the mysteries Gabby often finds herself involved in as a crime-scene cleaner. Then an old friend of Riley's goes missing. Gabby suspects one of Riley's buddies might be behind the disappearance. When the missing woman's mom asks Gabby for help, how can she say no?

The Scum of All Fears (Book 5)
Gabby St. Claire is back to crime-scene cleaning and needs help after a weekend killing spree fills her work docket. A serial killer her fiancé put behind bars has escaped. His last words to Riley were: *I'll get out, and I'll get even*. Pictures of Gabby are found in the man's prison cell, messages are left for Gabby at crime scenes, someone keeps slipping in and out of her apartment, and her temporary assistant disappears. The search for answers becomes darker when Gabby realizes she's dealing with a criminal who is truly the scum of the earth. He will do anything to make Gabby's and Riley's lives a living nightmare.

To Love, Honor, and Perish (Book 6)
Just when Gabby St. Claire's life is on the right track, the unthinkable happens. Her fiancé, Riley Thomas, is shot and in life-threatening condition only a week before their wedding. Gabby is determined to figure out who pulled the trigger, even

if investigating puts her own life at risk. As she digs deeper into the case, she discovers secrets better left alone. Doubts arise in her mind, and the one man with answers lies on death's doorstep. Then an old foe returns and tests everything Gabby is made of—physically, mentally, and spiritually. Will all she's worked for be destroyed?

***Mucky Streak* (Book 7)**
Gabby St. Claire feels her life is smeared with the stain of tragedy. She takes a short-term gig as a private investigator—a cold case that's eluded detectives for ten years. The mass murder of a wealthy family seems impossible to solve, but Gabby brings more clues to light. Add to the mix a flirtatious client, travels to an exciting new city, and some quirky—albeit temporary—new sidekicks, and things get complicated. With every new development, Gabby prays that her "mucky streak" will end and the future will become clear. Yet every answer she uncovers leads her closer to danger—both for her life and for her heart.

***Foul Play* (Book 8)**
Gabby St. Claire is crying "foul play" in every sense of the phrase. When the crime-scene cleaner agrees to go undercover at a local community theater, she discovers more than backstage bickering, atrocious acting, and rotten writing. The female lead is dead, and an old classmate who has staked everything on the musical production's success is about to go under. In her dual role of investigator and star of the show, Gabby finds the stakes rising faster than the opening-night curtain. She must face her past and make monumental decisions, not just about the play but also concerning her future relationships and career. Will Gabby find the killer before the curtain goes down—not only on the play, but also on life as she knows it?

***Broom and Gloom* (Book 9)**
Gabby St. Claire is determined to get back in the saddle again. While in Oklahoma for a forensic conference, she meets her

soon-to-be stepbrother, Trace Ryan, an up-and-coming country singer. A woman he was dating has disappeared, and he suspects a crazy fan may be behind it. Gabby agrees to investigate, as she tries to juggle her conference, navigate being alone in a new place, and locate a woman who may not want to be found. She discovers that sometimes taking life by the horns means staring danger in the face, no matter the consequences.

Dust and Obey (Book 10)
When Gabby St. Claire's ex-fiancé, Riley Thomas, asks for her help in investigating a possible murder at a couples retreat, she knows she should say no. She knows she should run far, far away from the danger of both being around Riley and the crime. But her nosy instincts and determination take precedence over her logic. Gabby and Riley must work together to find the killer. In the process, they have to confront demons from their past and deal with their present relationship.

Thrill Squeaker (Book 11)
An abandoned theme park. An unsolved murder. A decision that will change Gabby's life forever. Restoring an old amusement park and turning it into a destination resort seems like a fun idea for former crime-scene cleaner Gabby St. Claire. The side job gives her the chance to spend time with her friends, something she's missed since beginning a new career. The job turns out to be more than Gabby bargained for when she finds a dead body on her first day. Add to the mix legends of Bigfoot, creepy clowns, and ghostlike remnants of happier times at the park, and her stay begins to feel like a rollercoaster ride. Someone doesn't want the decrepit Mythical Falls to open again, but just how far is this person willing to go to ensure this venture fails? As the stakes rise and danger creeps closer, will Gabby be able to restore things in her own life that time has destroyed—including broken relationships? Or is her future closer to the fate of the doomed Mythical Falls?

Swept Away, a Honeymoon Novella (Book 11.5)

Finding the perfect place for a honeymoon, away from any potential danger or mystery, is challenging. But Gabby's longtime love and newly minted husband, Riley Thomas, has done it. He has found a location with a nonexistent crime rate, a mostly retired population, and plenty of opportunities for relaxation in the warm sun. Within minutes of the newlyweds' arrival, a convoy of vehicles pulls up to a nearby house, and their honeymoon oasis is destroyed like a sandcastle in a storm. Despite Gabby's and Riley's determination to keep to themselves, trouble comes knocking at their door—literally—when a neighbor is abducted from the beach directly outside their rental. Will Gabby and Riley be swept away with each other during their honeymoon . . . or will a tide of danger and mayhem pull them under?

***Cunning Attractions* (Book 12)**
Coming soon

***While You Were Sweeping*, a Riley Thomas Novella**
Riley Thomas is trying to come to terms with life after a traumatic brain injury turned his world upside down. Away from everything familiar—including his crime-scene-cleaning former fiancée and his career as a social-rights attorney—he's determined to prove himself and regain his old life. But when he claims he witnessed his neighbor shoot and kill someone, everyone thinks he's crazy. When all evidence of the crime disappears, even Riley has to wonder if he's losing his mind.

Note: *While You Were Sweeping* is a spin-off mystery written in conjunction with the Squeaky Clean series featuring crime-scene cleaner Gabby St. Claire.

The Sierra Files

Pounced **(Book 1)**
Animal-rights activist Sierra Nakamura never expected to stumble upon the dead body of a coworker while filming a project nor get involved in the investigation. But when someone threatens to kill her cats unless she hands over the "information," she becomes more bristly than an angry feline. Making matters worse is the fact that her cats—and the investigation—are driving a wedge between her and her boyfriend, Chad. With every answer she uncovers, old hurts rise to the surface and test her beliefs. Saving her cats might mean ruining everything else in her life. In the fight for survival, one thing is certain: either pounce or be pounced.

Hunted **(Book 2)**
Who knew a stray dog could cause so much trouble? Newlywed animal-rights activist Sierra Nakamura Davis must face her worst nightmare: breaking the news she eloped with Chad to her ultra-opinionated tiger mom. Her perfectionist parents have planned a vow-renewal ceremony at Sierra's lush childhood home, but a neighborhood dog ruins the rehearsal dinner when it shows up toting what appears to be a fresh human bone. While dealing with the dog, a nosy neighbor, and an old flame turning up at the wrong times, Sierra hunts for answers. Her journey of discovery leads to more than just who committed the crime.

Pranced **(Book 2.5, a Christmas novella)**
Sierra Nakamura Davis thinks spending Christmas with her husband's relatives will be a real Yuletide treat. But when the animal-rights activist learns his family has a reindeer farm, she begins to feel more like the Grinch. Even worse, when Sierra arrives, she discovers the reindeer are missing. Sierra fears the animals might be suffering a worse fate than being used for entertainment purposes. Can Sierra set aside her dogmatic

opinions to help get the reindeer home in time for the holidays? Or will secrets tear the family apart and ruin Sierra's dream of the perfect Christmas?

Rattled (Book 3)
"What do you mean a thirteen-foot lavender albino ball python is missing?" Tough-as-nails Sierra Nakamura Davis isn't one to get flustered. But trying to balance being a wife and a new mom with her crusade to help animals is proving harder than she imagined. Add a missing python, a high maintenance intern, and a dead body to the mix, and Sierra becomes the definition of rattled. Can she balance it all—and solve a possible murder—without losing her mind?

Holly Anna Paladin Mysteries

***Random Acts of Murder* (Book 1)**
When Holly Anna Paladin is given a year to live, she embraces her final days doing what she loves most—random acts of kindness. But one of her extreme good deeds goes horribly wrong, implicating her in a string of murders. Holly is suddenly thrust into a different kind of fight for her life. Could it also be random that the detective assigned to the case is her old high school crush and present-day nemesis? Will Holly find the killer before he ruins what is left of her life? Or will she spend her final days alone and behind bars?

***Random Acts of Deceit* (Book 2)**
"Break up with Chase Dexter, or I'll kill him." Holly Anna Paladin never expected such a gut-wrenching ultimatum. With home invasions, hidden cameras, and bomb threats, Holly must make some serious choices. Whatever she decides, the consequences will either break her heart or break her soul. She tries to match wits with the Shadow Man, but the more she fights, the deeper she's drawn into the perilous situation. With her sister's wedding problems and the riots in the city, Holly has nearly reached her breaking point. She must stop this mystery man before someone she loves dies. But the deceit is threatening to pull her under . . . six feet under.

***Random Acts of Murder* (Book 3)**
When Holly Anna Paladin's boyfriend, police detective Chase Dexter, says he's leaving for two weeks and can't give any details, she wants to trust him. But when she discovers Chase may be involved in some unwise and dangerous pursuits, she's compelled to intervene. Holly gets a run for her money as she's swept into the world of horseracing. The stakes turn deadly when a dead body surfaces and suspicion is cast on Chase. At every turn, more trouble emerges, making Holly question what she holds true about her relationship and her future. Just when

she thinks she's on the homestretch, a dark horse arises. Holly might lose everything in a nail-biting fight to the finish.

Random Acts of Scrooge **(Book 3.5)**
Christmas is supposed to be the most wonderful time of the year, but a real-life Scrooge is threatening to ruin the season's good will. Holly Anna Paladin can't wait to celebrate Christmas with family and friends. She loves everything about the season—celebrating the birth of Jesus, singing carols, and baking Christmas treats, just to name a few. But when a local family needs help, how can she say no? Holly's community has come together to help raise funds to save the home of Greg and Babette Sullivan, but a Bah-Humburgler has snatched the canisters of cash. Holly and her boyfriend, police detective Chase Dexter, team up to catch the Christmas crook. Will they succeed in collecting enough cash to cover the Sullivans' overdue bills? Or will someone succeed in ruining Christmas for all those involved?

Random Acts of Guilt **(Book 4)**
Coming soon

Carolina Moon Series

***Home Before Dark* (Book 1)**
Nothing good ever happens after dark. Country singer Daleigh McDermott's father often repeated those words. Now, her father is dead. As she's about to flee back to Nashville, she finds his hidden journal with hints that his death was no accident. Mechanic Ryan Shields is the only one who seems to believe Daleigh. Her father trusted the man, but her attraction to Ryan scares her. She knows her life and career are back in Nashville and her time in the sleepy North Carolina town is only temporary. As Daleigh and Ryan work to unravel the mystery, it becomes obvious that someone wants them dead. They must rely on each other—and on God—if they hope to make it home before the darkness swallows them.

***Gone By Dark* (Book 2)**
Charity White can't forget what happened ten years earlier when she and her best friend, Andrea, cut through the woods on their way home from school. A man abducted Andrea, who hasn't been seen since. Charity has tried to outrun the memories and guilt. What if they hadn't taken that shortcut? Why wasn't Charity kidnapped instead of Andrea? And why weren't the police able to track down the bad guy? When Charity receives a mysterious letter that promises answers, she returns to North Carolina in search of closure and the peace that has eluded her. With the help of her new neighbor, Police Officer Joshua Haven, Charity begins to track down mysterious clues. They soon discover that they must work together or both of them will be swallowed by the looming darkness.

Cape Thomas Mysteries:

Dubiosity (Book 1)
Savannah Harris vowed to leave behind her old life as an investigative reporter. But when two migrant workers go missing, her curiosity spikes. As more eerie incidents begin afflicting the area, each works to draw Savannah out of her seclusion and raise the stakes—for her and the surrounding community. Even as Savannah's new boarder, Clive Miller, makes her feel things she thought long forgotten, she suspects he's hiding something too, and he's not the only one. As secrets emerge and danger closes in, Savannah must choose between faith and uncertainty. One wrong decision might spell the end . . . not just for her but for everyone around her. Will she unravel the mystery in time, or will doubt get the best of her?

Disillusioned (Book 2) *coming soon*
Nikki Wright is desperate to help her brother, Bobby, who hasn't been the same since escaping from a detainment camp run by terrorists in Colombia. Rumor has it that he betrayed his navy brothers and conspired with those who held him hostage, and both the press and the military are hounding him for answers. All Nikki wants is to shield her brother so he has time to recover and heal. But soon they realize the paparazzi are the least of their worries. When a group of men try to abduct Nikki and her brother, Bobby insists that Kade Wheaton, another former SEAL, can keep them out of harm's way. But can Nikki trust Kade? After all, the man who broke her heart eight years ago is anything but safe...Hiding out in a farmhouse on the Chesapeake Bay, Nikki finds her loyalties—and the remnants of her long-held faith—tested as she and Kade put aside their differences to keep Bobby's increasingly erratic behavior under wraps. But when Bobby disappears, Nikki will have to trust Kade completely if she wants to uncover the truth about a rumored conspiracy. Nikki's life—and the fate of the nation—depends on it.

Standalones

The Good Girl
Tara Lancaster can sing "Amazing Grace" in three harmonies, two languages, and interpret it for the hearing impaired. She can list the Bible canon backward, forward, and alphabetized. The only time she ever missed church was when she had pneumonia and her mom made her stay home. Then her life shatters and her reputation is left in ruins. She flees halfway across the country to dog-sit, but the quiet anonymity she needs isn't waiting at her sister's house. Instead, she finds a knife with a threatening message, a fame-hungry friend, a too-hunky neighbor, and evidence of . . . a ghost? Following all the rules has gotten her nowhere. And nothing she learned in Sunday School can tell her where to go from there.

Death of the Couch Potato's Wife (Suburban Sleuth Mysteries)
You haven't seen desperate until you've met Laura Berry, a career-oriented city slicker turned suburbanite housewife. Well-trained in the big-city commandment, "mind your own business," Laura is persuaded by her spunky seventy-year-old neighbor, Babe, to check on another neighbor who hasn't been seen in days. She finds Candace Flynn, wife of the infamous "Couch King," dead, and at last has a reason to get up in the morning. Someone is determined to stop her from digging deeper into the death of her neighbor, but Laura is just as determined to figure out who is behind the death-by-poisoned-pork-rinds.

Imperfect
Since the death of her fiancé two years ago, novelist Morgan Blake's life has been in a holding pattern. She has a major case of writer's block, and a book signing in the mountain town of Perfect sounds as perfect as its name. Her trip takes a wrong turn when she's involved in a hit-and-run: She hit a man, and he ran from the scene. Before fleeing, he mouthed the word

"Help." First she must find him. In Perfect, she finds a small town that offers all she ever wanted. But is something sinister going on behind its cheery exterior? Was she invited as a guest of honor simply to do a book signing? Or was she lured to town for another purpose—a deadly purpose?

The Gabby St. Claire Diaries (a tween mystery series)

The Curtain Call Caper (Book 1)
Is a ghost haunting the Oceanside Middle School auditorium? What else could explain the disasters surrounding the play—everything from missing scripts to a falling spotlight and damaged props? Seventh-grader Gabby St. Claire has dreamed about being part of her school's musical, but a series of unfortunate events threatens to shut down the production. While trying to uncover the culprit and save her fifteen minutes of fame, she also has to manage impossible teachers, cliques, her dysfunctional family, and a secret she can't tell even her best friend. Will Gabby figure out who or what is sabotaging the show . . . or will it be curtains for her and the rest of the cast?

The Disappearing Dog Dilemma (Book 2)
Why are dogs disappearing around town? When two friends ask seventh-grader Gabby St. Claire for her help in finding their missing canines, Gabby decides to unleash her sleuthing skills to sniff out whoever is behind the act. But time management and relationships get tricky as worrisome weather, a part-time job, and a new crush interfere with Gabby's investigation. Will her determination crack the case? Or will shadowy villains, a penchant for overcommitting, and even her own heart put her in the doghouse?

The Bungled Bike Burglaries (Book 3)
Stolen bikes and a long-forgotten time capsule leave one amateur sleuth baffled and busy. Seventh-grader Gabby St. Claire is determined to bring a bike burglar to justice—and not just because mean girl Donabell Bullock is strong-arming her. But each new clue brings its own set of trouble. As if that's not enough, Gabby finds evidence of a decades-old murder within the contents of the time capsule, but no one seems to take her seriously. As her investigation heats up, will Gabby's knack for

being in the wrong place at the wrong time with the wrong people crack the case? Or will it prove hazardous to her health?

About the Author:

USA Today has called Christy Barritt's books "scary, funny, passionate, and quirky."

Christy writes both mystery and romantic suspense novels that are clean with underlying messages of faith. Her books have won the Daphne du Maurier Award for Excellence in Suspense and Mystery, have been twice nominated for the Romantic Times' Reviewers' Choice Award, and have finaled for both a Carol Award and Foreword Magazine's Book of the Year.

She's married to her Prince Charming, a man who thinks she's hilarious--but only when she's not trying to be. Christy's a self-proclaimed klutz, an avid music lover who's known for spontaneously bursting into song, and a road trip aficionado.

When she's not working or spending time with her family, she enjoys singing, playing the guitar, and exploring small, unsuspecting towns where people have no idea how accident prone she is.

Find Christy online at:
www.christybarritt.com
www.facebook.com/christybarritt
www.twitter.com/cbarritt

Made in the USA
Columbia, SC
21 November 2020